D0187976

THIS LIFE

A NOVEL

QUNTOS KUNQUEST

A Bolden Book

AGATE

CHICAGO

Library of Congress Cataloging-in-Publication Data

Names: KunQuest, Quntos
Title: This Life / Quntos KunQuest.
Description: Chicago : A Bolden Book/Agate, [2021] |
Identifiers: LCCN 2020040108 (print) | LCCN 2020040109 (ebook) | ISBN
    9781572842823 (paperback) | ISBN 9781572848481 (ebook)
Subjects: LCSH: Prisoners--Fiction.
Classification: LCC PS3611.U56 T48 2021 (print) | LCC PS3611.U56 (ebook)
    | DDC 813/.6--dc23
LC record available at https://lccn.loc.gov/2020040108
LC ebook record available at https://lccn.loc.gov/2020040109

9 8 7 6 5 4 3 2 1

Author photo by Zachary Lazar

Bolden Books is an imprint of Agate Publishing. Agate books are available in bulk at discount prices. Single copies are available prepaid direct from the publisher.

Agatepublishing.com

FOREWORD

by Zachary Lazar

I HAVE BEEN FRIENDS WITH Quntos KunQuest for such a long time—almost eight years now—that it's strange to look back to when we first met. It was in 2013 at Angola Prison, where Quntos has been incarcerated since 1996. I had come there as a journalist to cover the rehearsals and production of a passion play, "The Life of Jesus Christ," performed by the inmates, and Quntos was part of the sound crew. He also wrote some music for it. He was a rapper, he said, but Angola disapproved of hip-hop, unlike country, gospel, and rock, so he had to find ways to work that didn't draw much notice, teaching himself a little guitar, a little keyboard, enough to play into a digital recorder with programmable beats and sound loops that he could rap or sing over. He wanted to write stadium songs, he told me, songs for a huge crowd, which he likened to building an outfit around a pair of shoes or a necklace, a simple central concept as the focal point of a larger composition. He was tall and everything he wore was white—white sweatpants, white hoodie, white New Balances—his sunglasses either on or down in front of his ears so the lenses cupped his chin. He said he loved books: romance novels ("Don't tell no one") and history. He was weird, he said, an outsider, an artist, and he sometimes had trouble getting his message across—people would start to agree with him before they really considered what he was actually saying. They agreed to agree, not even thinking about what they were agreeing with. We started talking more about books—he had been reading Machiavelli, and he said that most people don't go deep with something like that, they just look for the main point, not the nuances or the development, and "what you do small, you do large," he went on, meaning that people look at their whole lives and the lives of others with the same haste and shallowness.

After I wrote my magazine piece, I mentioned to Quntos I was trying to write a novel about a man serving life at Angola, and he told me he had written a novel like that himself—he would send it to me, he said, and I could "steal" from it anything I wanted. I told him I wasn't going to steal anything but I was interested in reading his book. It arrived in my mailbox almost 20 years into his sentence, in November of 2015, the manuscript carefully handwritten in ballpoint pen, which made it a work of visual as well as literary art. What I mean is that he transcribed for me by hand a copy of his 343-page novel. When he needed italics, which he used sparingly, he would switch from print to cursive.

The story depicted an ensemble cast of characters enacting the power dynamics of prison, represented by rival crews of rappers. The action was interspersed with vivid set pieces describing daily life at Angola, written in many registers, from the African-American slang of the dialogue to the rich mix of formal and colloquial English of the narration. It was dramatic, elegant, and funny—funny in a way only possible for someone who in real life has maintained his sense of humor and joie de vivre after more than 25 years in prison.

After the first time I read it, I felt compelled to send it to my agent and my editor. It has been a long journey since then. I sent the book around for almost a year before I finally got an encouraging response from a publishing house owned by a famous rapper. They said they were interested in Quntos's novel but they would need a typed manuscript, so I asked one of my students if he would be willing to type it and he said yes, so then I sent in the typed version in September of 2016, and in mid-November the rapper's press came back and made an offer, with money involved. We had to educate ourselves now about logistics. For example, would Quntos have to publish under a pseudonym? How would we manage the contract and the advance and the royalties? Were there other forms of jeopardy we weren't even foreseeing? I was concerned that the prison authorities would find ways to punish Quntos for publishing a book set at Angola, even if the publication was legal. (I had learned that it was legal from a lawyer friend, who did the research.) It was a bad winter. Sometime in January, after a lot of back and forth about the book's title, about the difficulty of selling copies when the author couldn't make public appearances to promote it, the rapper's press stopped responding to me. A new president of the United States took office, the white nationalist who'd garnered more than 60 million votes. I wrote the rapper's press one last time that February. They withdrew their offer later that day.

There's much more to the story, but in one sense at least the story has a happy ending: After all this time, Quntos's novel has found its proper home, Agate, where Doug Seibold had the eyes to see and the ears to hear. As the critic Jerry Saltz once said, art is for anyone; it's just not for everyone. Readers of this novel will not find what they expect, because any novel that is a work of art bears the imprint of its maker, and makers, because they are people, are singular. Knowing them takes time. Knowing them is surprising. This knowing and these surprises are what make art valuable, even in a time that casts doubt on the very idea of any value that is not monetary but spiritual. Quntos has been incarcerated since he was 19 for a $300 carjacking in which no one was physically injured. He is serving a life sentence for this one act. *This Life* is a vivid portrayal of what the severity of a life sentence means, but that's not the reason you should read it. The title explains why you should read it. It is for the clarity and insight and enormous dignity with which Quntos KunQuest conjures the singular human lives in his story.

THE INTRO

CHAPTER ONE

THE A.U. STEPS INTO THE dormitory. Bewildered. Uncertain. A strange sense o' walkin' outside o' hisself. He keyed into everything aroun' him. The air so thick it presses against his skin. The dull, almost spooky glow from the lighting overhead is dingy yellow. It can't even push away the shadows that hang in the deepest crevices and corners, got him feelin' shook. Been like that since the turnkey slammed the door, locking him inside.

So much done already happened. He jus' numb to it, all this shit: his trial, conviction, and sentence. The time he already gave up sittin' in the parish jail. The hundreds of miles ridin' in shackles and chains in the back of a sheriff's van, the windows tinted and covered with some shit like chicken wire. Guarded by wack-ass correctional officers puffin' cigarettes and blowin' on stained coffee cups. Bad jokes and shaky laughs like he ain't know. If anything unusual happened, they wouldn't have hesitated to shoot. That triptriggered sump'n he wa'n't tryna think about, but he knew: this was his slow descent to the bottom of the barrel.

All of it got him even more numb now where he stands. The numbness like ain't nothin' there. He looks around, without feeling, at his new surroundings. He is an admitting unit. An A.U.

There is a bunch o' fans blowing all around. Everywhere he look he see convicts. Oldheads. Youngsters. Mostly Black, a few white dudes. Most of them wear either gray cotton joggers, jeans, or blue jeanshorts, and tanktop tees or color t-shirts. Different dudes walk past the newjack with their headphones blaring. They steal glances. Size him up. To them, he's a fresh fish.

Boom!

The sound is followed by the noise of a bunch of people yelling and screaming, beatin' on the walls, slammin' chairs on the floor. His muscles tense up. He turns quickly toward the direction of the disturbance and confronts a complex of plexiglass partitions. There are about 30 dudes wildin' out in the TV room. They're watching an NBA game.

The A.U. walks over to the mahogany-skinned sister in a navy blue corrections uniform. She sits behind a small square table. She is the only C.O. in the dorm. He hands her his paperwork while checkin' her nametag. *Sergeant Havoc.* When she opens her mouth to speak, he notices the two gold teeth on either side of her top bridge.

"You're in bed 22," she says and logs him on the head count.

"Where that's at?"

She raises her head and studies him, cold-eyed. "The numbers are painted on the sides of the beds."

The A.U. looks to his left at the bed closest to the table. He nods and turns to walk off.

She calls out, "Hey!"

"Yeah, what up?"

"The showers close at 9:00. If you go'n take one, you need to hurry up," she snaps. Her whole vibe vaguely akin to rancor.

"I'm cool," he says. Distracted. His senses gorge on these new surroundings.

At that, he walks toward his bed. Sergeant Havoc watches him with knowin' eyes.

The A.U. moves through the dorm wit' his head up. He notices pockets o' two or three players huddled in different parts of the resting area. None of 'em are making eye contact. Well, maybe a few of them. Most are leaning in and shoo-shooing with each other.

Most of these niggas are cowards, he says to himself. Disdain. He finds out his bed is little more than a cot. He sits down and places his few things on the floor beside him. A 'vict, a' old convict, walks up and stands in his aisle. Homedude is about 40, 45, wit' a' old-school shag, a salt-and-pepper beard, and bad teeth.

The 'vict says, "Check this out. The walk orderly oughta have your mattress down before lights-out. You need to remind the keyman, though. Your boxes probably won't come 'til the morning. So— "

"—Wait a minute," the A.U. cuts him off. "I didn't ask you nothin'! What you want wit' me?"

"Well, hol' up—"

"—No! You hold up! I don't need yo' help. Ya best bet is to back up off me."

The 'vict got this strained look on his face. He opens his mouth to speak and thinks better of it. He turns and walks away.

The A.U. is fuming. Who do they think he is? He's rememberin' all o' those stories he heard in the parish jail. *Ain't nobody g'on fake me out*, he reminds hisself. He won't tolerate no games. He 'bout his business!

His blood pressure starts buildin'. *That's right!* This is the mindset he's more used to. *It's time to set it off in this bitch!*

He jumps up and yells all kinds o' shit at the top of his lungs. Dudes filin' out o' the TV and game rooms look at him like he's crazy.

A couple o' cats unplug the fans so they can hear what he is yellin' about. As the hum of the fans die down, they can hear him better, like a lead guitar shredding through a break in the music.

"Yeah, that's what I said! And I'll represent that! . . . I ain't lookin' for no pot'nahs! I don't need no friends! Don't mess wit' mines, I won't mess wit' yours, understand me! My name Lil Chris! If anybody got a pro'lem wit' me, I'm down for whateva! . . . Wheneva! . . . Remember that!!"

As the ringin' of his shouts settles on the air, everybody goes back to what they was doin' to begin with. Nah . . . these cats ain't the gladiators he's painted into the scene. Better look again.

Like water, air ain't still.

Wind whirls through. The wall-mounted fans start back buzzin'. He stands there wide-eyed. The voices, their echo and hum. So many people in one place, but the area is open.

His third eye workin' overtime. It reaches to sense what his muscles can't possibly know. It sees there are things he'll need to peep. This need to know, he'll get the hang of it.

In the weeks ahead, he'll learn that while this used to be the bloodiest prison in the nation, all that has changed. The challenge of the penitentiary is more mental than physical now. Most of the savage cats that still ride are boxed away in the cellblocks and extended lockdowns where the conditions are barbaric for real. The dormitory that Lil Chris walked into is part of what is called population. Most of these inmates focus on trying to make it back to the streets. Or, at the very least, to make their stay here more comfortable, if that's possible. The dominant perspective is that position is everything, and much too important to squander on incidental conflict. Position is always at risk where the administration has rats, squeals, trinkies, informants, or whatever in every corner. And they tellin' everything. Period. Juggling these is a preoccupation in itself. No, he won't receive a direct answer from these quarters. He'll soon grasp this.

The prison's security scheme is unit management. This has made those subject to its clutches very, very sly creatures, indeed.

Very few of the challenges Lil Chris will face in the coming times will he approach head-on.

Lil Chris figures out early on that the only place to find solitude, a chance to hear hisself think, is on his pillow, beneath his covers.

In Shreveport, Louisiana, where he grew up, the weather was often this same numbing, apathetic cold in the winter, a dry cold he inhaled thoughtlessly, that frosted his breath right in front of his face. A stiff cold that held him like a blanket in the still-life the city becomes until the scorching hot summers.

Even now, he can picture his early years in The Bottom, one of Shreveport's oldest, roughest neighborhoods. His older sister, Michell, nursed a crush on Oreo. That one's signature bald head, dark skin, and gold teeth. One of the infamous Bottom Boys. Them ones among Shreveport's oldest, most organized street gangs. His beginnings.

Him only a few months past his 13th birthday, with that small band of lil street kids he started out with. Hot wires and joyrides to pass the idle hours. His mother practically as young as him. Off workin', crisscrossin' the country wit' this business that did inventory for large supermarket chains. "Accucount," or something like that.

He grew up in his grandparents' house. Big ole whatnot shelves crowded wit' porcelain statuettes, potted plants with running vines, and framed family pictures. Elaborate displays of cherished old china dishes. Always the smell of cooked food. At the best of times a whiff of homemade fruit preserves kept in thick glass jars with the two-part sealing tops. Loud, boisterous voices. More akin to what you'd hear in wide country fields, yellin' back and forth, instead o' the close confines of a workin' class A-frame set on a hill, sittin' on stacked cement cinder blocks. His Baptist grandfather. Pious. Stalwart. His grandma a stern homemaker, but always wit' a relievin' laugh, a ready smile. She also worked as a janitor for one o' the middle schools out in Motown, West Shreveport. Granddaddy always chased some hustle or another. A truck store, sellin' sweets and pickled pig feet. Watermelons or some shit. There was Michell and his younger sister, Nett, along wit' his Aunt Carrie and her two kids, Carlos and Kim. A' old school family, a full house. He among the youngest. Runnin' aroun' underfoot, trampling Grandma's flowerbeds.

His nest was one of love. From home he gained classic Black values and a basic education. And God. Still, he chose the streets. His moms was a bookworm, but his pops a' ex-con. It was in his blood. And life was real.

So there was the streets: the pace, the pulse, the rites of passage. The pressure of it all. Crime. He picked the elements apart without thinkin' 'bout it. Learned his lessons well and quick. By the time he turned 15 he was sump'n serious. Flanked by a different group of youngsters, some older than him. All ready to follow his lead. His confidence was boosted by survivin' a short but hard stint in juvenile for weapons possession.

Back in his own hood, Lakeside. Streets a mixture of black and white. Tar backroads lined by ditches on both sides. Paved concrete thoroughways, curbed and sidewalked. Rows of frame houses, almost all fronted by picture windows. Low-rate market. Mortgaged or rented. Honest, hard workers' dwellings weevilled by crack houses. Everybody struggling. Some much more than others.

The block, peopled by prayers and sinners. Churches and liquor stores switchin' up on every corner along the avenue. Scented by tree sap, treaded acorns, sprinkled pecans. Discarded liquor bottles and corner store feedbags. Baby diapers. Dog, cat, and chicken shit. Consumer brand smell-goods. Cologne and perfumes and sweat.

For a kid like him, running the back alleys, gulleys, packed dirt trails, and railroad tracks aroun' that grid, life was so free that even pain didn't cost much. And trouble ain't seem so bad.

There was plenty of it, too. Coming of age, he ran the gamut. Fist fights on the ball courts and gravel lots. Dice games in abandoned garages and under carports. Sneaking girls in his grandparents' back door. Front yard brawls, family friends and old folks yellin' for them to, "Break it up and get your tails home!" Guns. Crack rock.

As he came up in it, he seized every opportunity. Religious about his respect. No qualms. Blasted on all enemies, from another hood or the next street over. More times than he could count. Couldn't even tell you how many he actually hit.

For the most part, he was good wit' it. A long way from when he used to sleep curled up with a Bible. There was sump'n rewardin' about squeezin' the trigger. Making off with stolen goods. A fat blunt or a phat ass. His bad deeds never froze him in the moment—just later, when he had to face their sad, red, crying eyes. When confronted by his own conscience after dark, in the quiet of his thoughts. Or when forced to offer up an explanation.

Guilty as charged, he thinks to hisself as he lies there on his narrow prison cot. Somewhere in the back o' his mind, he always knew prison or death awaited him. Far from cringing, he embraced those probabilities as nothin' so much as gangsta shit. His issue. As far back as he can remember. The black sheep. Probably woulda chosen death, at some points along the way, even by his own hands. But he lives. Survived it all, and for what? The penitentiary?

Yeah, he knew what would come. Just didn't know it would feel like this.

July 11, a few weeks short of his 19th birthday, he left the streets. First-degree murder. Now sentenced to life imprisonment. He knows he gotta do something. Sure that he'll figure it out. Eventually.

Till then, he'll be thinkin'. And holdin' his shit down.

Lil Chris wakes up. It's deathly still in the dorm—only the fans are hummin'. All the lights are out, except for the dim blue lights that illuminate key spots in the livin' area: the toilets and showers, the TV and game rooms, the telephone and microwave station. All a lil bit brighter than the low-lit sleepin' area.

Outside of snorin' and the occasional fart, er'body quiet. Lil Chris turns his head at the sound of jinglin' keys. It's Sergeant Havoc makin' her rounds.

For the first time, he really peeps her out. She's maybe five-six, small waistline—maybe 120 pounds. Legs like a stallion. Nice apple bottom. Extravagantly manicured nails and ghetto-fabulous hair. A walk like a fashion model. She passes right in front o' him. She keeps her eyes trained ahead, fakin' like she don't see him checkin' her out, his head spinnin'. Damn!

Where is that notepad at? Lil Chris rolls over to grab his pen and paper. He begins to write the first thing that comes to his mind, then scratches it out.

He reaches for his pack of tobacco and rolls a cigarette. Lights it and takes a drag.

He starts to write again as he blows smoke.

Long and strong
> *Take a pull . . .*
Nicotine enter my brain. Full . . .
> > *I'm a mask*
Prosecution heavy, mind on my task.
> > > *Contemplatin'*
To hell with the past, hear me?!
I'ma make the world take heed,
> > > *Recognize, player it's Lil Chris*
Keyed on a masterplan
> > *Penitentiary got me thinkin'!*
Ranking every goal
> > *While gettin' swole.*
I'ma orchestrator.
> > *Stay wit' my mind on my biz*
> > > *Makin' sure niggas know*
> > > > *What time it is . . .*

CHAPTER TWO

Metamorphosis
   Transmutation. My principle of transition.
          Jewel scarab;
      Egyptian dung beetle . . .
   Transcended from humble beginnings.
   A lowly living bred majestic mature.
I was born under the sign of the twin—
   Mistress Cleo prophesied my rise
         In a hip-hop magazine.
   Anubis Wepwawet,
      Open up my way.
   It's the dawn of my comin' forth by day.

He watches.

Fifteen or so of them walk through the door. They seem to get younger and younger every trip. Even the most generous estimate of how many of them will ever leave this place alive is one or two. Three, tops.

Still, he watches.

Studying them is an art. A little something he's picked up along the way. Rise can push his boxes off the welded metal pushcarts used to transport footlockers along the concrete floor, in a dormitory of 64 men and a C.O., and within 30 minutes he'll have assessed every one of them's makeup. He'll know who's dangerous and who's soft, who's got sense and who can't think, who's playin' games and who wants to be left alone. And, most importantly, which of these fools he's willing to allow inside his zone.

Of the group of A.U.'s he's watching at this moment, a couple are repeat offenders—they'll go down the walk and blend right on back in. The worst of these will keep the homies they haven't seen in two or three years up all night. Jabbering about how they were out there doin' it! Thuggin' it up. While those that never left hold grudges against them for throwing away the one thing that all of them crave the most—another chance.

The rest of these fresh fish are the disoriented. The upstanding citizen who slipped, crossed the line, and got caught up. The big-timers who thought the world was theirs. The drug addicts who forgot about the world. Worst of all, the children of the ghetto. Few of them even had a clue. All of them think that they'll be home in three to five, but the truth is now they've been added to the count. Eighty-five-percent of them are predicted to die here in the joint.

"So, last night was most of y'all's first night in a prison cot, huh? If you were like me, you didn't sleep much. I bet you I can tell you what your first waking thought was this morning." Rise surveys the room, makes occasional eye contact. "Yeah, I know what you were thinking: *Damn . . .*

"By now, you have been poked, turned, pinched, questioned, in-structed, laid in, rolled out, shaved down, and locked up. It's all part of the process. You've been lodged into the system. I'm sure the sheer reality hasn't even hit most you yet. You're in shock and you don't even know it. You haven't had time to think about it, have you? Too many other things to take in, right?"

Rise walks among their chairs. A slow, steady gait, almost a strut. Not that he has anything to strut about. His disposition is one of awareness. Here, lately, no situation can overwhelm him. He's got time under his belt. He's in tune with this environment. Still, he chooses his next words carefully.

"This particular session is called Orientation. The administration has set it up so that you can be—well, I'll say, so we can basically give you all a rundown on what you've gotten yourselves into." He's trying to reach them. "You are sitting in the Louisiana State Prison, at Angola. My name is Oschuwon R. Hamilton. Most of the brothers here know me as Rise. If any of you need to get at me, that's who you ask for: Rise. Now, we are go'n try to move through our respective spiels and it would be wise of you to pay attention. There are a sum of choices you'll need to make. You need to make a conscious decision on how you are go'n walk this joint. There are a lot of pitfalls.

"Most of you, for whatever reason, will go down the walk and get with your homeboys. I know, I know. You ain't scared." Rise looks at the clean-shaven 16-year-old in the back row. "But don't be surprised if your homies are the main ones to try to play you. You need to focus on establishing your own individuality. Set your own feet. Validate yourself. Mostly, it's not what you do that these cats respect. It's what you don't."

Rise walks back up to the podium and looks over the room one more time. "I'll be back a little later to talk to you about education. For now though, we have a number of people here to help break down what's go'n be your Angola experience."

Rise signals for Reverend Andrews to come up and speak. A tall, slim, somewhat funny-built man around 50, Reverend Andrews is one of the more prominent preachers among a considerable number of inmate ministers that walk the compound. He stands in, shakes Rise's hand, and gives him an embrace, shoulder to shoulder.

Rise heads for the back of the room, his attention already turned away from what's going on up front. Living in his head, again. Prison'll do that to you. One never gets the chance to recover from the many isolated tragedies that riddle the life of the prisoner. So they walk, striving to stay engaged. Soul-jahs with open wounds determined to hold their position on the board. Not so much ignoring, but rather absorbing. Learning to live with the pain. Always thinking five moves ahead. Always moving forward. Always progressive. Always feeling that even in the midst of a crowd, one is always alone.

The cell was dark. In the distance Rise can hear the jingling of keys and echoes of laughter. How can they be happy? How can joy exist in a world that has brought him so much pain?

He's a go-getter, though. All his life he has had to fight opposition. But those agents were always on the outside. Out there where Rise could see them. Where he could attack 'em. But now they're settin' it off inside of him. His instincts are sharp, his defenses are up. Who are they? Where is the heat comin' from? He can't simply identify his target and swing it out. But the presence is there. He can feel it. All he can do is lie there and suffer.

And then there is this bird. A sparrow. . .

"Man, you see that lil dude in the back row? Kid, that's a pretty lil ole dude, ain't he. Ain't it, man? . . . Rise!" A foppish convict, leaning over the serving counter Rise has blindly withdrawn to.

"Huh?" Rise stirs absently.

"Rise!"

"What?"

"You don't hear me?"

"What, Puff?! What you want?!" Rise finally focuses. Irritated.

"I'm talkin' bout that lil boy in the ba—"

"What? What about him?" Rise zeros in with mounting menace.

"No, I was just sayin'—"

"Sayin' what?" Rise gives the room a quick once over from the vantage of the counter, to see who's seeing. "Say. Come 'round here right quick, Puff."

Puff follows Rise around the counter and back into the shed's food preparation room.

"Right over here, man. C'mere," Rise says in a calm, nonchalant voice. As soon as Puff comes within an arm's reach, Rise steps into his shirt and back-hands him. Bows him in his left rib and hems him in against one of the refrigeration units. Puff's breathing gets hoarse, ragged. Eyes bucked wide open. Oh, now he understands. Yeah, he got sense now.

"Don't ever come at me like that. You *know* not to bring that to me."

"Man—" It looks almost as if there is a shadow of a frown on Puff's face. Rise moves his grip up from his shirt to his neck. He squeezes. Puff squirms. Gags, tryin' to get a breath. He tries to push Rise off, but to no avail. Puff's pulse pushes insistently under Rise's thumb.

"What," Rise growls. "You got a problem with something I said? Huh? What?"

Rise leans in and gets right into Puff's ear to keep the disturbance contained as he delivers his next statement, vaguely aware of someone or another addressing the gathering of A.U.s from the podium out front.

"I *know* you ain't forgot I was the one you hid up under a while back, when you decided you wanted to change your life? I was the one that backed the wolves up off you when your ex-ole man wasn't tryna hear that, too—wasn't I? And, now, you go'n come to me like you tryna turn somethin' out? Wreck someone else's life? And you already know I don't respect that foolishness. Now, I would be down bad if I was to give that lil brother a black diamond and tell him to handle his business, wouldn't I?"

"But, Rise, I—"

"Hold that down and step off." Rise shoves Puff toward the door. He stumbles over a footstool on his way out. "Go get yo'self together, boy." As Rise's breathing subsides, they call for him over the P.A. system to return to the floor, and he addresses the group.

"The second-century stoic philosopher and Roman emperor Marcus Aurelius wrote this book, *Meditations*. He wrote about fire, the heaping of trash, and the flame's appropriating qualities. He compared all of this to the will of man in the face of opposition. I have my own analogy, very much influenced by his. I've come to think of God as a blacksmith. We are the metal. The fires of the furnace are the trials of life. The blacksmith's hammer has two heads, tribulation and triumph. With this hammer, the Creator delivers blows of elation, disappointment, grief, joy, depression, dejection, fulfillment, and sorrow."

Rise assumes they're not following him. Still, he presses on with his point. "The things we go through in life are what shapes us to become the people we are. The good and the bad are the faces of perspective. Behind these two faces, life changes as life changes us. At the other end of the smelting process, once we are lifted from the fire and molded by the blows of the hammer, only then are we ready to be placed in the water. The water of the spirit. And, no, spirit isn't an institutional religion. It is a concentrated search for an understanding and knowledge of self, conducted inside whatever guidelines and discipline your spirit identifies as truth. Now, you may not understand any of what I'm saying. But, along the way, you will. I want you to laugh when it bites. And by all means, holla at me. For now, though, I'll holla at y'all. That's all we have for today."

As the A.U.s stand and file out of the visiting shed, the A Building, Rise walks over to the youngster that was in the back row. The kid stands about five-ten. He's reddish brown, heavyset, and slew-footed, with long braids. His mug is authentic.

Rise steps to him. "Say, big boy, what they call you?"

"My name Lil Chris, nigga. What, you know me from somewhere?"

Vicious attitude. Gotta love that. Rise immediately recognizes this kid's potential. He's a soul-jah. Rise is impressed, but it only takes him a split second to give Lil Chris a stonegrilled nod. "Nah, lil brotha, I don't know you. You just remind me of someone I grew up with. Maybe I'll see you around. Peace out."

Lil Chris stares at Rise for a moment. As if he's tryna figure something out. He just turns and walks off. Not a misunderstanding. Not a making of acquaintance. It's kinda like they just sized each other up. Rise watches as Lil Chris moves out and swings the corner.

Damn, we in the joint, lil brother, Rise thinks. He picks up his things, stops to speak to a few people on his way out the door, then steps out into the sunshine on his way to the dorm.

He passes the cellblocks where all the hardheads at, mobbed out on the yard. He's got a couple of close ones he knows he needs to reach. He stops at the fence to holla at them before pushing out.

This is his world, for now. He passes by a couple of free folk on the walk. Including Sergeant Vernelic with her fine you-know-what-I'm-sayin'. He's going to have to get at her a little later. On the D.L.

This is his world. He passes by the law library and makes a mental note to stop through there later on to check out this Fifth Circuit case that just came down. As the gym comes into view, he reminds himself to hold to his commitment to stay in shape. Gotta sneak a workout in some kind of way. Prison is the wrong place to get sick.

This is his world. Here comes Major Mercury moving up the walk. Rise speaks, but the officer just passes on by. Must have problems or some shit. What's the problem? Rise is the one in jail.

This is his world.

After making it through all the security gates and checkpoints, and waiting for the keyman to open the door, Rise finally walks into the dorm. He heads to the desk to see if he has mail.

No mail.

Damn.

When he gets to his cot, he sits down. Before he kicks his shoes

off or gets his shower things together, or anything else, he grabs a pen
and paper to scribble out a few lines.

A quick 16.

A hot one

    To the dome. My only brother

        By my mother and my father; true love

            A hot gun

      released. Strikes the floor.

          Rings still.

     Blood pourin'

        God, tell me this ain't real.

  Ancient life leavin' young bones

    Soul departure.

    Journey home.

      God called for him

        Look!

Trigger my journey over. How can I ever forget about
all this livin' that we planned for

  With you, I buried everything I stood for

  Dead End. Anna Street Clic. I'm givin' it up.

I'm no longer thuggin' it up.

  I'm thuggin' it out.

See, 'cause now I know what strugglin' 'bout.

        Hard labor.

I ain't trippin'. Momma raised a

  Young go-getter

Taught me from my days as a tadpole

Son, you play now, you starve later

Me as a man-child

    Reared in a single-parent household.

Driven.

I was locked up in a cell

 When I heard about my brother passin' over

 It was my thirst for life that brought me over

 And pulled me through.

 It was at this point I began to change

 God, I thank you for the tribulation.

 Metamorphosis.

CHAPTER THREE

I open up the door to today
Lookin' for tomorrow,
Only to find yesterday.
What can I do broke?
—L.P.

SLEEP RELEASES RISE IN A sudden instant. As if all at once, his dreams clip closed and awareness clicks in.

In his ears, he can hear the subtle murmurs of a small group of Muslim brothers up front in the game room who've already started their morning prayers.

He raises his arms straight back and stretches. Breathe. Then he slowly raises up from his pillow and doubles forward to reach for his feet. Stretch. Breathe. Next, he pulls his legs beneath him in the lotus before again laying forward, his arms reaching overhead. Stretch. Breathe . . .

On autopilot, his legs swing down to his slippers on the cold floor. With his toothbrush and other effects in hand he heads for the shower area. Mentally, however, he's still picking through the different elements of the dream that just released him, to see if he can salvage any messages from his unconscious.

After washing up, Rise makes for the empty early-morning TV room. He flicks the channel to CNN. This done, he begins his Wu-style Tai Chi regimen.

Lil Chris is snatched from sleep by the sound of dusty metal footlockers sliding over creaking iron bedsprings. All around him there is movement. The floor beneath his cot rumbles with it. The dawn washes the resting area in new light from the dormitory's glass façade.

The first thought that comes to him is, *Damn, I missed breakfast, again!*

He forces himself to roll out o' bed to face the mornin'. His head feels stuffy. His throat is sore. His nose is stopped up. He's already mad and frustrated. Though, he can't blame nobody for not wakin' him up. Like a fist to his gut, he realizes he's alone.

He stands up to pull his locker box from under his cot. He fumbles with the lock before opening it up to grab his hygiene bag. He shuffles into the shower area, his anger mounting, his body aching and cold. Seven sinks and every one he stops to stand over is coated with unsightly slop and mucus, or full o' stagnant murky water. The smell of stale toothpaste and bad breath all up his nose, almost causing him to retch.

Lil Chris turns on the hot water at the big cast-iron industrial and fights the thought of the germs risin' toward him on the steam. *I'm a gangsta*, he reminds hisself as he begins to brush his teeth, glaring at his reflection in the polished metal mirror.

As he brushes his tongue, he leans over and gags until he coughs up yellow mucus. He cups water in one hand to flush it up his nose and blows it out loudly. He cleans his ears and throws his head back to gargle, then spit. He splashes water in his face a couple times before lookin' at his reflection, again, in the mirror.

There.

Everything's cool now.

He got it out of his system.

Rise gathers the last of his things as he prepares to leave the dorm. Once situated, he sips the last of his morning cup of coffee and watches the resting area come alive.

He assesses them as they wake up, compares what he knows of their past to the men they've become. Takes inventory of the effects of long-term incarceration. Watches men who were once cocky and athletic now struggle to sit up in bed, their bodies retaining the weight of their late-night snacks and comfort foods.

He sees the drug addicts who've always been drug addicts reach first for half-empty packs of cigarettes. In silence they puff in their covers and focus hard to devise a way to get that early morning high.

All about him are men in stationary transition. He acknowledges the changes in some who have found the love of a woman after years of challenging boys for their booty. The freakiest climb back into bed. While most others were gone to breakfast, they were peeking at the lady guard from some isolated corner and masturbating, imagining her participating in some twisted sexual rite.

Really, no harm done. For the most part, these snakes are now toothless. They tried everything they could think of. Nothing worked. They still woke up in this place. Ultimately, they learned to depend on their bossman and defer to the supervising officers. A balance of humility and humiliation that makes captivity somehow palatable.

Rise gathers his things and heads out of the dormitory. For now, he's housed on the East Yard, in one of the four dorms of Spruce at the end of the walk. The pedestrian traffic he merges into is made up of skilled labor. Compound workers, clerics, and vocational students.

He passes by orderlies pushing pushbrooms. Some have gone out to the yard already. He only half-notices them with their five-gallon buckets, beyond the fenced-in walkway, grazing and picking up cigarette butts. Others jog the fence line. The ledges are dotted with prisoners as they see to their business. Shift workers enjoy time off.

He moves past Cypress and Magnolia, on up through Ash, the East Yard's three other housing units. The scene over here is laid back, at least comparatively. A great many of these guys are the broken. Truth is ugly. Even the crafty and goal-oriented are in some ways invested in security's interest. To a certain extent, this is the case all over the prison farm, but nowhere as much as it is on the East Yard.

"Work call!"

The supervisor, Lieutenant Corrick, passes by Lil Chris where he sits numb on his cot. Tall, wily, middle-aged, and white, Corrick walks along the rows, absentmindedly kicking the iron cots of those who are still asleep beneath their covers. It's the same routine every weekday. At least on his shift. He pushes, they drag.

A young female cadet works her way up the opposite side o' the dorm. She's kickin' each offender's cot with relish and yellin' for them to "Get they asses up!"

She kicks. *Clang*!

She stops at a cot about two rows up and to the left of where Lil Chris is sittin'. The guy beneath the cover, Monroe Black, doesn't budge.

She boots the bed again, twice. "Hey, inmate," she yells. "I ain't got time for this! Y'all act like fuckin' children!"

Clang! Clang! She kicks again.

"Bitch, I'm up! You ain't gotta kick my bed like that!"

The cadet stumbles back a step, taken off guard. Monroe Black springs up, throws his covers aside.

Lieutenant Corrick rushes over to the commotion. Lil Chris stands in his aisle. He can see where this is headin'. As Lil Chris heads out, he hears Corrick attempt to handcuff Monroe Black. A percussive slap follows. Out of the corner of his eye, he catches a glimpse of Corrick staggerin' back, arms flailin', as he stumbles over a footlocker and crumples to the floor.

The concrete floor rumbles. When Lil Chris reaches the door several other supervising officers rattle past him. Clanging keys, squawkin' radios, bootfalls. This is the West Yard. The fieldlines of Walnut and Hickory. And Oak and Pine, where a bunch of fuckups are housed. They have job assignments but have yet to convince security that they're East Yard material.

Lil Chris steps out onto the walk. A number of other prisoners mill about, wit'out direction, though most eventually head for the gate and out onto the prison yard. Most are in white t-shirts, stained beige from dirt that refuses to come off in the wash, faded blue jeans, and noisy wetboots.

The sky overhead is still gray. Beyond the fences and guard towers, over the trees behind them, there is a riot in the eastern skies. Red and purple herald the sun's arrival. A pink firmament and milky blue border the uprising. The blue cools as it trails out over where the fieldworkers have lined up on the ground below.

"Bitch ass nigga, you think Ms. Bailey lovin' you, don't you?"

"Hell, yeah, mayne. That's my baby."

Lil Chris stands stone-faced among them. Four lines side by side. Seems everyone is talkin'. Except him.

"Yeah, well you know what your baby did this morning, huh." The other men jabber on.

"Yeah, he know what that bitch did," someone else says. "She got Monroe Black jumped on."

"Ah, man, I 'on't wanna hear that shit. My bitch thorough."

"All you niggas is fucked up," a deep gravelly voice puts in from the line next over, to the right. "A bunch o' you weak muthafuckas stood right there and watched the free folks whoop that man."

"Bitch-ass niggas."

Silence.

"Fuck Monroe Black," someone mumbles grudgingly. "That ain't my homeboy."

Having waited at the gate for security clearance, Rise has finally made it inside the Education Building, up the stairs, and into the adult basic education classroom he's been assigned to teach in.

After writing the lesson plan on the blackboard and laying out the worksheets, he's awarded a moment of contemplation before the day starts. As he often does in these instances, he turns off the lights and grabs the earth globe. Pulling up a seat behind his desk, he sets the model before him.

He studies the landmasses and oceans.

One of his childhood friends, Marlon, contacted him out of the blue a while back. He had to appreciate the thought. It meant more than he can express.

Rise places his finger on the globe. On top of the place where the two of them grew up. Shreveport, Louisiana. He traces a line down to Baton Rouge where Marlon went to school, at Southern University. Imagines a few short miles to the northwest where he's been held since Marlon's school days.

Angola.

This is where his travels have stopped.

Now, he slowly traces his finger from Baton Rouge to Philadelphia to London to Amsterdam and, finally, to Accra, Ghana, where Marlon said he was in his letter. Serving in the Peace Corps.

Rise pulls a drawer open under the desktop and takes out a pen and pad.

His hand remains poised over the paper for a timeless moment.

But then he places the pen down and closes his eyes. He lays his head back onto the headrest.

After he clears the roster at the work gate, gets counted, and marched out double-file to the tool room, Lil Chris waits in line to receive his long-handle ditchbank blade. He lays it over his shoulder like so many others before him. He returns to the line and waits to begin the long march to the day's worksite.

The linepusher rides up on his horse and hands his work roster in a leather satchel to the prisoner headline. The headline takes his place at the front of the fieldline. One of his assignments is to set the pace for the nearly 200 inmates in line behind him.

The linepusher kicks his horse off and the headline begins the walk. A water cooler or two go'n be picked up somewhere on the way. The convicts on trash detail bring up the end of the line. They go'n be runnin' here and there to pick up litter.

On two horses a lil ways behind the fieldline are the gunguards. Armed to the teeth with handguns and fully automatic assault rifles. Yet, even in the presence of all this firepower, a bunch of strangers, hardened criminals with sharp tools and shit, the scene ain't even tense.

It's just another day in prison. Just like the ones before it. Much like the ones to come.

CHAPTER FOUR

I got dibs on the next 16
    I
               Guarantee a classic.
                  Homie, watch this.
               Got a thing for some hot hits,
                        86 this!
    I'ma spit sick.
            Ever heard a crook politic?

IT WAS ANOTHER HOT DAY.

They had walked for about a' hour straight. Most o' 'em were soaked wit' sweat by the time the fieldline got to the worksite. The linepusher assigned a number to each prisoner goin' by his spot on the roster. The headline marked the cuts out with a garden hoe. The workers fell in on the cuts.

Every 15 to 20 minutes, the linepusher yells, "Swing it down!" At this, the workers move on down the dirt road to another cut to be worked. It's a process. Once the workers get their rhythm, it sets in. It's Wednesday. The middle of the week. Two days from the weekend. Two days from rest and free time. Close, but not close enough. The frustrated youth are restless.

Out of nowhere, a drumbeat. Listen. There's an echo in the bass. A bass and a click. If you listen closer, you can make out that somebody is beating on his chest. And clicking their teeth. That'll last for about five minutes, but then the linepusher will yell, "Swing it down!"

Damn.

Gotta catch another cut.

Once they get into their cut and get their rhythm going, it starts again. First the beat, then the click. This time, the worker is beat-boxing.

The rhythm plays in they chests while they work. Makes the work more tolerable at first. They're movin' to what the beat makes 'em feel. Yeah, the work is g'tting' done, but they're not workin'. They are coordinatin', movin' with a math that counts time and motion. A line-worker's dance to shake off the strain o' hard labor. One voice calls out,

"You ain't heard of another like me,
Son get it ghuttah 'awfly'
Ghetto sick, crack avenue
Keep 'em hollin' ill street blues
Split fools, wit' hollows that follow bad moves, huh
Heard of me?
Tell 'em, 'cause this could get ugly, huh. . ."

Damn, he fell off . . .

The natives entertain this thought for a while. Almost everybody in earshot is thinking the same thing: *Come on with that, mayne!*

Now, after every cut rotation, they've started to congregate. Eyes look-a-who'n. The voices start in.

"Say brah, don't stunt."

"Bring that on back, man."

"Look! Help him finish his cut."

"Don't worry 'bout it, dawg. The chump go'n be yellin' 'swing it down' in a minute. Wait till after the next cut."

"Yeah. Hit it, get it up, and quit it."

"I'ma break y'all off a lil somethin' too!"

"Uh-oww! There they go!"

"Come on wit' that, mayne!"

Before anyone notices it, nobody's tripping off the work. The hip-hop heads fall in and get out in rhythm. Most make it back to the cypher at the same time, and all you see is a bunch o' beatniks standing in a loosely made circle bobbin' their heads. One after another they take turns spittin' mad flow. Crazy lyrics. Some 16-bar verses. Some wild out for like ten minutes. That's a long time to be talkin' nonstop, huh?

Now, after every cut there are about 20 brothers in the crowd. Rappers, beatmakers, and spectators. They wide open.

Lil Chris tries to ignore the pull of the cypher. He's stayed to hisself for the first three weeks in the field. The only reason he eventually said something to his cut partner is 'cause he was nicking hard one day and the dude offered him a cigarette.

Kid is an alright looking dude. Kinda fly with his, to tell the truth. He's the type you have to allow to open up. The majority of them are like that. They play their hands close to they chests until they can learn their surroundings.

Dude's name is PowwWoww. High-yellow cat. He's Black, but claims he has Native American relatives that still live close to the soil. The C'ster feels like he's lying about that part. Although, he does have that tall, slender build, with high cheekbones. That in-between hair. But he can't tell Lil Chris nothin' about In'jun tradition? Survey says? Lame!

Anyway, PowwWoww has the gift of gab. He keeps his hands in something. Today, he has a couple o' sugar bags of that sticky-icky.

And he's determined to get Lil Chris "out there." Pull him out o' his shell. He don't know he's messing wit' a real smoke dragon.

"Say, big boy."

Nothin'.

"Say, man. Ah . . . Lil Chris."

Still nothin'.

"Come on, kid. I know you hear me."

Nothin'. PowwWoww just stands in the cut, staring at him. After a minute, the C'ster says in an agitated, high-pitched voice, "What you want me to say? I'm standin' right here next to you. Of course, I hear you! Talk, nigga!"

"Oh, my bad, ma—"

"What you want?" Lil Chris interrupts him. He hates when these cats come at him sideways. Try to start a conversation. Unlike most dudes, Lil Chris doesn't seem to be holding any punches. He speaks his mind. At least, he does whenever he decides to speak. This is what PowwWoww digs about him.

PowwWoww smiles. Goes on. "You get down?"

"What you mean?"

"On the bud side."

"What? . . . Oh, you mean, ah . . . Hell yeah!" Lil Chris comes all the way out the bag on him.

PowwWoww is tripping off him. This cat Lil Chris is a real live wire. Gotta feel him.

"Chill out, man," PowwWoww says.

"Don't play no games wit' me."

"I ain't pl—"

"Well, roll it up then."

"Damn, nigga!" PowwWoww laughs. He's really tripping off this dude. "Alright, come on, you got papers?"

Lil Chris goes in his pocket and pulls out his pack of Bugler tobacco. He fishes the rolling papers out of the pouch and hands them to PowwWoww. All the C'ster can think of is that he hasn't been in that zone since he caught this case. Almost two years ago. As far as he's concerned, PowwWoww can't roll the shit fast enough.

Lil Chris checks him out. PowwWoww must have stuck two of the papers together. What he rolls is longer than the regular Bugler paper. He purses his lips and chomps down on the paper. This holds it snug while he rolls the rest of it up with his fingers.

"Damn . . . That's a—c'mon, mayne. Quit playin' wit' me." Lil Chris is about to bug up on him.

"Hold up, big boy."

"That ain't no square! That's a toothpick. Is you serious?"

"Don't trip. This is how we doin' it down here." PowwWoww takes the cigarette tobacco from Lil Chris and rolls a cigarette. Then he stops to think.

No, since he kinda feelin' the C'ster, he decides to keep it real and give him the "OG homie loc" treatment. PowwWoww goes in his pocket and pulls out a box of Black & Milds. He gives Lil Chris one of the individually wrapped brown bombers.

Lil Chris takes the cigar out of the wrapper and goes to licking on it.

"Man, why you spittin' all over it?"

"You . . . ? I'm wettin' it. You go'n roll a blunt, huh?"

"Hell, no. You know how much money you can get for the amount of bud it takes to roll a blunt? $200."

"Oh, I thought that's what you gave me the cigar for," Lil Chris says, perplexed.

"Nooo. Be cool. It's enough in this right here to get yo' head straight."

"Well, stop talkin' and put it in the air."

PowwWoww looks around to see who's birddogging. In the pen there are no secrets. Somebody always sees you. Even when you don't see them.

He waits until the chump yells, "Swing it down!" Then he takes the Black Lil Chris has lit and was puffin' on. PowwWoww places the joint in his mouth and lights it with the tip o' the cigar. He takes two long drags and passes it to the C'ster.

Lil Chris takes the burner and pinches it between his thumb and index finger. Brings them to his already purple lips. One long drag. It burns the back of his throat. He almost coughs, but holds it in.

They are walking to their next cut. Another long drag without exhaling. He puts the hot end to one nostril, pinches off the other, and sniffs the smoke coming from the cherry. *This boy is a real smoke dragon.*

He holds it. Holds it. Pressure builds up behind his chest. Head kinda dizzy, spinning . . . He exhales. Can feel the fire leavin' his lungs. One long gush of breath and smoke is all gone. No coughin'. And then . . . nothin'. Damn.

Lil Chris falls in his cut. Bends into the work. *Mayne, this dude a real buster. I know he didn't phade me like that. I wonder if this cat's playin' with me. I oughta split his head with this swing blade. Damn, the headline must've marked this cut too long . . . long . . . wonder what's wrong with that fool. Man, I'm gettin' tired. I ain't finished yet . . . yet? Okay, just a little more to go . . . more to go . . . more to . . . go. Man this shit fire! Dammmmmn.*

He's blowed. Barely tilted. Wholely spliffed out. Standing there trying to act like he's not. Failin' badly.

"Say, Lil Chris, let's go over there." PowwWoww is lookin' in the direction of the cypher.

"Nah, kid. I don't wanna be aroun' all them suckers."

"A lot o' them dudes is real. Man, you trippin'. Let's go." Poww-Woww strikes out walking towards the crowd.

The linepusher calls a 15-minute water break. What the hell. The C'ster moves on, a few steps behind his new rolldog.

The closer he draws to the crowd, the more the beatin' and hummin' is pullin' at his mindset. Lil Chris is feelin' the vibe they got goin', but these ain't his people. He didn't come here to get cool wit' these cats.

He stops to get some water out o' the water cooler. Balancing his plastic white cup, he steps to the outer edge of the cypher. Sips. Intends to just stand there, but the rhythm pulls at his chest. He bobs his head to the beat. Zones all the way out. He takes a few more steps forward. He can barely hear the cat that's rapping. He moves in even closer.

By now, he's in the middle o' the crowd. They're packed in tight, shoulder to shoulder. Heads bobbing in syncopation to the beat. Lil Chris feels someone pokin' his arm. He turns to his right and finds PowwWoww, reachin' him the Black & Mild cigar.

He takes it. Hits it. Dizzy. Head spinning. The pipe tobacco in the bomber pulls smooth. It's got an alright taste and the smoke smells good. Plus, the nicotine is really boosting his high. He's really feelin' the rhythm now. As he exhales gray smoke, he realizes that he has internalized the beat. He can feel it vibratin' in the pit of his stomach. Even in his arms. He can even feel the water vibratin' through the cup in his hand. He takes another toke off the Black. Starts to hand it back to PowwWoww, then pulls it back. *Uh-uh. Gotta tax him for bringing me over here.* With this thought, Lil Chris steps in farther until he finds himself in the center o' the cypher.

It's dusty. The wind blows, picks up sand and sweeps it over the crowd in their dirty state blues, dingy shirts, and work boots. Lil Chris cannot so much see the people but rather feel the press o' the crowd behind him. He's got his head down. Everybody's tryna hear what's being said. More than a few eyes are cast curiously in the C'ster's direction. But he ain't even trippin' off the crowd no more. The heat is oppressive. It's burnin' up. He's sweatin' buckets, but all he can hear, or see, or feel is the music.

He's vibin' with these cats. Before he knows it, the dude next to him is rappin'. Spittin', too. Nice flow. Kinda Jay-Zish, but nice, still. Lil Chris isn't even thinking about rappin', but after this guy tosses around 16 bars, he comes right on in. Second nature.

"Uh . . . Uh . . .

Long and strong
Take a pull

Nicotine enters my mind. Full
   I'm a mask
Prosecution heavy.
   Mind on my task,
Contemplatin'
     To hell with the past. Hear me!
I'ma make the world take heed
        Recognize, playa. It's Lil Chris
Keyed on a masterplan.
Penitentiary got me thinkin'
     Rankin' every goal, while gettin' swollen
I'm an orchestrator. Stay with my mind on my biz.
     Now, go make sure they know what time it is . . ."

At this last statement, the crowed breaks out into whoopin' and hollerin', saying Lil Chris is the best they heard in a long time. Poww-Woww is right behind him. Pats his shoulder and talks shit. He knew this was a live nigga. Lil Chris, though, is just puffin' the Black. Takin' the whole scene in, thinking.

"Hold up, hold up," Lil Chris says. On his MC shits like a true master o' ceremony. "Bring that beat back! Gi' me somethin' to work wit'. Yeah . . . " The beat starts again. "Yeah, Lil Chris in this bitch.

"They got a brother doin' bad
     tryna worry me. Sad!
They've taken my livin'. Young!
Momentarily numb
   To feelin'
Given the profile of a hoodlum
Straight void o' compassion; a bum
Mashin' in scum,
    Poverty stricken in slums
The press'll have you stressin'
Drama givin' occasion; my dilemma
Media moppin' the situation wit' bias venom.

Pitiful how penny hustlers get caught up
    In political dollars
Cloutless
    Now I know!
        What a costly lesson.
Doubtless
    Now, I show flashes of a scholar.
Who'da thought white collars
    Conversate with ballers and shot callers
Revelations are ransom
    Got me sittin' handsome
Fronted; given what I wanted
    Livin' blunted. I never stunted
The state is holdin' me hostage and the
Only thing that'll grant me liberation
    Is the knowledge
        I obtain.
Underrated. My college?
Consequently . . . I been trained.
Now, I'm searchin' for my degree in pain
It's a struggle thing
    The strain, mayne. Reality?
Is barin' down on my back
But, I won't pay attention
'Cause I can't let my high go."

Lil Chris puts *everything* he has into recitin' that particular 16 bars. He channels all of his frustrations, his dejection and depression, his hopes and dreams, his resolve, his faith, his energy, down to his last reserves, into spittin' that verse. From the time the verse jumps off, all you can hear is his voice and the beat and the hum. For that moment in time, he pulls them all in. Speaks words that they all are feeling, but ain't articulate enough to express. He provokes their thoughts. Gives life, in the form of idea. All this with one verse. The power of one voice. He gives them a sure refuge inside of themselves.

After he finishes, there is nothing. Silence. They haven't heard him, per se. But they've experienced every syllable, every word he spoke. In the distance, another voice pierces the silence, bringing them all back to the order of the day.

"Swing it down!"

CHAPTER FIVE

The Clock is so conceited
It doesn't think of anyone
But itself.
The rest of us
Have just been falling in step.
I dare you to let go and live.

THE CAST IRON BARS SLIDE open as Rise steps into the MPO, the main prison's nerve center. He goes to the control booth to check in for the workday with Sergeant Angelwing.

He's in one of his funks this morning. Feels cloudy. But he's learned that it's possible to feel one way and think another. With this in mind, he climbs the stairs to the second floor wing of classrooms, all the time seeking that familiar attitude inside himself. That place where he can reside above his emotions. Still human enough to feel them, to experience them, but clear enough to focus over them. Free to function.

Lil Chris feels jumpy for some reason. He banishes the thought. That ain't gangsta. Continues to nibble on his Snickers bar.

Just outside the fence from where they are walkin', an inmate trustee passes by driving a riding lawnmower. Gray-headed and buff, like maybe he used to lift heavy weights. Probably still does.

A bird is chirpin' somewhere off in the distance. The air is balmy.

He and PowwWoww slide through the Walnut/Hickory gate. Get jammed up at a security station where they checkin' for passes. Lil Chris is spookin'. He just knows the gate man is gonna bust them for cuttin' work call. He's had misgivings since PowwWoww popped up in the dorm after breakfast and talked him into hidin' behind the hobby shop until the fieldlines finished checkin' out.

After getting passes signed for the law library, they shuffle forward a few steps at a time. The prisoners in front of them take off their belts and shoes and empty their pockets before they step through the metal detector and show their passes to the gate man.

Off to the side, he notices another line. More inmates in kitchen whites and denim coveralls. They move nonstop through the West Yard gate from Oak and Pine side like this checkpoint don't apply to them.

A group of 'em catch his attention. They're no different from the rest. Except, as they come up on PowwWoww coming out of the metal detector, they tense up. Look like dogs heeling or some shit, this strain on their faces as they slip by him and through the gate, careful to avoid any incidental contact. Lil Chris frowns, confused for only a second before he has to turn his attention back to his boots and belt and the key sergeant standing at the gate. Fleetingly, he marks the smirk in the gate man's smug expression.

Rise shivers slightly as Ms. Waverly moves past him in the narrow spaces between the rows of student desks. The soft fabric of her blouse brushes his torso. She isn't wearing perfume, but the smell of her coats his lungs. And, for that brief instance when she was close, there was this clear sense of the warmth and weight of her soft mass. But far from lingering on that, he's already bending to hear what one of his students is asking about a math assignment.

Where is Mike? He thinks despairingly. He went around the corner by the club offices for a cup of coffee like 30 minutes ago. Rise glances at the doorway, hoping to find his inmate colleague standing there holding steaming styrofoam cups. Damn shame they have to bum that type of shit. Rise believes, strongly, that the inmate clubs should be donating to the education department. That wouldn't be a handout. More like a reimbursement. Most of the club heads were students at one time or another. Most of their membership still are. Yet, teachers are usually the most underappreciated. Disrespectful mu'fuckas.

"Quarterly testing is coming up," Ms. Waverly is saying. "So you all really need to be working over your needs assessment charts. Let's pull those lower battery scores up."

"Say, Rise." One of the older homies a couple desks down signals for help. The old guy stares, perplexed at a fact/opinion worksheet. *Damn*, Rise thinks. *Why?* One of the hardest things to teach a grown man is the easy difference between fact and opinion.

"You had this down when we went over it yesterday," Rise reminds him, looking over the man's incorrect answers. "How did it get away from you?"

"Man, this shit is crazy," the man stresses. "I thought about what you said. I even went over it in the dorm last night with a few fellas."

"Okay, so you been on it. What's the problem?"

The old guy exhales, exasperated. "Well, you said a fact is something can be proven. Ah, with evidence. And that opinion is just what somebody think."

That's not all of it, Rise thinks. But what he says is, "Uh huh. So what's the problem?"

"Well, I ain't talkin' slick or nothin'. But how can opinion just be what people think? One of the people I talked to last night said that with the right evidence you can start with any opinion and make it a fact. Even a lie. And, I think that's true, too, 'cause that's how the D.A. put a lot of us here in prison."

Rise looks at the old man for a second.

"Okay, big bro," he says. "Let's grind this out."

Lil Chris and PowwWoww stand at the MPO's bars, waiting to get into the Education Building. Lil Chris feels some type o' way about somethin' that happened along their route.

When they passed by the kitchen, PowwWoww stopped in the cut to talk to this wobbly lookin' dude in skin-tight jeans. The skin of his cheek and chin shone like he cleaned it with Magic Shave powder.

Anyway, the whole time they were runnin' it, the dude kept reachin' out and touchin' PowwWoww. On his arm. His elbow. Rubbin' on his shoulder. All the while he was standin' right there with the two of them. They wasn't talkin' about nothin'. The shit just didn't feel right. He files the impression away as the bars slide open, affordin' them entrance into the building.

While everyone else falls into a line leadin' to yet another security station, PowwWoww darts through a door to the right. Lil Chris follows. They go no farther than the stairs down to the entrance to the Law Library, where PowwWoww peeks in and throws the deuces as if to say hello, then turns to head back the other way. As he passes by Lil Chris, PowwWoww mumbles, "Act natural. It's cameras in here. Come on."

At that, he follows him down the hall, up the staircase to the second floor, and down a hallway with four or five classrooms packed with a bunch of fools sitting at desks like they in high school or some shit. Before they get to the end of the hall, PowwWoww stops and pushes through a door that leads to a nice-sized restroom.

"Watch the door," PowwWoww says as he unbuckles his belt.

"Watch the door?" Lil Chris echos, incredulously. "Mayne, if you gotta shit, I'ma go back and wait in the law library."

"Mayne, chill out," PowwWoww says, chucklin' while he shoves his hand down the back of his pants. He comes back out with his hand cupped and steps over to the sink, fishing in his pants pocket with his other hand. The air in the restroom has gone musky. Got the C'ster battling a mixture of revulsion and curiosity.

PowWoww comes out of his pocket with a small plastic bottle of hand sanitizer. By the time he finishes playing with whatever it is in his hand, Lil Chris feels someone push against the door.

"Hol' up," Lil Chris says.

"Who dat?" PowwWoww says.

Neither of them talking loud, but the room's acoustics amplifies their words. Rather than answer up, whoever it is knocks two times.

"Let him in," PowwWoww says.

Lil Chris stands aside.

Black dude. Black, black. Heavy set. Low cut. He walks in and angles straight over to PowwWoww. Not a move wasted.

PowwWoww comes out of the sink with what Lil Chris can now make out as a slim roll of money wrapped tight in plastic.

When he hands it to big boy, he asks, "It's all there?"

PowWoww's face goes cold. "You serious?"

Tension.

Big boy comes out his pocket with a roll of something wrapped in black electric tape. It's thicker than a white boy dick. Where PowwWoww gon' put *that* at?

They make the trade. Big boy leaves.

PowwWoww pulls out some greasy-ass lip balm.

Lil Chris blurts out, "Mayne, you a punk or some'm?"

"Okay, so lets go over it, again," Rise says as he glances at the doorway. Mike still hasn't shown up with the java, but just before he looks away he spots two young dudes passing by. One of them is the kid from orientation a few weeks back. *Damn*, Rise thinks. *Lil daddy in school, already?*

"Fact ain't just what can be proved wit' evidence," the old man says. "A fact is something that is true whether you think it is or not."

"Right," Rise confirms.

"A fact ain't just what can be proved wit' evidence," the old man continues. "A fact is the evidence."

"Now you got it," Rise agrees. "Furthermore, the D.A. is not on the scene when the crime happens. Their job is to collect the facts and draw an opinion about what the facts mean. In court, the facts are like cards in a poker game. They are what they are. You have to build the best hand from what's there."

"Uh-huh. The D.A. can line the facts up like that, to make a lie look like the truth."

"Right, again, big bro," Rise says. "The winner is usually the one who can see the best hand. And, that ain't always the one who has the best hand, my man. That's why those math exercises are so important, too, big bro. Those numbers ain't just for counting. It's not just about memorizing your time tables. With math we gain discipline in our thinking. We learn to see what we can't argue with. And, what we can. The number and the variable. Fact and opinion. Why they say men lie, women lie, numbers don't lie."

The man just looks at Rise this time. With unspoken gratitude. He finally gets it. "The old folks use to ask," he begins, "if a tree fall in the woods and nobody there to hear it, do it make a sound?"

With that, Rise stands up straighter. Mike just showed up with the coffee.

The day drags on painfully slow. Thankfully, his work assignment is an enterprise from which he can draw some sense of fulfillment. The student prisoners often leave him drained. He's learned that it is possible to teach an old dog new tricks, but the effort is hard labor.

Presently, he's been at his desk for some time talking to Gary Law. G, as he's simply referred to, is a political prisoner. He's a casualty of the south's turbulent reorganizing program, a living reminder of the consequences of the nation's move from the oppression of Jim Crow to Civil Rights inclusion.

It is said that prison preserves the inmate like a time capsule. Gary Law is no exception to this. He's aged well. After 37 years of incarceration, no feature remains of the 16-year-old who had to fight his way off death row. However, as a benefit of healthy choices, G is a surprisingly fit, dark-skinned, robust version of his old self. The only things about him that betray his age are a carefully groomed salt-and-pepper beard, his old-school shag haircut, and the contrasting depth of his striking blue eyes.

As G talks, Rise's mind drifts. He can see the sun set beyond the second-story window. Where G stands in front of the window, his face and torso are partially silhouetted in Rise's vision. When G moves slightly to the left or right, the sunlight flashes directly into Rise's face. The winking effect can be strenuous on the eyes, but the occurrence is . . . stimulating.

"You understand what I'm saying," G asks, penetrating Rise's thoughts.

"Yeah, I feel you," Rise replies dismissively.

"You see," G complains. "That's what I'm talking about . . . "

Rise drifts back into the heat of the sunset. The sky is ablaze with reds, pinks, whites, and the hottest yellows. His mind naturally begins to concoct lyrics.

I watch the sunset

Through my second-story window

> *Blue sky. Kinda cloudy out.*

Penny for your thoughts . . .

He looks to the sky for more insight. The horizon is pitch-black, jagged and severed along the shadowy treeline. A reddish pink is predominant among the sunset.

"Rise! . . . Rise!!!"

"Huh?" Rise jumps and almost falls out of his swivel chair. "What's up, G!"

Gary Law doesn't like to be ignored. He leans over the desk, all up in Rise's grill. When G gets excited it's hard for him to talk around his dentures. The result is a small spray of spittle with every word, which Rise catches in the face.

Rise looks up as Sergeant Angelwing and Major Mercury walk into the classroom, along with Captain Casper, whom most prisoners call Big Will.

"Big Will," G says, a ready smile plastered across his face. "How y'all doin' this evening?"

Rise trains his face to stonegrill, hiding from G more so than the officers. Doesn't serve to show this man he respects how much disdain he feels to see G shuffle every time security comes around.

"Making sure you not hidin' out in here with one of my female officers," Big Will says. "The two of you ain't hangin' around tryin' to trap, huh?"

"C'mon, Big Will," G tucks his head a bit, frustrated. "I told you that was a' isolated incident. The women in this building are some of the most professional officers you have." He tries not to look at Sergeant Angelwing, but can't help to steal a glance.

What's up wit' this, Rise wonders as Sergeant Angelwing writes he and G's names down on the stickout count. He especially doesn't like the way Major Mercury is watching him.

"Okay, you can go back to whatever you were doing," Big Will says as he and the other officers leave the room.

"What up wit' that?" Rise asks.

G holds up a finger, careful to let the security guards move out of ear shot. "They found Bolo yesterday in the Literary Arts office, hugged up with Ms. Green. Walk right down on 'em."

"Oh, so that's why Bolo's in the dungeon," Rise says. "I just got word this morning he was sending for me. No one said why."

"They walked Ms. Green down the walk in handcuffs," G says with some consternation. Ms. Green was one of the club's sponsors, and a friend. He turns his attention back to Rise.

"What's your problem, son? I'm tellin' you something' you need to listen to . . . You're a leader, youngster. Not because I see it in you or because you've managed to educate yourself in those cellblocks. You're a leader because the people chose you. Because they identify with you. The eyes of those hardheads watch your every move. The old 'victs respect your mind and your jacket. But, you gotta get it together. You wander off at times. I've watched your eyes and noticed you checking out in a crowd, surrounded by well-wishers—and snakes. Rise, you're gonna have to stabilize yourself. Stay focused. You remember a while back, I spoke to you about the zeitgeist?"

"Yeah, the spirit of the times." Rise just wants G to know he's paying attention. If only barely. Still chewing on the Bolo situation. Wrestling, a bit, with G's code-shifting.

"Okay, well the spirit will tend to suck you in and thrust you into position. Whether you're ready or not. Irregardless to what you want. The zeitgeist is upon us, now. You need to be aware of this."

Now, Rise is listening. "What are you jibbin' 'bout, G? I told you. No movement without me. Okay. Now I see. You had an agenda from the moment you broke the door seal."

Gary Law knows his people. Reads well. He smiles inside at Rise's selective alertness. The boy is a dreamer. Often times the same thing you come to love about a person becomes the thing you hate. The very thing that draws you, if not watched, will push you away. Choose to accept a person, gotta take the good with the bad.

Gary Law forges on with the reason he actually came to speak with Rise. "The Skies Over Gaza has been taking the initiative to unify the heads of various inmate clubs under one board. The purpose being to concentrate energies and resources towards one goal: parole eligibility. As it stands, a Louisiana life sentence means life. The decision has been made to take over P.C.P.A." G watches Rise closely for his reaction.

"You mean the chess—"

"Yeah. The Prison Chess Players Association."

"Why?" Rise is the picture of composure.

"Because it's a rat's nest and a haven for predators. Not to mention, in the past they have been a constant opponent to any efforts to unify inmate organizations."

"Uh huh, I see."

"Okay . . . " G falters a bit. "So I know you see the logic in that, but—"

"But you already knew all that prior to today," Rise interjects. "So, why the take-over?"

"The chess players have become our main disturbance. They're causing too many problems with our efforts to unify this prison population."

Rise ponders this. "What kind of campaign would it be?"

"Bureaucratic," G is quick to answer. "No muscle."

"Why am I just finding out about this?" Rise wrestles with this. "More importantly, why am I being told after the decision has already been made?"

"Rise, now, remember, for all your influence, to most of the guys you're still just a youngster." G shows some chagrin here, but presses. "S.O.G. operates on a need-to-know basis. And, to be honest, until the decision was made you didn't need to know."

"Then why tell me now?"

"Because, you have been selected to participate. Security will definitely try to protect them. But against who? You and a few others aren't known for this type of maneuvering. They won't see you. Plus, afterward, the club's presidency will be your post." G watches, still.

It's times like this that Rise is reminded that Gary Law is not one of the broken ones. Far from it. For decades, G was one of the most respected voices on the prison farm. A known revolutionary. In the 60s and 70s sense of the term. Dreadlocks and rough rhetoric. Not to mention buff from powerlifting, and known to throw his weight around.

His plight was well known: falsely accused of a murder he didn't commit. The whole incident undeniably connected to the southern school desegregation program. Amnesty International recognized him on its list of political prisoners. But his support on the streets was feeble at best. Never really mainstream. Over time, the community he spoke for so powerfully allowed his memory to fade. Had some notable mentions in a few books. A couple soul songs, lamentation and a cautionary tale. For all that, he was practically alone.

The turning point was his late 80s campaign to gain a pardon from the governor. All of the evidence of police tampering and collusion, witnesses to the hours-long beating he suffered during interrogation, and only 15 years of age at the time. It was all laid before the state's governor and pardon boards on petition to correct the injustice. The legal lynching, they called it.

They ultimately denied him. Worse, the governor told the newspapers they denied him because after decades in prison, G still hadn't earned a G.E.D. No one mentioned that during that time officials wouldn't allow him to enroll in the prison's education program. That he'd had to educate himself in those death row cells they'd refused for years to release him from. That he was only still alive because of a moratorium on death sentences in the late 70s. As if a downgrade from death to a life sentence was lenient enough for the likes of him. After all that, G changed his tactics. Adopted a new strategy. Stopped openly fighting a system bent on crushing him.

No. Not one of the broken ones. Far from it.

Rise gives him nothing. "Okay, G."

"Do you know what this means?" Gary Law asks him.

"Yeah, it means you all have finally decided to deal me in," Rise says matter-of-factly.

Gary Law stands and looks directly into his eyes. He holds his gaze for a moment. "The zeitgeist," he says. As he turns to go, he adds, "The spirit of the times, my boy. The spirit of the times."

Rise is left to listen to his own thoughts. He hadn't sought out
S.O.G. They came to him. The spirit of the times? Maybe a sign of the
times. He can handle this.

He rolls back from the tan and chrome desk in his swivel chair.
The desk's metal compartment drawer squeaks as he pulls it toward
him. He pulls his notepad off a small stack of mathematics papers he
needs to grade. Cuffs a pencil out from among the thumbtacks, staples,
and paperclips.

He pulls back up to the desk. Lays his notepad open to a fresh
page. Props his left elbow on the desk as he leans forward, places his
index finger on his temple, his thumb at his jawline. His grandfather
used to focus in this position. It's a reflex for Rise.

He strums the desktop with the fingers of his right hand and ro-
tates the pad so the paper is almost upside down. He's left-handed.

He picks up the pen and begins to write:

We stood I and I
Two men beneath the sun
Free minds in a captive land
    Conscious
He spit when he spoke
    And a spray of his spittle did touch my lips
        I'm overcome by
    My sense of awareness
        He gave me truth.
Rise
Have you any passion inside left
    For this rugged ride
Your proof of purchase ain't at issue
    Perfect your walk. Be your . . .
Wages of labor recompensed
    From this system of servitude that we've been

Toilin' under . . .
Trigger my journey over.

CHAPTER SIX

Don't be so foolish
 And hold on to—these games you like to play.
 'Cause I've been takin' my time.
   To make you feel comfortable enough
     To say what you gotta say.
 Do you have something that you would
     Like to tell me, girl?
 'Cause I've been
     Obsessin' about you
     Wonderin' what to do
       Over and over to
     Finally get through to you
     I see how you look at me
 Your eyes are sayin' what you really
     Wanna do wit' me

And I . . . I've been
Thinking about you.

He waits on the shift to change. Of course, the C'ster would never admit it. Not to nobody. But he is really feelin' Sergeant Havoc. It's a real trip to him how his whole mindset changes when she works the dormitory. Lately, they've been havin' him twisted. Because she's been assigned to another dormitory way on the other end of the walk.

Lil Chris being the G that he is, he violates and walks down to the other end. Stands on the dormitory ledge. Just to get a glimpse of her. His problem is biological. He's barely over 20. Hormones bouncin' all over the place. Shit on the inside workin' against him. His problem ain't discipline. It's scientific. He has a biological need to get his swerve on.

The dormitory ledge is full, from one end to the other, with young cats and old 'victs. Some sittin', some standin' up. Some stand in the yard. Some are on the ground, leanin' up against the elevated walkway as she passes by.

He sees Sergeant Havoc look out on the thick sprinkling of bodies in the prison yard. Some tall. Some short. Some slim. Some big. Some are strikin' poses with their shirts off. Some still filthy from the day's field labor. Some stand by themselves, tryin' to be seen. Some stand in a crowd, tryin' not to stand out.

Wait, did she just see him looking at her? Where he's standin' here by the iron pile? Shirt off? She turns her head away, real quick-like. Trains her eyes straight ahead.

Somewhere in the background someone calls her name. Others, too, are sayin' hello or some other lame shit. Anything to get a smile. She turns her head back for a sec to quiet 'em down. A slight head nod. A smile or some shit.

Right now, his wheels are turnin' up there. He follows her trek and sees that she's assigned to his dorm tonight. He's got 12 hours to say whatever it is he has to say. He chews on this when she steps into his dorm to relieve the officer on duty.

Lil Chris walks in the dorm pulling his shirt over his head. He struggles to keep his composure. He already filled out a pass to go to the gym and left it on the desk. His intention had been to go out on the yard and watch Sergeant Havoc walk down the walk, see which dorm she's in. Then come back to pick up his pass and head out. Believe, he couldn't get back to his dorm fast enough when he found out where she would be for the night.

She sees him standin' in the back of the throng surroundin' her desk. Waitin' for her to finish fillin' out the logbook so she can sign their pass for the night's outing. She steals a few glances at him as she looks up to give or receive the small slips of paper.

Damn, look at her eyes! What the hell kinda color is that? Ah nawl, I got to get at her, Lil Chris thinks to himself. *She go'n just have to send me. Tonight, girl. Tonight, I'ma speak my mind.*

All the other men have cleared out.

"How you doin' Sarge?"

"Fine. What's up with you?" She returns.

"I'm straight." *A little too emphatic. Damn!* "I mean, I'm cool. Just another day in the joint," He recovers. "So you chillin' wit' us, tonight?"

"Yeah," she smiles. "I'll be here with you, tonight."

Did she just give him a little under-eyed glance? *Boy, that's cold. I know she just didn't do me that,* Lil Chris thinks.

He's tongue-tied. Damn. All he can manage to get out is, "Uh-huh." *Come on, soul!*

Sergeant Havoc leans back in her chair and folds her arm across her chest. She looks up at the C'ster and says with a straight face, "You stay out of trouble, tonight, ah . . . Mr. Lil Chris."

He smirks. "Anything could happen at any time 'round this muthafucka."

"Yeah, you right about that," she says with a smile.

The door swings open for callout. Lil Chris leaves without a word goodbye.

They are all crowded at the entrance gate to the main prison's gym. Some have come to work out. Some to play ball. Some to shoot pool. Some are here just to congregate and hook up with they boys from the other yard.

However, the main thing on e'rybody mind is checkin' out this new cat from off Walnut and Hickory side. Most of the pocket conversations goin' on are whispered impressions about big boy with the nice flow and the fresh fish complex.

Lil Chris don't even notice all the frequent hawkin' and peekin' aimed at him. If he does, he's gotten used to it and ain't paying attention. He has this environment all figured out now. Roughly two months in. He sees that 80-percent of these cats don't want no part of trouble. The majority are cowards and the few solid dudes remaining are really focused on givin' their time back and touchin' the streets.

There are a few real threats and he understands that he just has to keep his circle small and his grass cut. In other words, as long as he limits his number of associates and keeps his business in order, he'll be good. Whatever is for him, good or bad, bring it. As long as he can see it approaching, it's not a problem.

The old 'vics tend to say that this ain't "penitentiary," it's "pay attention." Lil Chris is the proverbial kind of G that everybody knows. So, in this sense, he's in his element. Got his footing. Ready for whatever. Got a feel for them, now it's time to make sure they feel him. Huh?!

At the moment, he's standing on the wall with his two rolldogs, PowwWoww and Wayne. The three of them are cut partners. PowwWoww to his left and Wayne to his right at work call. They state down: state-issue blue jeans, brown brogans, and blue button-downs. Most of the cats with time in wear free-world clothes. Basically the same type of work gear, but state issue is just that. It's manufactured in prison, by prisoners. Even a state-issue white t-shirt has a distinct look. Such being the case, Lil Chris and his folks are uncomfortable as hell. But whatever comes easy for a go-getter. They all face forward, a brick wall against their backs.

For his part, it ain't what he got on. It's how he wears it. Lil Chris got his afro picked out, his blue button-down riding open, white t-shirt hanging, and he's sagging his jeans so hard his belt is on his thighs. His pant legs bunch over the top and around the heel of his loose-laced, untied state bros. As usual, he's g'ed up from head to toe. His face oozin' self-confidence. And he's only two months in? Standin' there lookin' like, "Dammit, I'm fly."

The keyman comes to open the gate. After a few others, he calls for Lil Chris's housin' unit to walk through. It's time to get his shine on. Once again.

Rise has been in the gym for the last hour or so with his two friends, Pam and Peggy Sue. Two 60-pound dumbbells, cast iron with that. Solid. Brownish grey and ugly. He likes to rub and kiss on them between sets. Fifteen reps or more. He's doing the burnout portion of his chest, shoulder, and bicep routine. Sweating it out. Loving the heat and adrenaline high.

He looks up and sees the crowd pouring into the gymnasium for evening callout. He sits and watches. Waves his fist from time to time when a familiar face looks his way. Pounds his chest to signify lion love when one of the true homies comes through the booth entrance.

He spots the young brother, Lil Chris, that everyone has been talking about. *Lil daddy just got here and he already makin' noise.* Rise knows he could be a soul-jah.

He turns his attention back to his exercise. Takes a breath and exhales as his left arm curls Pam to his left shoulder. Inhales as he uncurls and brings Pam back to his side. He exhales as his right arm curls Peggy Sue to his right shoulder. Inhales as he brings her back to his side. Repeats the process. *Repetition. Make it burn. Work through it. Gotta be able to move on with the pain. Keep going till you can't go no more. Gotta break through the pain threshold. Breathe to help cope with the pressure.* He zones out . . .

Gotta breathe, he tells himself. His whole body trembles. All of his muscles are tense. The back of his head, neck, and upper back are tight from straining, stress, and pressure. He tries to remain calm. Sits in this little box. But every so often his pulse increases, his breathing becomes ragged, and he goes into physical and emotional convulsions.

He throws silent tantrums. Tosses his head back and shakes it side to side, up and down. Flails his arms and legs out. Kicks and punches and clutches his throat and chest. Through all of this, he barely even whimpers. He doesn't want to alarm anybody on the cellblock. No one need know of these demons he's wrestling with. But it hurts. It hurts all over. And nowhere at all.

He's scared. He pulls himself together. *Gotta stay cool.* He knows if he loses it, he might never get it back. Gotta keep his composure. He thinks of the people he's seen that have gone crazy in these cells. He remembers the pity he felt looking at them.

No! Not him. They can save they sympathy. He knows he's a fighter. *To hell wit' 'em.* His heart is beating so hard and fast that it feels like it could burst his chest open. But how can that be? How can his heart be beating when it's broken? So broken. It'll never be whole again. He's sure of this.

The tier orderly slides a tray of food in the cell hatch. *Gotta eat*, he tells himself. *Gotta have strength to live.* He keeps telling himself to eat, but when he thinks of functioning, he begins to shake so hard the spoon bounces off the tray and onto the filthy floor.

Then he sees the bird again. A sparrow. How did it get in the cellblock anyway? Maybe his love has been reincarnated. His eyes and forehead burn as tears strain forth. Never drop past his lashes. He blinks them back. Too real to whine.

Now he knows he's trippin'. He'll never see his love on this side again. He understands that. A calm descends on him with this acceptance. He still has a long way to go, but he's on his way. *Gotta live two lives.* For the both of them.

He looks at the spoon on the filthy floor. His mind is starting to clear and rational thoughts are starting to prompt and provoke him. He glances at the bird again. Closes his eyes and begins to thank God for the hurt and the pain and the tribulation. His forehead wrinkles with thought. He looks back at that sparrow, so small sitting up there on that air vent.

Though he doesn't recognize or taste the food, he begins to eat as much of it as he can with his hand. His chest shudders and his face squinches up. He mumbles softly and incoherently. He begins to shovel the food, whatever it is, into his mouth. Determined to complete this simplest of tasks.

Need food for strength, and strength to live. Gotta live two lives. Gotta function. He notices that bird again as he forces down the last mouthful.

Gotta function. Now, breathe. Breathe. Breathe . . . Acceptance . . .

The cast iron clangs against the metal on the weight bench. He can hardly gain his breath. Can't muster enough energy to curl either arm anymore. His whole upper body is on fire as he drops the 60-pounders to the floor, shaking the gym.

His head is light. Almost spinning. He feels good. *Breathe.*

Rise is about to fill his water jug and leave, but he sees the cypher over by the water bucket. He decides to walk over and see what the new jacks are working with.

Lil Chris ain't even spit yet. He's basically chillin'. They got some vibrant cats up in here. He's just vibin' on their flavor. Once again, PowwWoww got him in that zone. PowwWoww has proved to be a solid dude. Him and Lil Chris done started thuggin' together on the daily. Both of them are like way too gansta. PowwWoww likes to get Lil Chris loaded and just listen to him flow. He draws a sense of pride from bein' able to say his rolldog is the dopest lyricist on the river. Anyway, Lil Chris has been peerin' out the eye of the cypher trippin' off the cat curling the dumbbells. Dude was over there wiggin' out.

All o' the sudden, they switch the beat. The homie 2 Times beats on the tin bleachers. He brings a live complicated drum track, uses his fist for the bass kick. A bush comb doubles for the snare and the hat. The way that bush comb lick echoes all over the gym puts the C'ster's semi-sedated mind in a trance. Then somebody starts humming the bass line to that old school 2Pac, "Ambitionz Az a Ridah."

About four more people pick up the hum and it goes to soundin' like a' incantation or some shit. Spiritual. Soul-stirrin'. The effect has Lil Chris standin' there wit' his head tilted back and his eyes closed. The music is inside of him. Vibrates in his stomach. He sways with it. Nods. There's this mug on his face that has him frownin' so hard his bottom lip pokes out.

By this time, everyone in the area is lookin' at him. The spectacle of it all. Curious grimaces on their faces as if they're twisting on a Rubik's cube. By this time Rise has climbed up on the top row of the bleachers. He's sitting close to the edge. From this vantage point he's able to see right down into the center of the cypher, where the rappers are standing. There has got to be like 75 inmates or more surroundin' here. And he can see that all eyes are on Lil Chris.

PowwWoww grabs Lil Chris by the shoulder and says, "That's you right there, kid. Go head, bless 'em."

The beat and hum done married each other. Not too loud. Just loud enough to sit aroun' his flow. But Lil Chris ain't trippin' off none of that. He feels the clang of the bush comb lick echo in his head. As he steps to the middle of the cypher he pictures himself comin' in behind the legendary Tupac hisself. Gotta bring it. He bobs his head with the hum, gets his timin' together.

Pickin' up on the one, he lets his voice boom:

"Shots rang out, the spot's
        hot, blades and heaters do damage
Who can manage without they Glocks cocked
Smoke screens!
        Evidence of the days we blaze. Hazy
Got me reminiscent of crazy ways
                Was wicked
        On the block where the regulars kick it
        Spot it and hit it
        Profit off the top when we get it
So if you thinkin' about steppin' to get your caps on
Strap on one o' dem nice-sized 'g' things
        Or be content on gettin' yo' nap on . . . "

At about this time, Rise hops down to the floor and steps in, leaving
Lil Chris staring at him.
    "My God!
        Navigate my steps
                Make 'em pure and precise
    Sure to entice moves, inducin' profitable life
    Reciprocity's hard, they ain't givin' us nothin'
    Can't they see my peoples tryna have somethin'
                        For real, though
    Exploitation's the norm
        Playin' on my niggas' need for cash
    I can hear 'em laugh when they come
        Capture me. Slave livin' fillin' my days
        Now, I'm stressin'. Got kids to raise
    Oh, you ain't know
            We breed
                Seeds in the struggle.
                        Hustle for what they need
        Lead my freed homies

Down to scuffle and bleed.
Apparitions of my lost ones
Hauntin' me now
Beatin' me down
Look at me mob
Mugs and frowns
Sittin' heavy wit' my disposition
Talk to my ghost wishin'
They ain't have to leave, me y'all
I can recall how we rolled and balled.
Reppin' the set, throw it up
Nothin' mattered by my g's and dawgs . . . "

Right here, they switch the beat a little bit and one of the dudes
starts to hum the bass line to Mystikal's "Here I Go." It takes a few
bars for everyone else to catch on. The change-up makes Rise fall off.
The crowd doesn't know it, though. It's pandemonium! Everybody is
like, "One more round, one more round!"

The cypher is officially a classic. Rise is one of the most recognizable rappers in the can, a living legend for the showings he's put down
over the years on the river. Lil Chris ain't no joke, though. The boy is
a beast.

A couple o' people have mumbled conversations in the background, but that will die down when the lyrics start. Everyone looks at
Lil Chris and Rise expectantly.

Suddenly, Lil Chris steps up with his arms raised out in front of
him. Waves and rocks to the Mystikal bass line. Concentrates on the
bush comb lick for his timin'. He laces the beat:

"Now when they caught
My nigga slippin' in '93 it fucked me up
Nothin' but BG's surroundin' me
Layin' deep off in the cut
Come up
Money and murder

We done slipped and hit a gangsta lick
Ain't nothin' but the hustlah in me
     That make my mind tick
Now, I know of a OG, he taught me how to
       Make my mail
Nigga don't ask for no credit
   I ain't got nothin' but dope for sell, playa
Comin' up, and it's like that, livin' phat.
   Carry two 44-calibers in my backpack
These hustlin' and strivin' days
   Kept a playa paid
In many ways
   I'm a slave for my trade
Still I stayed
   A young "G" tryna keep his game tight
Hearing' voices tellin' me 'Lil Chris get ya muthafuckin'
      Money right!
I was addicted to hustlin'
   Nigga, you know that fast money
     Equals cash money minus strugglin'
Recollect what the fuck I'm talkin' bout, nigga
   And burn a pouch, will ya . . . "

Rise comes in:
"Dried tears got my face
    white and ashy
  Sweat tracing da stains
Suffer pain tryna maintain
   Dream o' life at its peak!
I seek out truth
   Speak out o' youth. Evolution
From sheltered innocence to disillusioned.
Meant to be scorn

But I live in the storm
                    My yesterday's neighbors
Probably torn, no conceivable future,
Past detrimental. Mental hopeful
                    But still discouraged
Tryna
          Fathom they purpose
                    Please, tell 'em it's worth it.
We all was adolescent and lively
                    Until the killin' started
Scarfaced influence rendered focus distorted
Turned to powder
          Mitigated responses. The sirens infiltrated
Conspiracy presence; informants.
          Suffocated essence
Got us all searching for freedom, but hol' up!
How can we fight for manumission
          When we don't know what
                    Disenfranchised is?
All we know is we ain't happy here
My brother's suicide betrays the dissatisfaction
                    With which we live."

At this, Rise shoves his way through a stricken and mesmerized crowd. He leaves the building.

Lil Chris turns to PowwWoww and says, "Damn. That nigga dope."

When Lil Chris goes in, he sees Sergeant Havoc standing at the door talkin' to Captain Henry. Big white dude, late 40s or early 50s, probably played every sport offered at his old, back-country high school. Now, he's fallen victim to the Dunlap syndrome. His belly done lapped over his belt. Real cheesy shit.

Every shift got a ring o' supervisors that pressure they female subordinates into breakin' it off. It's just the way it is. Maybe she's tryna move up in rank, or maybe she wants an easy drop assignment, or maybe she simply wanna keep her job. Whatever her button is—be it price, vice, or fear—this con ring got ways o' findin' out how to penetrate her defenses in order to push it. Captain Henry is a ringleader.

Lil Chris done been peepin' him workin' on Sergeant Havoc for some time now. She still ain't broke. That's unusual. He's getting frustrated. She knows how to think.

"Alright, now, there, Sergeant Havoc," Captain Henry says. "Don't hastate to call if you need me."

"I told you. I don't want to be worrying you. Your regular rounds are good enough."

"Okay, but remember I offered. Don't be so quick to turn down a helping hand."

"I'm just trying to be self-reliant, sir. No need to trouble you about stuff I can take care of myself." With this, Sergeant Havoc turns and walks back to her desk. Leaves the captain standing at the door.

Captain Henry turns and walks away. As far as he is concerned, Lil Chris guesses, there is only one thing that could stop her from getting' involved wit' a' upstanding man like hisself: *She must be lovin' one of these inmates.*

Lil Chris passes right by Captain Henry, wearing an old school bucket hat low over his eyes. High as the price o' gasoline. Full of them trees. She sits at the desk, talkin' on the phone. He's the last in a line of five prisoners returnin' from callouts.

After Rise left, the cypher broke up, so he had a chance to get a quick workout in before leavin' the gym. Not to mention PowwWoww burned two more sugar bags wit' him. He's feelin' alright, indeed. Already thinkin' about what he's go'n say to her tonight.

She frisks each returnin' prisoner and gets their bed number to log them on her count. As Lil Chris walks up, she studies him. She gives him the strong impression she can tell that he's more than a little disoriented.

"Take that cap off and turn around," she says in her most professional voice. Seeing him like this seems to annoy her.

He turns around and holds his arms out. When she grabs his shoulders his muscles flinch, and she pauses. She keeps her head down and don't look at him, but she felt him. He knows. When she runs her hands over his chest and belly, aroun' his waistline, he moans. She can't so much hear it as much as she can feel the way it makes his body vibrate under her hands. She keeps her head pointed toward the dorm, hiding her face while she finishes. She rubs down his legs and pats his butt when she's through.

Lil Chris feels like a heavyweight champ. For that treatment he would go out the door and come back in four more times. For tonight, though, one is cool. He struts through the dorm feelin' kind of good, for real. Although he ain't been in the penitentiary more than two months, he spent roughly 19 months in the parish jail before being shipped down south. The slightest contact wit' a woman like what just happened, especially in his elevated mind state, is thoroughly enjoyable, to say the least.

When he makes it to his bed area, he slides his footlocker out and pulls his night gear and cosmetics bag out of the sheet metal boxes. He kicks off his boots and slides on his sandals. Takes his shirt off for good measure. Gotta get his floss on. Looks nice from all that field labor and working out.

He grabs his shower shoes and heads for the shower. Flexes hard as he passes by her desk. She don't look up. That's cold-blooded. He spins the bend and steps behind the shower wall.

When he finishes, 45 minutes later, she's still there, probably overhearin' loud conversations pouring out of the shower area. They talk about some of the stupidest shit. And argue about nonsense! She wouldn't have heard anyone address him by name, though, in all that time.

When he swings the corner, he's in sandals and cut-off shorts. No shirt. Still has a little water on his back. As he passes, she gets up to turn the blue lights on. It's about ten minutes until lights-out. Before long, the dorm is dark. Movement slows to a minimum. Work call in the morning.

For now, there are two people in the TV room and one in the game room.

Lil Chris sits on his bed with a pillow and blanket over his lap writing another verse. That cat Rise really made him feel somethin' tonight. He's tryna go deep wit' this one.

> I used to blow the buda smoke
> > Out my nose
> Murder, I heard her poppin'
> > Forgot to separate the weed from seeds
> My victim,
> > Backwoods covered with maple droppings
> > > Slow-burner for the thick smoke
> > > > Breeze wit' ease, when we hit 'em
> Scandalous
> > Can't handle this, I have to dismantle this,
> > > Roll a fatty for my reefer thoughts
> That backburner got me stressed out,
> > A nickel leaf wasn't big enough
> > > So I had to roll the whole pouch
> I'm queasy
> > Needy for mine, hustlin' ain't easy

No. That's alright, but not what he's reachin' for tonight. Not at all. He leans over the paper, tries to focus past the high. Inside the high.

Black Fubu boots and black pants step into view. When he looks up, Sergeant Havoc stands over him. Trying to read what he's writing. Now that he's aware of her presence, he can smell the faintest scent of her perfume, even wit' the fan blowin' from behind him. The fragrance has his head spinnin'.

"What are you writing?" she asks.

"Just a couple of thoughts," he returns.

"Is that a rap?"

"Yeah."

"That's the first time I've seen it written like that. When they quote raps in the magazines, they look different. That looks like poetry."

"I know what you mean. I've been writing music since I was 12. This style just developed over the years."

"How old are you?!"

Gives her a dumb look. "Why?" he asks.

"I was just wondering. You mentioned writing since you're 12, but if you don't want to—"

"20."

"Dang, you young. Can I ask you how much time you have?"

"Life."

"Ooh, that's sad."

His anger flares. "Get off from over me wit' that. Save ya' sympathy. I'll holla at cha."

"Damn." She's suddenly indignant. "Why you talk to me like that?"

"That's how you handled yourself."

Silence.

"Well, okay, my bad. I didn't mean to offend you—"

"You didn't," he cuts her off. "I just don't dig . . . People say shit that sounds right. That's fake. Keep it ghuttah."

Silence.

"Anyway," she looks around. Checkin'. He can tell she's starting to feel comfortable. She rolls her eyes and gives him a smirk. "What are you in for?"

"Murder. First-degree."

"Ooh. Did you do it?"

"Hold up. What is this? Twenty questions or some shit?"

Unshaken. "I'm sayin' . . . well . . . you in here, now—"

"Yeah, but if I was to ask you some questions about yo'self, you would try to handle me like—like . . . a sucka."

She just stands there and looks at him. "You don't know that," she says.

"Come on, don't play games wit' me." She's blowin' his high.

"No, seriously. I mean, normally I would. But, hell, who you go'n tell? You don't talk to nobody."

He studies her for a few heartbeats. Vaguely wonders what made her stop to talk to him. "Okay, well, who am I talkin' to, then?"

"What you mean? Man, you know who I am."

"No. What's your name? I'm asking a question." He looks at her. Proves his point. "You want to ask me all kinds of personal shit, but you don't even respect me enough to tell me your name. Come on, man—"

"Where you see a man at?"

"I don't know. What's your name, huh? Derrick Havoc?" He smiles.

They both laugh a bit and then look around to see if they woke anyone up. The fan's hum is pretty insistent, though. Kind o' loud. No one's even stirrin'. Lil Chris looks at her as if for the first time. Like, really looks at her. He's diggin' her, for real. *And*, he thinks, *she can see it*. But what she's doin' doesn't make sense. He intended to be the one approaching her. *Must've took too long . . .*

She bites her bottom lip. Stains her front teeth with cherry lip gloss. Looks around the dorm, again. He senses that if she tells him her name, it crosses some kind of line. She looks in his eyes. He stares directly back into hers.

"Veronica. My people call me Roni." She waits to see how he act.

"Roni, huh? I'm feelin' that, Veronica."

"Oh, you feel that, huh?" She stammers when she speaks. Damn.

"How old are you?"

"Boy, you don't ask a woman her age. I'm 25."

"Yeah? What's your sign?" He works a devilish smile.

"You crazy . . . I'm a Scorpio."

"Oh, okay," he says. Nods. "So *that's* what the deal is."

"So that's *what* deal?" she asks all uptight.

"Y'all freaky."

"Boy! I ain't freaky!"

"Shhh, shh! What you doin'? Chill out," he reminds her.
They both laugh.

On the other side of the penitentiary, Rise wakes up smiling. It's the middle of the night. He was just pedaling up that steep hill on Milam Avenue along the fence-line sidewalk next to the golf course. He was pumping his brother who sat on the seat behind him. They were on a royal blue and grey ten-speed bike with chrome and the racer handlebars.

When he got home he had some good clothes on. Some cream-colored Girbaud jeans. A dark brown, pullover polo shirt, and dark brown, pointed-toe dress shoes made of some kind of reptile skin. He is sure that it wasn't a dream. It was some sort of twisted prophecy.

He fishes under the cot as he sits up. He grabs his pen and pad from on top of his footlocker. Suddenly, somethin' that Pusshead said to him yesterday has rushed to his mind. He scrambles to scribble it down before he forgets it.

Ninety-percent of success is knowing *exactly* what you want. The other ten-percent is the how-to.

SECOND VERSE

One year, six months later

CHAPTER SEVEN

We do these things
 'Cause we have to
When we put in work
 It ain't personal
It's all about respect
   For the game.
If you gotta squab
 You gotta squab
    Don't just think about it
Or, get caught slippin'
 'Cause that nigga know the same thing.

THE WIND IS A COMFORTABLE breeze.

The mood is settled, yet the sky cries out. Moving grays play over clean patches of white, to stirring effect. Then the rain comes.

Underneath it all, the fieldlines toil. The linepushers refuse to call "headline." Not until the last vegetable is pulled from the dirt. The workers are weary of gettin' soaked, but most of 'em feel they need the mobility they have in population. Few would give up what little ground they've gained since leavin' the cellblocks. So they keep pickin'. Others, who don't have sense enough to strategize, continue pickin', because although they may deny it vehemently, they are followers by nature.

Lil Chris is among the laboring ranks. Like so many others here, he tends to closely scrutinize the minute, but doesn't understand enough to make out the bigger picture. Not yet.

The wind is stronger now. It whips at his blue state-issue button-down. The shirt is too thin to offer any cover from the chill. He shivers. Too mad to speak. Deathly cold, inside and out. He is conscious that these conditions are meant to kill something inside of him. He knows this because he feels whatever it is strugglin' to live. The whole time, he wonders how it is possible that this shit could be happening. In the same society that claims to have placed him here for breakin' the law. Modern day slavery.

Almost two years have passed since he arrived. He has heard it said often that the punishment should fit the crime. That the life sentence is justified when the prosecution has shown that somebody is incapable of functionin' in society. That there is absolutely no way to fix him. How could that apply to him? He cannot yet put it into words, but it is clear to him that something about the so-called criminal justice system is fucked up.

And the rain comes. It falls so hard it stings the skin. It beats down on their heads. It rains so hard the whole area takes on a gray tint.

As the workers march in, they have to hold the back of each other's shirts in order to keep up. The line is a loosely linked wreckage of its usually disciplined double-file order.

"Boy, you stay writing, huh." It's a statement. More so than a question.

"Yeah."

"Why?"

"I don't know. It's how I, you know, express a lot of things that be on my mind."

Lil Chris has not so much matured as chilled out. He's still a little wild, but he doesn't have the complex. He's been back and forth to the dungeon for minor shit, but he's managed to stay out o' any real drama. At least, up until now. In the joint, it is often said, anything can happen at any time. And it usually does. The trick is to not get caught off-guard.

"Well, look. Put ya pen down for a second. I need to run sump'n by you."

"Catch me later. I need to finish this thought before it get away from me," Lil Chris says. Looks up for the first time to acknowledge PowwWoww.

"No, I think you go'n wanna hear this. You need to be on top just in case sump'n jumps." PowwWoww is adamant.

"Just . . . let me finish . . . writing this . . . last . . . few . . . Alright, what you got?" Lil Chris asks, laying his pen down.

For the first time, now, the C'ster is really paying attention to PowwWoww. Whateva it is he has to drop, it ain't good.

"Say, C, some foul shit being said about our boy."

"Who dat? Wayne?"

"Yeah. They got some things in the wind that's go'n have to be dealt with."

"Like what!" Lil Chris starts to get twisted. This can't be nothin' good.

"The word is that they got a few cats playin' games wit' him."

It dawns on Lil Chris like black smoke. "What kinda—you mean . . ."

"Yeah. Booty bandits. They at him."

"Nah, I don't believe that," Lil Chris says. His face don't show it, but he's burnt. Like major.

"Don't act like no fresh fish, man. If it's in the wind it don't matter if it's true or not. The vultures circling."

Lil Chris frowns in disgust. "You talkin' 'bout what niggas think? I don't care nothin' 'bout what niggas think. In my eyes he a man."

PowwWoww gets frustrated. "You steady tah'm 'bout you, you, you. This ain't 'bout you or what you th—"

"Man I know wh—"

"No! You don't know. If you did, you would know that the lil homie gotta handle his business. It's all about *respect*. Even if it ain't true. If he don't make a showin', that's what's go'n hurt him. In the end, that's what's go'n be remembered."

Lil Chris calms down. "That nigga a man, PowwWoww."

"May be. But that ain't the issue. He have to make a showin'. Point blank. He gotta live amongst these dudes. This will follow him. Without respect, ain't no peace. People go'n steal from him. Talk crazy to him. Mess over him. Play ass games wit' him for real!" PowwWoww is adamant.

"Ah man, come—"

"You hear what I'm tellin' you?! If he don't face this thing head-on, he'll never have no peace. If he let this go, it won't go away. He go'n stay in some bullshit. The pride he do have will keep him fightin'. Constantly. That's how it goes. If he don't nip it in the bud, they go'n keep comin' at him. Minor nitpick shit. Until he breaks one way or another. Either he will have to hurt one real bad. Or, he'll start runnin'. And he run, they go'n run him until he gets tired. Next thing you know, he be a—"

"Go'n wit that, PowwWoww!" Lil Chris is trippin'. He's never given this any thought. He's known the wolves were there, but all that exists outside his world.

His homeboys, though, are his team. He doesn't have but a few.

Loyalty, duty . . . he doesn't even think about these things. They're second nature. Now, they fucking with Wayne. He 'bout to wig out.

"A turn out. What? This is the joint," PowwWoww mashes his point home. "The big house. Ain't nothin' nice. And everybody gets tried sometime."

"Not me! I wish a ni—"

"Man, we need to get at Wayne. Quick."

"Well, let's go then," Lil Chris is already up and walkin'.

"Hold up, m—"

"No, ain't no hold up," Lil Chris calls over his shoulder. "Catch up! We 'bout to take care o' this."

With that, they go lookin' for Wayne.

There is a knight on D-6 and another on F-6 that should have long been captured.

There is a bishop on E-5, as well as a rook on C-1. The H file is open, except for the white king on H-8 and his pawn on H-7. There is another white pawn on F-7. The white queen is on G-6, stacking the white rook on G-8 . . .

It's black's move. His house is in order. There are three pawns, from A to C across rank 2. The black king sits comfortably on B-1. Gotta have your house in order.

Wayne studies the board. The game should have been over, but he likes to play with his food before he eats it. He already cleared out the whole of white's king's side of the board, then sacrificed his queen to a pawn on F-6 just to give his opponent a false sense of hope. Wayne punishes trash talkers severely. Otherwise, he would have already beat the beginner and put him out of his misery.

The dude Wayne is playing is typical. So typical. Six-three, around 200ish. Fat, Black, bald, dusty, loud. All muscle and no brain. The guy is unable to reconcile the admiration he has for Wayne, who appears to be considerably weaker than him and all. That is, if one goes by appearances. So, he's using the chess game as a sounding board to shoot all kind of foul remarks Wayne's way. So typical.

As Wayne ponders his next move, Lil Chris and PowwWoww walk into the game room. Something about Wayne's calm demeanor slows and settles them for the moment. Plus, the two of them know they need to keep a low profile. They're out of bounds. In Wayne's dormitory. Both of them full of cannabinoids. Riding dirty.

Wayne sees four moves ahead. He's playing his opponent for just one logical move and then another mistake.

Wayne's opponent, for his part, focuses on PowwWoww and Lil Chris. He knows Wayne is their homeboy. He's going to really act bad now. He intends to drive all three of them by handling their boy Wayne like a chump. For him, this is the height of aspiration. Mental gymnastics. So typical.

"Come on, chump. What, is you scared?! Dat's why I hate playin' you lil boys." He frowns and glares at Wayne. Really about to mash on him. Hard.

Lil Chris pulls a chair up to the table. Sits where he can see both sides of the board. He doesn't understand much about the game. He's just readin' on instinct. Looks back and forth, from the chessboard to each player's face. His disposition is cool, calm, and collected. Exaggerated nonchalance. The reefer they rolled, slim like toothpicks, is what did it. The indo' pinhead he and PowwWoww just finished has his head swirlin'. He just sits and chills. And listens.

"Look! What time is it? You need to do something! Oh, you can't think under pressure, huh?"

Wayne doesn't say a word. No response. He concentrates on the last two pieces he needs to consider. The white bishop on E-3. Problem piece. It needs to be lured out of the way. And the black rook on F-1. Significant. This will be the anchor piece for his strategy. He jumps one of the black knights from F-6 to E-8. Never takes his eyes off the board.

The guy grabs the white queen and lines it up with the bishop, places it on G-5.

Lil Chris takes the white queen and puts it back on G-6. Impulse. He points insistently at the black bishop and says, "You in check."

"What?!"

"Discover check," Wayne says without taking his eyes off the board.

"Say, my man," the guys says, talking to Lil Chris. "Stay out my game."

PowwWoww, who's been leaning against the plexiglass behind Wayne's chair, shifts from one leg to the other.

The guy looks back to Wayne and the board. Says, "Speak up, fool! What you want me to do? Read your mind. You better learn how to talk!" At this, he moves the white rook up to block the check, places it on G-7.

"Touch and move," Lil Chris says, a little too quickly, but still calm. "He gotta use his queen. Move that bitch!"

"Don't worry about it," Wayne says, more to Lil Chris than to his opponent.

The guy mean-mugs Lil Chris. With a boot in his mouth he says, "A'ight? I done told you. Get out my business."

The C'ster doesn't respond.

Wayne starts, "Look, brother, don't worry—"

"Well, play then! Your move," the guy cuts Wayne off. "Coward! I don't need you tellin' me what to worry about."

Wayne keeps a level head. Like he don't speak English. Or rather, bullshit. That rook moved up to G-7 was the one logical move he had anticipated. Now, he needs to run the bishop out of position. He'll let him keep his queen.

He takes his other knight from D-6 and drops it on F-5, thus putting double black offensive on the white rook blocking check. Two knights. Plus, one of them is threatening his white bishop. All this with one maneuver. Tantalizing. Wayne can actually taste the turmoil and confusion in his opponent's mind. Watch, he'll do something stupid.

"See, that's what I'm tah'm bout, right there, lil boy," the guy says. "You had me, but you ain't got no killa instinct. *Oh*, that's right! You a coward." He laughs hysterically.

PowwWoww looks around to see where the freeman's at. He catches the keys all the way in the back of the dorm, eating tuna fish sandwiches with another prisoner, who incidentally runs a store out of his footlocker.

The dude in front of Wayne is still laughing and putting his finger in Wayne's face. Yelling, "You a coward, lil boy. You ain't got no killa instinct!"

Lil Chris just sits there with his elbows propped on his knees, resting his chin in his palms. His face shows no emotion.

The dude leans over the board and says, "Now, watch this, chump." He moves the white bishop down to capture the black rook on C-1. He says, "You through, lil boy . . . Busta!" Giggles. Cackles, really. And glares at Wayne.

Still, Wayne says nothing. He keeps his eyes glued to the board. Okay, he was able to successfully run his opponent's white bishop. The guy's capture of the black rook was overly aggressive. Dislodged him. He's playing into Wayne's hands. Best thing to do now is go ahead and remove the white bishop, thus eliminating that problem altogether.

"Black king captures white bishop on C-1," Wayne says with almost no emotion at all.

The guy moves the white queen up and says, "Check."

Wayne moves his king back to B-1 to sit comfortably out of the line of fire.

Now, the guy frowns and really studies the board for the first time. He tries to figure out what his best move would be from this point. He feels that as long as he has his queen he can win. He studies the board a moment longer. Too pigheaded to consider the possibility that his own house may still be in danger. He decides to move the white king from H-8 to G-8, in order to free up his rook to attack.

Wayne hops his knight from E-8 to F-6. "Check."

The guys moves his king to F-8. Probably doesn't want to block his rook again.

That did it! He fell for the okey-doke. This was the mistake Wayne was waiting on him to make. A mistake Wayne saw ten moves ago. Wayne moves the black bishop to D-6. Finally he holds his head up. He looks the guy right in the eye. With a smile on his face, Wayne nods and says, "Checkmate."

The dude stands up from the table. Before he can say anything, Lil Chris swings up and hammers him with a strong right. The guy hits the floor and folds up.

The C'ster doesn't say a word. He just commences to kickin' him, stompin' his face. The guy bleeds all over the concrete floor.

Eventually, PowwWoww gets his attention. Signals. Lil Chris steps over the guy's prone body and tracks his blood to the door. He walks out of the dormitory like nothing ever happened.

By the time Major Brooks and five other officers catch up with Lil Chris, he's already packed and ready to ride out.

The guy he touched up told the authorities that he didn't know why Christopher Darell struck out at him.

CHAPTER EIGHT

People say one thing

  And mean another
. . . If we could
    take a chance with each other
          But, we can't, though,
                Can we?
And so we play the game
    Actin' all strange
    Everything changes
        Now, we can't take it
              Nothing is the same.
And so our bond breaks
Forever didn't last
          For always.

THEY SIT AT THE TABLE staring at each other.

She's wearing light brown felt jeans that hug her phat apple bottom, flat tummy, and ample hips. The summery red blouse, cut low to show off her girlish bosom, undermines his resolve. Been seducing him since she walked into the visitation shed. Some matching red and brown, open-toed wedges complete the outfit. Adds to her height and overall erotic mojo. She's sexy and curvy, but not what you would consider a brick house. Her mystique is not that insistent. Or provocative. Her beauty, style, and appeal are more subtle. Delicate. Sensual. Her skin is peaches-and-cream, with a coffee-brown sprinkle of freckles. Her hair is long, rich black, French braided to the back with red highlights. And, her eyes—this girl's eyes are a deep, sparkling hazel. Breathtakingly gorgeous. Without question. Gorgeous.

Shonda.

He is as he always is. Not really conservative. Just him. His everyday-everyday. White t-shirt, loose fitting blue jeans, blue and white Adidas shelltoes. But there is so much going on in Rise's mind right now. He's strategizing. Refiguring. Analyzing the ills of life. Considering damage control. Dissecting the characters that surround him. Gauging their capabilities. Grading their initiative. Choosing where best to invest effort.

He looks at her and wonders how he could think of anything else in her presence. Life is way too hectic. Too complicated to allow even one moment to pass without careful scrutiny. So much of his life has just . . . passed by. So much of this existence has been dictated to him. Someone else was always making the decisions in times past. Someone else has always had the power, *his* power, in their hands. His having been swept up in a world that wouldn't even wait for him to grow up.

Shonda reaches out and takes Rise's hand. "Oschuwon. What's up with you, boo? It always seems like you're somewhere else. Sometimes I wonder if you even want to see me. Do you miss me at all when I'm gone?"

"Shh. You know that's nonsense," Rise reassures her. "I miss you from the moment you leave till the time you return."

"Then, why are you always so distracted?" Shonda is plaintive. "I don't just visit this place for you. I come 'cause I need to get away from the—"

"Well, *I* can't get away." Rise cuts her off. His words cut into her. "I'm fightin' to live in here. I—" He considers what he's doing, what he's about to say. "I'm sorry, love." He sees the hurt and frustration in her eyes. "I apologize, baby. I didn't mean to take it—"

"No." Now, Shonda interrupts him. "That, too. I'm here for that, too. I'm trying to help you, Oschuwon. But I need you to understand me. I need to understand you. Stop drifting away from me. Tell me. What's going on?"

Shonda looks to Rise for some kind of confirmation that she's gotten through to him. He purses his lips to suppress the impulse to speak. She hates when he does that.

She looks around the visitation shed. At all of the little kids running and hopping and jumping. At all the security personnel walking through the building. All constant reminders that her Oschuwon can't come back home with her when she leaves. At the many families, mostly minorities from all over the state, and even some from out of state, who have travelled way back here in the woods. For no other reason than to see their brother, their daddy, their son. Determined to maintain family ties, even under the extremely uncomfortable conditions they have to endure just to make it to the very tables they sit at now. So much spite. So much emotional exhaustion. Then, the very people that they come to see are often so aggravated that they don't make for good company at all.

So many obstacles to happiness.

In a fit of frustrated defiance, Shonda shifts in her chair. Moving toward Rise, she says, "Forget it, then. Uh, Rise, look." She grabs his arm and pulls it around her. "Just hold me, baby."

Rise feels Shonda's soft warmth as she leans on him and wiggles until she's comfortable. Smells her scent. Sweet, sweet recourse. "That's all you wanted, anyway," Rise laughs. "Ya lil freaky tail."

He looks down on her head. Sees her the way he did at 11, so many long years ago. He barely noticed her at first. She used to hang out with his sister, Shonetta. Both of 'em used to wear them wild unruly ponytails and get off into everything.

Shonda and Shonetta were both at the house when the incident happened. They were in the back room playing when they heard pots and pans crashing and clanging. Sounded like they were falling to the floor or being thrown around the kitchen. The small house was little more than a wood frame lifted off the ground on cement blocks. The standard home in the hood.

Rise was out back, fixing up a blue and chrome Mongoose bicycle. He had just got the flat tire repaired when Shonda and Shonetta ran out the back door crying.

"What's wrong wit y'all?"

Neither of the girls could speak past a mumbled word or two.

"Oh . . . Ricky done made it home, huh," Rise said, totally understanding what was going on. "Y'all go on aroun' to Shonda's house and stay inside."

Rise, who everyone still called Won back then, watched as the two girls ran out of the backyard and through the trail that led to Shonda's. He was in no rush. He didn't understand why his moms always allowed Ricky back, considering the way they fought, and after she went through so much to put him out. It had been years now. His moms and Ricky fought so much that it no longer evoked a sense of urgency in him. He used to get jittery. Afraid he would be next. But his moms never let that happen. She wasn't Ricky's punching bag; she was a worthy, sometimes active opponent in these confrontations. Although most often she came out the worst for it.

Rise got so angry after these episodes. That anger gave way to a feeling of being powerless and helpless. And helplessness to desperation, at times. He was desperate to stop what was happening to his moms. As a former Black Panther, she had taught him so much about self-worth and confidence and social responsibility. She had made him feel he was exceptional. Not only that, she nurtured a sense of belonging in him, made him feel part of a golden lineage, impressed upon him the notion that his life had purpose. That he was obligated to discover and fulfill his design. To see her in a relationship that was the very opposite of everything she taught him to be cut him deep. Of course, at his age, he did not understand enough to fully comprehend this contradiction. He felt it, though. He wanted it to stop. He was desperate for it to stop.

Rise stirs. Shonda picks lint or something off his shirt. She feels so good leaning on him. Right now, though, he's too distracted to entertain her. Even after all these years, his mind is still aflame with memories.

"You okay, baby?" Shonda asks.

"Yeah I'm cool, shorty."

Her head is nestled in his chest. His arm rests protectively around her. Enfolds her. They sit in silence watching the goings-on in the visiting shed.

Delayed effect. "I'm not short!" She pouts as she playfully punches him in the stomach. His chest rumbles under her as he snickers, but his mind is in turmoil.

He pictures himself all those years ago, matter-of-factly walking up the steps and opening the rear screen door. He almost feels the weight of the stainless steel, vise-grip pliers in his hand, the ones he'd been using on the bike. He was so intent on seeing about his moms, he'd thoughtlessly carried the tool into the house with him.

Everything happened so fast. He merely reacted.

When he stepped inside, it was as though he could feel them scuffling. It spoke to him through the plank board floor moving beneath his feet. As he turned out of the washroom into the dark main hallway, he caught sight of Ricky dragging his moms by her foot through their bedroom doorway. At first, all he could do was stand there watching the rug bunch up beneath her. She kicked at him with her free foot, trying to break free.

She was half-dressed. She still had on her tan work pants, stockings, and her black belt, but her blouse was gone. Only a black bra, and one of its straps had popped.

Rise was a real skinny kid at 15. Tall and lanky. When Ricky looked up and saw him standing in the hallway, he reached down to grab at his moms's arms. She swiped at his hands, scratching him as she spit in his face. Ricky started kicking her and punching her, like he was fighting a man. Right in front of Rise.

His moms never screamed. She gritted her teeth, grunted, and continued to struggle.

He called out, "Ma!"

Through the tussling, she managed to say, "Won, get out o' here!"

Rise didn't retreat. For some reason, he couldn't. He took measure of the scene. Saw his mother on her back, refusing to lie still. Scuffling. Swinging back as best she could. He felt the weight of the steel tool in his hand. But he also felt so powerless.

Then he heard the solid thud of Ricky's licks finding their mark, flush in the center of his moms's bosom. The impact of the blows pushed an uncharacteristic sound from her lips. Sharp, high-pitched. A whimper. A distressed whimper had escaped her lips. A subtle sound, but it struck Rise like a scream. Desperation gave way to resolution. Rise began to move. It is said that the journey of a thousand miles starts with one first step. Movement is the dividing line between what could have been and what is. Rise moved.

He walked over to where they were getting at each other. He tried exactly one time to pull Ricky away from his moms.

Ricky swung wildly, knocked Rise into the wall. The sheetrock caved in behind him. That's when Rise wigged out. He commenced to beating on Ricky's head with those stainless steel vise grips.

Ricky grabbed Rise. Started choking him. Rise took his time and got a better grip on the handle of the wrench. He struggled to stay conscious. Ricky had both hands around his neck, pressing in on his throat. Rise gagged, panicked. He raised the vise grips and swung, and kept swinging. He didn't stop until he couldn't lift his arm anymore. That's when he finally heard her ruined voice. His moms had been screaming so loud, and for so long, she had gone hoarse.

"Fried fish and grits," she says.

"Fried fish and grits?!"

"Yeah! What's wrong with that?" she asks. So demure and innocent.

"I'm cool with that if that's your thang."

"Well, yeah, it *is* my thing," she rushes to answer. "Or, excuse me, my *thaaang*. Y'so country. This whole *state* is country." She feels like playing. So sassy.

"Man . . . "

"'Man?' Where yo 'man' at?" She corrects him. Smiles.

"I'm sayin', you ain't went and got pregnant on me, huh?"

She gasps. His question has caught her totally off guard. He sees her hold her head down for a moment as if she is suddenly aware of all the people standing around them. The white-top counter where they're standing, waiting to order something to eat, is waist-high. She plays with the little salt-and-pepper baggies that are in the pan in front of her, sitting next to the toothpick dispenser. He watches as the heated feelings wash over her, ignited by the implications of his question.

When she musters enough courage to look up at Rise, her eyes are searching, but he turns to talk to some guys. He feels her studying his face, but he's masked. No emotion. Suddenly, he glances down protectively to where she's standing at his side.

He tries to smile, reassuring her, but his cheeks and lips only clench. The expression can't break past his stonegrill. No emotion, except for his eyes, straining to tell her he's waiting on her answer. He turns back to the people he's talking to. She smiles.

After a moment, the crowd Rise consults with disperses and he embraces the last guy to leave. She's close enough to hear their parting exchange: "To touch without feeling is the ultimate sin," the guy says. "Far worse than blasphemy," Rise replies.

With that, the last guy leaves. This isn't the first time she has heard this exchange.

Just as she is about to ask what they mean by it, the concession worker walks up to her and asks, "What are you having?"

"Fried fish and grits."

He knows he confuses her. He aggravates her. He knows she's passionately in love with him.

She notices things about Rise that have been getting by her. Not just the physical features that signal aging and maturation. But also his demeanor. This dispassionate approach to almost everything.

He remembers the terrible crush she's had on him since she was nine years old. She wanted so much to be his one and only. His wife. Even back then. She and Shonetta have been friends for as long as either of them can remember. Rise, being four years older, has always been fiercely protective of them both. Still, she's always had her own designs concerning what type of relationship she and her Oschuwon would eventually have.

When she was ten, she hung up on other girls' faces whenever they called for him.

"*Won ain't here!*" That's *if* they got that much.

Oh, and it wasn't a secret. She made her feelings known on several occasions. He never took advantage of them. He was careful not to embarrass her. When she threw tantrums for all her frustration, he would placate her.

She was Shonetta's company, but somehow she was always on hand to offer any assistance her Oschuwon might need. It was in her bedroom that Rise hid out for three days after he served his momma's boyfriend.

That day, she'd had a bad feeling. A foreboding. When he came running up through the trail, she stepped out into the opening to meet him. Later, it was her phone he used to call his momma. When he found that his moms was still twisted about the whole situation, Shonda walked behind him, even though he repeatedly told her to go home. She followed him all the way to the police station the night he turned himself in.

Oh, she was a little soul-jah. She wouldn't let him see her shed a tear. But afterward, she was broken. She cried for days, Shonetta told him.

She's been with him ever since, through the highs and lows. The system claimed them both. Him, and her because of him. She was in the stands when the juvenile court gave him juvenile life, meaning until he turned 21. She was also at the first visit to the boy's home and reform school, when he and his momma reconciled after three years. That was when they shared their first kiss. She pecked Rise on the cheek. She was 14.

They began to write to each other after that. She recognized early on that the place was hardening him. She rode with his moms and Shonetta when they visited. Sometimes he just sat up and frowned the whole visit. He did this so much that she ended up bugging up on him. She tagged him twice in the face before his momma managed to pull her off him. He never swung back or defended himself. He just sat there like a statue and withstood the onslaught of her frustration.

This really gassed her up. She couldn't calm herself down. Eventually, the guards stopped the visit. She was lucky they didn't pull her off his visiting list. Shonetta and his momma knew she was in love with him. They let it go unsaid.

In a letter she received from him three days later, he opened up to her. He had written and mailed it the night after he'd seen her. He wrote about the corruption inside the facility. About how the guards invented all types of techniques to torture the young prisoners at their whim. About the way the whole set-up fostered conflict and enmity between the juveniles. How it was nothing for two of them to be pitted against each other like young gladiators while the guards stood and watched.

Rise was forced to grow up in this environment. At 18, because of his stature and prowess as a fighter, he was looked up to by most of the youngsters locked up with him. The facility checked all the letters he mailed, leaving the envelopes Scotch-taped but unsealed. This made it easy for his momma to read all his letters to Shonda before passing them on. Shonda knew this, but since his momma never brought it up, neither did she.

Still, Shonda noticed during their visits that his momma renewed her conversations with him about what manhood meant, its strange rites of passage for Black boys. She and Shonetta sat silently at the table for hours listening to these exchanges. She saw that Rise responded enthusiastically to this uptick in the attention he was getting from his momma.

His momma sent him literature from all kinds of enlightening authors. He was intensely drawn to his momma. His sense of self-confidence grew. He became so respectful. So protective of them all. He wanted to know everything that was going on with them. He began to speak of the streets and freedom again. Everything looked as if it were going to be all right.

Then, out of nowhere, there was a riot at the facility. In the aftermath, several young prisoners and correctional officers were injured. One officer was killed. Rise was tried and convicted for the guard's death. Given life. Transferred to the state penitentiary. All in a whirlwind of consequence.

Rise remained closed-mouthed and silent through the whole process. He had been within two years of his release date. Now, he would face a true life sentence. He was 19 years old when he first set foot on this prison farm. Louisiana's prison city, Angola.

"So, you go'n answer my question or what?"

"What question?"

"Come on, man. You been actin' like a punk all visit. All sad-eyed and such. What's up with that?"

"I'll answer your question when you answer mine," she replies.

"What question?"

"Why you questioning me? Who you supposed to be, my man or something?"

Rise just sits there with his mouth open, staring at her with a look of utter bewilderment. A detailed picture of the perplexity that has seized him.

She gives him a pucker-lipped smile. "That's what I thought. Get it on back, then, and, uh, baby . . . close ya damn mouth." She reaches over to place a piece of the chocolate she's been eating on his tongue.

CHAPTER NINE

Creation!
> I ain't lyin'
>> I swear I hear
>> The beauty of the Nile
>>> From my cellblocks.
> Starin' through my bars
>> Contemplation
> Invaded visions of virtual nautical shocks.
>> My adversaries bangin' on my walls
>>> Who did it?
>> I ain't guilty, no!
` > Feelin' cheated, I fall.
>> Crocodiles draggin' me.

Oh!
> The agony of accusation

My uninhibited pleas.
Shake the heavens
Why y'all lyin' on me?
Maat!

HE STANDS AT THE CELL bars, runnin' it:
"Picture the world
outside of my cell bars, light rain
Doin' 'bout 80 on the interstate
Blowin' out my carburetor.
I got a 7-9 Chevy
With a 454 engine
And I'm tryna get it
Spinnin'. Kick in!
America's Nightmare in the tape deck
Spile 1 talkin' to me.
I'm mashin'
Streetlights passin'
Spirit o' the homies in the backseat
Pushin' me
Muffler blastin'
Car jumpin', cylinders pumpin'
It's all good
Got an insurance settlement
Moved out the hood. Premature
Cash flow splurgin'
Done put a dent in my wallet
Now, holla at me.
I can't call it
I need a hustle
Man!
I'm bent. The life of an alcoholic

> Wit' a weed fetish
> Roll seeds and all.
> Poppin'; I'm burnin' holes in my clothes
> That ain't stopping me, though.
> I'll probably roll.
> About four blunts
> Str-8 skunk
> Wit' a shot of Jack Black
> Puffin' it all
> Smoke film, stainin' the wall
> Who can relate, this is how we ball
> What?!
> Die!"

They love it so much they beat their applause on the wall-mounted iron desks in each cell. Lil Chris done been in these two-man cells for five weeks now. The dungeon. Administrative segregation. The middle ground, between drops. No cosmetics. Hygiene is wrecked. They shower and rub soap under they armpits. No radio. No television. Nothin' to read besides religious papers, law work, and personal mail. Cell confinement for 23 hours and 45 minutes a day. Exactly 15 minutes to shower.

The disciplinary board took 90 days good time, gave him eight days extra-duty, and sent the C'ster to the working cellblocks. The inmate counsel told him he lucked up 'cause he could have been sent to Camp J or some other extended lockdown. One-man cells. Twenty-three hours a day for months—even years—in a cage.

PowwWoww has been having the homies smuggle tobacco, deodorant, soap, candy bars, Black & Mild cigars, and of course two or three sugar bags of bud a week into the cellblock for Lil Chris.

Word got out that Billy Black snitched and told them that the C'ster snuck him, slid him, and stomped him. That's why they ain't even blow the yard. They just came straight to Lil Chris's dorm. That's how he got an aggravated fight instead of a rule-ten simple fight. For the footwork. He stomped him. The free folks also charged Lil Chris with Billy Black's medical fees.

Billy Black got his issue. PowwWoww, who's from New Orleans, couldn't even get to him when they sent him back down the walk from the dungeon. Lil Chris's "round the ways" from Shreveport put the boy in a *Soul Train* line. Everywhere he rolled his property, somebody from the home team rode him out. They put the word out on the homie hotline. The C'ster wasn't even hanging with his rounds when he was in population. He was seen as a stand-up nigga, though. So they stood up for him. The Port City homies touched Billy Black at every camp he transferred to. Until he went ahead and caught a one-man cell on a protection tier. He'll be there until Lil Chris makes it out of the blocks. That's how that goes.

Now, Chris is on the backlog list waitin' on a bunk to open in one of the workin' cellblock units. Until that happens, he'll be doing what he's doin' at the moment.

"If given a nickel
    for my troubled thoughts
I'll reveal humble petitions
      To powers that be
Stand in agreement for the fury it brought
    Cold part about it
    I was righteous, this whole affair
        Is shady.
What manner of man
    Could hand
      True reproach to a prophet!
Tell me his heart is pure
    Stop it!
I ain't tryna hear your practical probes
Ill-intended to fish me for the meanings
    Of epistles I wrote
      Ponder parables

I got issues
   Y'all don't hear me, I'm worried
      I ain't see the pen for months
      Shaken by what was spoken
  My distracted dreams hindered
            Habitations.
Unable to reach back
      I was copin'
    Mode of action was open
Squeeze off like
    Demagogues
Utterances spoke with flashes of age
    Must be changin' my ways
Hear me populace
    Nah, they ain't right!
Break to the city of habitation
    And pray for vindication
      In seven days!
        Maat!"

"Damn! Who was that?"

"I think that was cell 7?"

"Say 7 . . . cell 7!"

"Wow!"

"Say, mayne . . . that was you?!"

"Uh-uhn. I think that was, ah . . . 8! Cell 8!"

"Nawl, dog. That wasn't me, but I know who it was."

"Say, ah . . . Lil Playa . . . Lil, ah!"

"Don't try me, nigga! You know my name. My name Lil Chris!"

"My bad. My bad, lil homie," Bama says, in his high-pitched, almost childish, breathy voice. "Don't take it like that. I wouldn't never disrespect you, ya heard me? I just was tryna find you. What cell you in?"

"I'm in 9," Lil Chris says.

Another voice from further down says, "No, that wasn't Lil Chris. That dude in cell 8 lyin'! That was him!"

"That's rattin'!" Someone shouts.

Everybody breaks out laughing.

"I knew you was a rat, Kay Ray!"

"Don't play wit' me wit' no rat jacket, fool! I'm tellin' you right now, don't play wit' me like that!"

"Boy, ain't no secret! You know you been eatin' cheese. Don't stunt now, potnah! You done did that."

Everybody gets quiet. Pregnant silence. Listenin'.

They 'bout to trip.

"I done told you, whoever you is, don't play wit' me like that—"

"You know who this is," the voice cuts him off. "This Sanrock! Now tell me you don't know me."

"Sanrock? Nawl, I don't know no Sanrock," Kay Ray responds. "Where I suppose to know you from?"

"Oh, you don't know me, huh?" Every word spoken is crystal clear. Piercing the silence.

They're listening. Everyone.

"So, that's how you go'n play it, huh?"

A snicker comes from up front. A giggle in the back.

"Alright! Didn't you work in the captain's office? You was a clerk or somethin'."

"Yeah, but that don't mean . . . "

Somebody says, "Ah, man!" Condemnation.

"Hold up, y'all! Hold up," Sanrock says. He's tryna keep control of the situation. He loves exposin' these chumps. "Y'all be cool. Peep. Check this out," he says insistently. "Kay Ray, you was in Pine 1, huh?"

"Yeah."

"Well, I was in there, too. You sho' you don't 'membah me?"

"No. I told you I don't know you."

Silence.

"Check . . . In '99, around September, they found a shank in the air vent in the shower—"

"Mayne, that was umpteen years ago!"

"Yeah, but you remember, huh?" Sanrock asks portentously. "Chill out. You was messin' with that homo, ah TinaBoy, huh?"

"Yeah! He was for me."

"Or was it that y'all was for each other!"

"What?! Fool, you know who I am? I'm Kay Ray—"

"—I know who you is! I was workin' in the shower area. I caught y'all flip-floppin' back there!"

The tier erupts. Cats is shakin' the cell doors and beating down! Real boisterous laughter. All kinds of laughs sound out. If what was said wasn't all that funny, the laughing itself was infectious.

"You 'membah me now, huh!"

No response.

"You 'membah y'all set me up?! You know, by right, *both* of y'all was supposed to be for me, huh!"

No response.

"So you put that black diamond on my drop, and turned around and played the people on me, huh! That's rattin', huh? Ain't that rattin'?"

Some snickering in the background. Bar fighting. Plain and simple. Bar fighting. Some stray giggles, then silence. They'll be throwing shit on each other when they make it to extended lockdown.

"Say, cell 8!" Bama calls from cell 10.

"What's hap'nin'?" he answers. Bama can hear the smile in his voice.

"Was that you, my man? I'm just tryna find out 'cause if it was, I liked that! You ah . . . ah, you es'spressas yo'self good."

"What? Rappin'? That wa'n't me, big bro. That was my cellie. Say cellie," he calls out. Beating on the bunk to get his cellie's attention. "Go'n head holla at them people, cellie."

"Say, Bama," his cellie says. "This me, man."

Lil Chris is in cell 9 paying attention. He knew it was cell 8 that was rappin'. But which one of the two in there? He listens to Bama to find out the name of the rappin' cellie.

"Who that!" Bama gets excited. "That's No Love, huh?"

Now Lil Chris gets it. No Love must be the second dude in cell 8. The rapper.

"Yeah!" No Love replies.

"Lil Chris! . . . Lil Chris! Say, lil bro!" Bama beats on the wall in cell 10. "Ain't you from Shreveport?!"

"Yeah. Anna Street. Thirty-one hunned block!"

"Lakeside," Bama exclaims. "That's yo homie, No Love! Y'all homeboys! No Love yo' 'round, Lil Chris!"

Ole Bama, he was one of the truest.

Another day in the cellblocks.

Thug life!

Rise walks through the door of the Main Prison Law Library, already tired. He's gotten plenty of sleep, but still he's tired. It's always like this when it comes to law work. Just the thought of it makes him weary.

He spots Gary Law stepping away from one of the dusty old shelves. The old guy looks alert and as resolute as ever.

"What's goin' on, G?"

"Everything's cool, lil brotha," G answers before clearing his throat. "You finally here to check out the new cases come down, huh?"

Rise dips his head a bit. G knows he hates this part of it. Which happens to be the most important part. His silent gesture is answer enough.

"Gimme a minute," G says. "I'll run you off a copy. Just lemme grab this criminal code for that man over there."

Rise takes note of the old 'vict sitting over by the typewriters. He's seen him several times before. Knows the type. The bald spot is an island at the crown of his head, surrounded by a halo of gray hair. The well-worn pair of reading glasses hanging from his neck on a faded brown shoe strap pulled from long-gone state brogans.

The old man could probably quote every noteworthy court ruling published in the last 20 years from memory. And he's probably sent every bit of 10, 12 lucky fools home. All out of the kindness of his heart and his commitment to just results. He just as likely is 10, 12 times bitter because not one of them ever looked back to lend him a helping hand.

G walks over and hands the man a green-covered, annotated volume of the state code of criminal procedures. That done, he heads for the computers and printers situated along the back wall. Rise joins him there.

As G clocks through the case law, Rise sits back in his chair. One guy kidnapped a girlfriend and boyfriend, then made the boyfriend watch while he raped the girl. Another dude killed his grandfather. Another one molested his nephew. Two or three more murders. Then an attempted murder.

This is exactly why Rise hates law work. It's not the studying, since reading and writing are second nature to him. It's having to read over the most heinous, despicable crimes imaginable, then having to consider his own actions in that context. The whole enterprise always leaves him feeling like a lesser version of himself for having the criminal act in common with these people.

He exhales expressively as G hands him the stack of case law. "Anything in particular I should focus on?"

"Actually, there is," G says. "U.S. Supreme Court. Another Strickland application. This one relevant to you."

Rise frowns. Strickland? Ineffective assistance of counsel. Nothing to do with his guilt or innocence. This would be about whether he had adequate legal aid. Always a really hard one to prove and will definitely take a lot of time and effort to develop.

Gary Law knows Rise's case. Been helping him with it for years. "Major?"

"Gonna take alot of work," G confirms. But, twice, he nods. "Yes, this could be major for you."

Rise braces himself. If this is what he's been waiting on, he'll almost certainly need a lawyer to represent it. A lawyer that will cost money. Money he absolutely doesn't have and doesn't know how he'll find.

Still, he clamps down on his misgivings and focuses on the only thing he knows for sure he can do.

Grind.

They really clicked.

Their first conversation lasted all through the night. They've been in the same places. The odd thing is, although they're both relatively young—No Love is 30, Lil Chris 22—they're still from two different generations.

No Love grew up under old heads. Got the game from the last playas and macks. The real ones. He was a humble student first. Had to pay his dues. Now that he's older, he has a sum of game stack to deal from.

Lil Chris was a ghetto star. Street fame. Spotlight. All-hood first team, first selection. When he was super young, the OGs used to stay running him off the corner. He couldn't hang out with the big homies. He wouldn't accept the subordination that was thought to be a young G's place.

He stayed in confrontations with dudes that were twice his size. Got scuffed up most of the time. Developed a name for hisself 'cause he kept comin' back. Long before he was strong enough to whoop 'em, they were already startin' to avoid him. Tried to ig him. Eventually, gave him some space. Yeah, they could whip him. But they knew he wouldn't stop. That's what's up.

Different paths have led him and No Love to the same point. They both are extremely self-confident. Both are given to pushing the envelope. Married to the rugged road. Without question or reservation, both would choose death before dishonor. Both draw people to them without effort, just their demeanor.

By the time Lil Chris was 13, he had a jump crew of misfits, young cats, and busters. All of them fiercely devoted to him. By 15, he was quite the young manipulator.

As was No Love. After he understood enough to step out on his own, he quickly made a name for hisself. He wasn't afraid to do what others only thought about. And was clever enough to get away with it. At least, most of the time.

Few people his age know him from the block. Most of his life done been spent in and out of some detention center or another. On the inside, though, it is a different story altogether. No Love is a legend. One of the most recognizable prisoners not only in the institution, but also in the system.

No Love takes to Lil Chris almost immediately. The cellblocks offer another type of hip-hop scene. Much like population's, but still very different. The whole setup is a lot like that old school television series *Highlander*.

The rappers fall into a circuit of sorts. They all have at least a little bit of hype. Some have a lot. The exceptions are those writers and brand-new cats who stay working on their tablets on the under.

Mostly, they move back and forth, from block to block. Raven, Tiger, or the main prison cellblocks. These are the working cellblocks, where prisoners still mix at work call in the field and on the cellblock yard at their leisure. There are also the dungeons and extended lock-down. Max. Where the only way prisoners mix is by yelling through cell bars or air vents, or during extended's rotating tier hours.

The majority of them are young dudes who've just come to prison. Wild. Constantly into it with security or each other. Misunderstand-ings. Blame it on respect preservation and principle adherence. Their peers call them ridahs, 'cause they stay packing their property. Pushing it to the dungeon: administrative segregation, which is the middle ground for investigations and everywhere you transfer to for disci-plinary reasons.

Whenever and wherever, they fall around each other, whether it's through the cell bars on the "highway," yelling from fence to fence if they are anywhere remotely close to each other, or clashing on the same yard. Best case scenario, it's always raw and rugged.

Especially if you've got two heavyweights. Two legends clashing would be talked about for years. Like old folklore. And the objective is always the same. They battle until one or the other grabs the crowd and emerges the victor. Thus, taking the other's props. His hype. His power. The more rappers a lyricist outshines, the stronger he becomes. Powerful.

It gets deeper than that, though. Much deeper. Many of the rappers and hip-hop heads have life sentences, or number sentences equivalent to life. It's nothing to be standing next to someone who's been sentenced to two lifes and 495 years. The prison farm's warden keeps upping the percentage of the inmate population expected to die here with every successive speech. Shit is real. They've all regularly sat in assemblies and heard this shit spoken over their heads.

So, of course, the environment is highly charged. The music it churns out is intense. And sincere. These are young men. Ages 17 to 38, sometimes older. They make up more than three-quarters of the population. The large majority of them are Black. Many of them come to prison frustrated, backward, and degenerate. The music speaks to them. Comforts them. Teaches them. Encourages them. To both the speaker and the listener, the music is a lifeline.

The battles are not what one would expect them to be. Yes, there is a large amount of "shoot-'em-up-bang-bang" gangsta and street commentary. But that's just at the broad entry level. If a rapper wanna be a member of the elite, he gotta step up his game. Legends and heavyweights alike spit poetic. They spit flames. Knowledge. Awakening. The realest say things that mandate studying and self-awareness to even understand, let alone to compete wit'. The legends provoke thought. They push people to keep up with them. The heads quote their lyrics in troublin' situations like Bible verses. Proverbs.

So what has developed is a bunch of young men soul-searchin' and playin' the library to keep up. The bar is high. The elite make up a small society and are separated into two primary orders. These two be lookin' through the masses for prospects and prodigies. They pull them and polish them up. Prepare 'em to be positive agents in the struggle. Then they push 'em back into the population to inspire, encourage, and enlighten. To help they people adopt the proper mindset needed to strengthen them spiritually, mentally, and emotionally. With the right morals. To also help them develop the necessary tools and reasoning faculties to study law independently and appeal the game.

This is the legacy that No Love is a part of. Since they've been talkin', he has not necessarily been givin' Lil Chris the whole rundown. He has more or less been hipping him to the bigger picture. Showing him how real go-getters hop. Alerting him to the possibility of another level to this shit, an enriched way of life to be pursued by the lyrically elite all around him.

"It's way bigger than rappin', lil bro," No Love says, and beckons him to come on in.

CHAPTER TEN

"Say, hall man!"

"Who that is?" somebody calls out. "Hey, who that is on the tier? . . . Hey!"

A slow, throaty voice replies, "Oh, man, that's umm . . . ah, ah, ya boy. You know. Ole boy be wit' that be-boppin'."

"Say, Bama!"

"Wow!"

"Putcha peeper out and see who that is."

"Alright!" Bama sits up on the bottom bunk and pulls his mattress back to reach a piece of glass about the length and width of a fingernail. It is mounted on the tip of a plastic white spoon. Old gum for adhesive. He leans against the cell door and sets the peeper just beyond the cast iron bars.

"Yeah, man, like I was sayin'. A great deal of my life has been spent craving. I'm hungry, straight like that. Sooner or later, they go'n have to let me eat."

Rise looks at the brother standing at the cell bars speaking. Sees the hurt and frustration in his face. Passion and disappointment play hand in hand behind the chests of most of the brothers in the system. If it weren't necessary to follow the unspoken guidelines that govern this mass cult of masculinity, then it would be commonplace to see brothers breaking down. Showing all emotion.

"I put in work for everything I got and all I am," the frustrated brother says. He waves his arm over the interior of the man cage that has him trapped. "You think I 'on't want more than this? Rise, I grew up in this place. I'm a hard-knock vet. I got a lot I could contribute to society out there in them streets."

"I understand fully. Don't get sidetracked. Stay focused. Content to prepare yourself. Without waver, homie. And, when the time comes, execute."

With this statement, Rise takes one last look at the man he's talking to. He looks him in the eyes. They are the only part of him that is distinct. Everything else about him is similar or identical to every other brother trapped in these blocks: dingy white jumpsuit rolled down and tucked at the waist, shower shoes, nappy hair, and ashy skin.

There is a stale stench on the tier because the brothers that can't get their homies to slide them deodorant have to put state soap under their arms, and that only works for so long. Their breath is straight, though. If they don't give you anything else, the state gives you toilet tissue and toothpaste.

Still, the eyes are the expression of the man. They tell you of his mental and spiritual condition, his health, his objective. His intentions. It is so very hard to train the eyes to deceive. Few are capable of doing this. The eyes tell where the man has been. Who and where he is. And where he's going.

Rise looks the man in the eye. The man in the cell places his fist to the cell bars. Rise meets his gesture with his open palm.

"Oh, that's Rise! Hey, Rise, come down some! Holla at the homie!" Bama, with his childlike voice.

"Who that is, Bama? That Rise?"

"Yeah! Flag him down here!"

"Say, Rise!"

"Look, man, I'ma let you get to yo' people down there."

"Yeah, they wildin' out for real, huh."

Rise has been on the cellblock unit for about an hour now. Being a tutor, he comes to teach the brothers who are in cells and out of reach of the learning programs. He can also see about the needs of his brethren. Sometimes, serving these needs calls for a little violating. Nothing major, just not allowing the threat of disciplinary action to stop him from answering certain calls that need to be met.

Rise understands that he is a power piece. In the system, everyone is a write-up away from the cells. No matter how much favor one may have garnered with the administration. Few in Rise's position understand this. Or, they don't acknowledge it. So when one of the real homies ascends to a position of comparable privilege in the institution, it's his responsibility to keep it solid with his team. To make sure that the benefits of his post are circulated through the general brotherhood. At the end of the day, you don't climb your way out of prison. You work your way out. So, the power piece does good to recognize that these are the only people who will remain when he falls out of favor. Which is inevitable if he's living right with his people.

On the other hand, it's on his team to protect his interest. Make sure that his path is not littered with nonsense and carelessness. They're supposed to restrain from asking him to pull off frivolous acts or transport major contraband. This is for pawn homies, lil soul-jahs with dues to pay.

Each day offers another set of issues and goals the homies want or need to address. Rise is the hand up. A voice with the administration when they need to be heard. A resource when for whatever reason a homie is dealt a bad hand. He's the mobility when they can't move. This is why they protect him. He's just a bolt in the machine, true. But a valuable one.

"Wow! What's up with the brothers?"

"What's happenin', Rise? I knew you was comin' 'round after a while," Bama answers. "I just was tellin' yo' two homies about you."

"What's happenin' with you, mayne?" a familiar voice asks.

"Is that No Love? I was just asking Black about you. I hadn't seen you in a minute."

"Yeah. I was on my way down the walk but I got somebody in my enemy jacket down there. I'm still tryna figure out who dat is."

"If you want, I can look into that for you," Rise offers.

"I 'preciate the offer, Rise. But you know you can't check my enemy jacket."

"Don't sweat me. Do you want me to see what can be done or not?"

"Ay-ay-*ay!* Al'ight, you got that, homeboy. Do ya thing. Like I said, I 'preciate you."

"Just be cool, and don't catch no more write-ups while you in here waiting. And stop thanking me for doin' what I supposed to do, anyway."

"Yeah, you right. It's supposed to be done, but ain't but a few playin' it like it go. So you gotta feel the ones that do."

"Say, Rise," Bama puts in, "you know they got Lil Chris in cell 9, huh? You need to holla at him, Rise. He cool people. He can say them raps, too."

"Yeah, I'm hip to the lil brother," Rise says. No Love's cell, where Rise is standing, is right next to Lil Chris's cell. Rise takes the few steps over to stand in front of the C'ster's cell.

He sees Lil Chris sitting in the bottom bunk, staring at the wall. "Whaz happening wit' you, lil bro?" Rise greets him.

"I'm cool."

"I know you ain't still in here from that lil car wreck you had a few weeks back, huh?"

"Yeah, they wrote it up aggravated. They wanted to send me to J."

"Nawl, lil man. If they wanted to send you to Camp J, they would have."

"Nawl, I'm just sayin'—"

"I believe I know where you at," Rise cuts him off. "These cells are a necessary evil, though. Don't sweat it. You need to concentrate on turning the cage into a laboratory and focus on building yo'self up."

Rise stops. Looks at Lil Chris. Lil Chris says nothing in response. Stares at the wall in front of him.

"You know," Rise starts again. "You can move that wall if you want to."

"Wit' what," Lil Chris says.

"Your mind."

"Look, my nigga. Don't play wit' me. I don't play."

"I may laugh, but I don't play either," Rise assures him. "All we have, right now, is our minds. But the thing is, that's all we've ever had. There is a deeper truth that abides. This will do for you for now," Rise trails off, more to himself. Adds, "What type of education do you have?"

"What?"

"Did you finish school?"

"Oh, yeah. My GED. I got it when I was 16. I was even in college for a minute."

"Good. Where did you study at?"

"Southern, on the Cooper Road."

Rise frowns. "Oh, SUSBO! I know where you at. That community college. A junior program."

"I don't know what it was, but I went."

"Okay. That's a start. Do you remember what you studied?"

Lil Chris smiles. "Yeah. Tashona. Danyell. Tammy. Kris. Oh, and Samantha—she was off the chain."

No Love, who's been lying in his bunk listening in, starts laughing.

"Alright, alright," Rise says. "I get ya point."

Silence. Rise studies Lil Chris, who's still studying the cell wall. After a long pause, No Love mumbles, "To touch without feeling is the ultimate sin."

Rise stiffens. Makes his mind up.

"Just . . . stay out of trouble, lil brother. I'll be around to see you when you get where you goin'."

Silence. Not a word from the C'ster.

Rise walks over and pulls a bunch of candy and a pack of Bugler tobacco out of his front two pockets. He gives them to Bama. "I got your kite. You need anything else just shoot me another one. I'll be up from time to time. You can holla then. I'ma talk to some people to see if anything can be done about your situation. Be cool, big homie."

"Okay, Rise. And, I 'preci—"

"Uh-uh, Big Homie. Don't ever thank me for doing what I sup-posed to do." Rise stops to look at him, as if thinking to himself. He says, "I gotta go. I love you, Big Bro. Holla when you need me."

As he walks past the cells, he speaks a goodbye to the brothers. "A'ight, Lil Chris, No Love. Y'all be cool. I'ma handle that." He walks a few steps further. He speaks to everyone he passes as he makes his exit. "Be strong, my man. Peace out, brother. Alright, alright, keep ya chin up, kid." He feels their pain.

As Rise stands by the bars at the end of the tier, waiting for the turnkey to come open the door, he looks back at the cells. *They're warehousing us*, he thinks. The C.O. finally comes to open the door. A few heartbeats later, he's walking out of the cellblock unit.

As he steps away, he says quietly to himself, "Indeed, far worse than blasphemy."

"Say Lil Chris," No Love shouts as he beats on the wall that stands between them. "Lil Chris! Where you at, mayne?"

"There ain't too many places I can be. What you want?"

"Where you at?! Stick ya head to the bars."

Lil Chris comes to the front of the cell, where the wall separating them pulls up short of the bars. If they stand real close, they can see each other's face.

This implies that the conversation is private. Though it doesn't necessarily mean that no one is listenin'.

"Say," No Love starts. "Rise a real nigga, man. Don't play him off like that."

"What you mean—'play him off?'" Lil Chris asks.

"Come on, kid. I was listening the whole time. The dude ain't lame, noo."

"I ain't say he was," Lil Chris is perplexed.

"No. It's a reason I'm telling you this. If he didn't have no intention of dealin' wit' you, he would have never told you to be still. He go'n holla. Expect that. But, if you wit' the foolishness, he go'n back up. You'll lose out in the long run. Trus' that."

Silence. Lil Chris doesn't respond.

Rise lays awake in his bunk, looking out the window. He's thinking about the homies from earlier that night. Going over the best means to remedy some of the problems they face. This is his burden. When he comes across adversity, whether it challenges him directly or indirectly, through someone else close to him, his spirit won't let him turn it loose. He has to attack it.

Often, he strategizes. Dissects each soul-jah's character in an effort to really understand them and their plights. Ain't but one struggle. He knows this. His thing is to figure out how best to help them. He's always been like this. It's the reason he's still in prison.

His thoughts turn to this young brother, Lil Chris. There is something about the boy's spirit. He feels drawn to this kid. As if in ministering to the youngster, he'll somehow correct a disservice he's done another soul in a past life.

He knows, just off instinct, that helping Lil Chris won't be easy at all. The kid is definitely gonna fight him. But, the prospect of releasing the boy's strength—that much power, liberated . . . It's too much to allow to lie dormant. He may need to be shook a little, but in a conscious state the lil brother stands to be a major force. The struggle needs Lil Chris.

And Lil Chris needs to struggle.

With this thought, Rise feels a creative drive. He reaches over and grabs his pen and pad. Begins to jot out a few loosely constructed thoughts:

Winds whisper

    Through the corridors of life

        With unseen forces

Combat boots stomp in cadence

    Dust rises.

Were nature to rebel

    In frustrated response

    To men's feeble attempts to defy universal law,

Then who would lend a hand to raise the sun?

    Who would water the soil?

Who would breathe on us

    That we should breathe, again.

To touch without feeling

    Is the ultimate sin

    Far worse than blasphemy

CHAPTER ELEVEN

I placed my hand
    On the concrete wall.
        Felt the heartbeat
The pulsatin'
    The passion
        The cellblock aura.
My cellblock state mind
    Utter despair, where I come from
Mingled wit' a conviction to overcome.
Explore my beginnings
    From a ghuttah mentality
But, peep my vitality, vibe wit' me
Follow the growth of a hooligan
    Come up from hard livin' without
        I was driven . . .

"Yo! Rack the door back!"

The cell door slides open and C-Boy looks up from the toilet bowl where he is crouched over, doing his white laundry. He can hear the boxes sliding down the tier. *Damn, I'm finna get a cellie,* he thinks to himself.

"Ay, ay, ay, lem'me push my boxes up to the front of the cell," C-Boy says as this new cat comes into view.

Whether he heard him or not is debatable, but this dude just continues workin' his property into the cell. Eventually, he lodges his two footlockers up front, by the cell bars.

"Say brah, you ain't hear me?"

Silence. The lil dude walks out the cell and comes back a few minutes later carrying his sheet bundle wit' everything that he didn't leave in the dungeon. As the door slides shut behind him, he swings his bundle up to the top bunk and busies himself with breaking the metal seals security placed on his boxes during storage.

That done, he takes up half the space on the cell floor, trapping a frustrated C-Boy in one corner while he's opening up his boxes and rummaging through their contents. A moment later, Sergeant Willis steps in front of the cell.

"Everything there?"

"Yeah."

"Well, sign these papers, right quick."

As his new cellie busies himself signing property papers, C-Boy glances in the open locker boxes. *Damn, that nigga got a box fulla stuff. Okay then, my nigga. I'ma let you make it . . . for now.*

"Say, where you from?" C-Boy asks when the C.O. leaves.

Silence.

"Man, I know you ain't deaf."

Silence.

"Look, if we go'n live in here together, we go'n have to communicate, my nigga. Understand me?"

Nothing. The dude fiddes with the seam of his white jumpsuit. He pulls something out, but C-Boy can't catch what it is.

"Say, brah," C-Boy starts. He's 'bout fed up by now. "What yo' name is?"

The youngsta looks up with a straight face and says, "My name Lil Chris. You get loaded?"

C-Boy smiles. Puts his hands to his mouth and yells out, "Say, Sarge! We need a mattress in cell 4!"

Luckily for the two of them, they both make good cellies. Lil Chris, born in '79, is a year older than C-Boy. Both are built on the same frame. About five-ten, not tall, stocky. Shuck-chubby, as they say in the south. Both have enormous egos and are pretty good with their hands. Yeah. It's good that they hit it off. 'Cause if not, then the cell wouldn't be big enough to hold but one o' them.

The best thing about it is that they're both out of Port City. Shreveport wit' that. Lil Chris is from Lakeside. C-Boy is from up on the Cooper Road, right around the way. So, although they've never met, they know some of the same people.

"Man, I'm tellin' you, your cousin, Tab, is my boo," C-Boy insists.

"Tab wouldn't fool wit' you, nigga. You a young buck."

"C'mon, mayne," C-Boy says, agitated. "Don't start the foolishness." He's sensitive about his youth.

"Well get on back, then. Don't play wit' me 'bout my people," Lil Chris returns.

One of the hardest things for Lil Chris to get used to is stickin' his hands in the toilet. The sink is little more than a shallow bowl with about five small holes in its base. Anything extremely dirty or greasy tends to cause the water to collect fast and drain slow, usually leaving grit and grime behind. So, as a necessity, the sink is only used for hygiene: washin' their hands, brushin' their teeth, and washin' dishes. Even then they have to fill the plastic containers up and dump them in the toilet once or twice to get most of the food and grease out of the way.

Everything else is toilet action. If they send their whites to the laundry, they come back brown. It's the toilet or to the shower with them, and in the blocks they only have 15 minutes to get in and get out. Then, there is work call to consider. When they come in the cell dirty and sweaty, it's ill advised to jump in the bunk and soil the sheets they have to sleep on. They can only wash sheets every four days. If the sheets are funky, so is the cell. Strugglin' to breathe in a funky cell? That's a quick way to fall out with your cellie.

Then, too, in the blocks, they can't just shower when they want to. They're in cell 4. If the shower starts at the back of the tier, they're stuck out until late. So, if they go out and play basketball during the morning yard, or come in dirty from work call, there is only one other option besides sitting on the floor for hours, what convicts call a bird-bath. To soap and bleach the toilet, strip down, and have at it. Good luck finding the bleach! And, after the bath is over, there is the issue of going back in the toilet to wipe up the mess with a floor rag.

C-Boy doesn't have a complex. He works out a lot so he takes two or three birdbaths a day. Lil Chris . . . well, Lil Chris has been in the cell for three weeks. He's spent the majority of his time sitting on the cell floor.

It's Wednesday. About noon. The cellblock fieldlines have just come in from the first half of the day's work call. Lil Chris is sitting on his footlocker next to the cell bars. C-Boy has folded his mattress back and is sittin' on the lower bunk's metal beddin' rack. Both of them are tired and hungry. Waitin' for noon chow carts to come down.

It's fried chicken day. Hopefully the cooks have not messed over the red beans and rice. Nothing worse than having to pick over a meal when there is a whole other half of work call left to be done.

Lil Chris has his peeper resting on the cell bars, but he's not payin' any attention. All of the sudden, someone yanks the small mirror with its toothbrush handle away from the bars. The C'ster looks up with a start.

"Damn, lil one, didn't I advise you to stay out of trouble?"

Before Lil Chris can answer, C-Boy says, "Ah man, whuz up, Rise?"

"Say, brah, can I get my issue back," Lil Chris says with a scowl. "You don't know me like that."

"Listen, lil brother—" Rise starts.

"—Damn, Rise, you know this nigga," C-Boy cuts in.

"What I ask you about that word?" Rise switches his attention to C-Boy.

"What word? 'Nigga'!" Lil Chris interrupts. "Damn. What kind o' shit is that? He tryna tell you what to say? How to talk? Come on, now."

A sober C-Boy says, "Nawl, man, check . . . he . . . he tryna help me elevate."

"What?! Fuck outta here!" Lil Chris is incredulous.

"For real, kid," C-Boy insists. "Straight up. I'm givin' you the uncut."

Lil Chris ain't feelin' him. He's g'tting' ready to set in on C-Boy for being what he sees as soft. By his standards, that's serious rib action.

"Yeah, you givin' him the real, but can he respect the real?" Rise says, adding a serious note, throwing a monkey wrench in Lil Chris's mix.

"A real nigga can't do nothin' but respect the real," Lil Chris shoots back.

"Oh, so that's what you is . . . A real nigga, huh? Another one of these real niggas—"

"No! Another nothin'. I stand alo—"

"Yeah, yeah, I know. I heard all o' that before. You stand alone. Yeah. Uh-huh, they got real niggas all over this camp. Real niggas. Niggas for life. Life's niggas."

"Go on with that," Lil Chris feels strangely uncomfortable. There's something in the way he says that word. "I'm serious, brah. Go 'head on wit' that."

"Uh-uh, nigga," Rise says with venom. "I wanna talk about what these cats do 'round here. I'm tah'm bout y'all that call yourselves niggas."

"What you mean, 'y'all?'" Lil Chris interjects.

"Yeah, you too. All y'all call ya'selves real niggas, huh? No? But, anyway. We see real niggas 'round this cut every day. They the ones that disrespect themselves and compromise their manhood. They jack off on the lady in the guard tower. Hide in the TV room, or the showers, gettin' off on the free lady sittin' at the desk. Either entertained or appalled, still offended by these fools. These real niggas. Stand-alone killahs, killin' theyself. Then they go get with they other real niggas and brag about how they got that bitch. Major accomplishment. Real niggas rat on they homeboys and get 'em sent south of Egypt. More than just gone till November. That nigga get his boy on death row then turn around and call hisself a real nigga. He rolled over and he wasn't facin' nothin' but a misdemeanor burglary, a parole violation, and he ain't wanna back his time up. But, you real niggas embrace each other."

"Say, man, don't put me in the same category wit' a rat—who you think—"

"No! You did that for me. Remember? You a real nigga. I don't know you. But, I know you call yourself a real nigga. Shit, that's the same thing they call theyself . . . And I *know them*! Been round them sorry mu'fuckas for years!

"The real niggas, I know, they the functional illiterates. The ones can't do sixth-grade mathematics. Can't read on an eighth-grade level. That's real. They got 13-year-olds smarter than them. Is that real? Ain't it, mayne? But, y'all stick together, though. All you . . . real niggas. Real niggas done just took over. Ain't no more fake niggas. All the niggas real.

"On the *streets*, you commit the most courageous feats . . . against each other. Stand in the middle of the asphalt and shoot it out. Automatics, high-powered assault rifles. But when two police come, yell

'Freeze!,' ya drop ya guns and run off. Then, meet back up and brag about how you ran off. Retreated! But ya got away, huh? Real niggas. The same ones that go back there to them Camp J cells and slang shit on each other.

"Well, I don't know about everyone else, but you real niggas disgust me. I'm sick o' you real niggas," Rise says. The look on his face says even more.

Silence. Lil Chris just stares, close-mouthed. Frowns at him.

Rise stands at the cell bars for a few more heartbeats. He decides to leave before the youngster can say or do something that will lock them into conflict. His words, it is what it is.

Rise turns to go and almost falls over this nerdy-looking inmate pushing stacked footlockers down the tier.

"Wayne," Lil Chris calls out. "Whuz hap'nin', nigga!"

The nerd stops and looks dispassionately toward Lil Chris's cell.

"Mayne, what you standin' there lookin' crazy for? Come holla," Lil Chris beckons, with enthusiasm enough for both of them.

The most life he's seen out of this one yet. Rise is nonplussed. Everything about the guy is nondescript. Average height, average weight, peach fuzz on his chin and upper lip. Some extra-conservative horn-rimmed glasses that may or may not have cost a little money. And judging from his posture and carriage, he may or may not be in a world of trouble moving into these cellblocks. *Wonder what's the connection between those two*, Rise thinks, noting the way they interact at the cell bars.

"Hey! Catch ya cell," the C.O. yells from the front of the tier by the keybox.

"What cell they got you goin' in?" Lil Chris asks as his friend turns back to the boxes.

"Cell 11," Wayne says before shoving off.

As Rise heads towards the front of the tier, he looks up to see Major

Mercury, Sergeant Bohannon, and a cadet. They have all apparently been standing there for some time.

What draws his attention, though, is Bohannon. A nice-looking white woman with big hair—damn near an afro. A brunette. Expressive, smoky-gray eyes. A mature woman with a tough body that speaks of her background in college softball.

Bohannon is a regular in these blocks, on this shift. Rise hasn't figured out what she finds so interesting about him, but there she always has a catty smirk on her face when he comes to make his rounds on her cellblock. This is his thought, or at least what he's trying not to think about, as he steps through the tier gate and out into the lobby with the three officers.

Boom! The cadet, a young, white lad, slams and locks the tier gate in one motion, rattling the cast iron bars. "Hey," he says. "What were you doin' in front that cell down there?!"

Rise turns to the green kid with a vaguely amused, bewildered look on his face, as if to say, "What are you, jokin'?" He knows he's not.

"I said," the cadet stresses. "What were you up to in front of that cell just now!?"

Rather than answer, Rise looks to Major Mercury and Sergeant Bohannon to see if they're going to call the kid down.

"This officer asked you a question," Major Mercury says in his slow drawl.

"Yeah," Rise returns. "And the two of you know I make rounds twice a week in these blocks. I was doin' my job down there."

"And what's that?" The cadet steps in his space.

"Teaching," Rise says, simply. Solid. Holding eye to eye with the kid. Refusing to shuffle.

"This officer says he heard you down there yelling about niggers," Major Mercury puts in. "What was that about?"

None of your fuckin' business, Rise thinks. But he says, "I was teaching." A bit more forceful. Always an ordeal to hear them say that word.

They've reached an impasse. Calm, Rise still hasn't allowed the cadet's energy to infect him. For some inexplicable reason, he spares a glance at Bohannon.

"Well, I've smelled weed smoke a time or two when I've passed that cell," she says. "Ah, Lil Chris and Calvi, C-Boy, right?"

That hurt. Can't deny it.

"Step in the closet over there," Major Mercury says.

Rise holds his composure as best he can. Sets his books and backpack on the sheet metal serving table and backs into the small utility closet. Mercury and the cadet crowd the doorway.

"Strip," Major Mercury commands.

Rise pulls his shirt over his head and immediately feels the closet's stagnant air on his skin. As he hands over his shirt he sees Sergeant Bohannon standing by his personal effects, thumbing through his notebooks.

Rise grits his teeth, slips off his jeans, and hands them over. As he stands there in his underclothes, the cadet scowls at him. Rise straightens his back, lifts his chin.

Major Mercury tosses Rise's jeans to the side and holds his hand out. "Hand 'em over."

Rise pulls off his tank top. Next he hands over his boxers. Finally, he slips off his socks and stands flatfooted on the cold, polished concrete. The chill working up through his legs has his ass shivering. Still, he stands straight and looks the officers in the eyes. Bohannon watches over their shoulders.

"Turn around," Major Mercury commands. "Hold your feet up. Squat down and cough."

Rise stoically complies. Then he calmly faces them again. Eyes the cadet.

"Turn back around, bend over, and spread 'em."

Rise doesn't move. Isn't going to.

"I said turn back around, bend over, and spread 'em," the cadet nearly screams.

Rise just looks at him, knowing that his turn to go lay in a dungeon cell has likely come around. He'll take his ride.

"Are you refusing a direct verbal order?" Major Mercury questions.

"You asked me why I was on the tier. I gave you a valid—"

"I said are you refusing a direct—"

"I've already submitted to a strip search."

"So, you're refusing."

"I'm not doin' it."

Silence.

"You want me to get the gas, sir?" the cadet asks.

Silence. They all just stand and stare at each other.

"Get your clothes on and get out of here," Major Mercury drawls.

With that, he tells Sergeant Bohannon to let him make his rounds. They leave Rise standing alone.

Once he has himself situated, he stands by the door and waits. After a few heartbeats, some keys come jingling down the staircase and Sergeant Bohannon pops out. She takes a moment to look Rise over, as if inspecting him, then unlocks the door and opens it just wide enough for Rise to slide through.

He doesn't move.

She opens the door wider and Rise takes his leave. As soon as the door bangs closed behind him, he exhales. He hadn't even realized he was holding his breath.

As he walks down the walk he's so mad he's trembling.

One of the orderlies stops by Lil Chris and C-Boy's cell. "Mayne, yo' homeboy Rise a mu'fucka. Check this out . . . "

"Hello," a rich, feminine alto answers before the recording kicks in.

"This is MCI. You have a collect call from—" Rise's voice, pre-recorded, says, "Oschuwon", "—an inmate at Louisiana State Prison. If you wish to accept the charge, say 'Yes' or press 5. If you do not wish—" The recording abruptly stops. Silence.

" . . . Your call has been accepted. Thank you for using MCI."

"Hello? Rise?" Shonda's voice is urgent.

"Yeah. How you doin' baby?"

"Your momma and I went to see the lawyer today. We gave him the papers you sent. He's gonna let us pay the rest of the money in monthly installments."

Silence.

"Rise?"

"Yeah."

"Well, say somethin', man. Let me know you—"

"I appreciate y'all," Rise cuts in. "That's really gonna be a big help for me."

"You know I'll do anything I can for you, don't you? You know that, right?"

"Yeah, Shonda. I love you for that. I kinda thought you would back up once Shonetta left for college."

"I'll never leave you. You know that."

"For sure. You're like a sister to me."

Silence. He knows what he just did.

"Oschuwon, why you always doin' me that?" she says. Her tone is sweet and plaintive, and also hurt.

"What's that, boo?" he asks. Feigning ignorance.

"I'm not goin' through this with you, tonight, Won." She's aggravated. "You need to stop that."

"Stop what?" The smile is audible in his voice.

Silence.

"Love, I told you," Rise starts. "I want more for you than I can give you. I want you with someone that's go'n appreciate and do right by you—"

"Boy!" She's exasperated.

"No. Listen. I'm caught up in this place. I know you love me. And I love you too. If I was out there on them streets it would be different. But, I ain't finna have you doin' this time with me while your life just passes by. I want you to live, love."

"I can't live without you."

"You are speaking with an inmate at a state correctional facility. This call is subject to monitoring and may be recorded," the voice recording interrupts.

CHAPTER TWELVE

My eyes drift past
> *The vantage point*
>> *Of what's immediately around me.*

I am
> *Transfixed*

No longer
> *Can these circumstances*
>>> *Confine me*
>> *I define my shine*
>> *My outlook*
>>>> *My . . . neue sachlichkeit*

My sense of being
> *My person*

I am
> *Transfixed*

I have transcended.

Rise stands up to address the membership. As he looks over the crowded room, he realizes, again, just how large this callout is. Too large. Some of them will have to leave, eventually. Others will mature with time.

Then there are always the plants: the rats, the heat, the squeals, the stool pigeons. Those few agents placed in the room to stir up problems. The few who remain from the old group, still there to promote division. They report back to the security personnel that sent them. In another prison environment they wouldn't be tolerated at all. Another time. Another state. Not so here. Here, gotta let a couple of them stay. But they're harmless when you know they're there. Useful, even. Long as your house is straight and you know exactly who they are. All the unknowns must be flushed out. Or, better yet, made to dismiss themselves.

Banished until a time when they can be accurately identified.

Most important, though, are the jewels. The prodigies. Coals that the heat and pressure of the struggle have made or will make into diamonds. Still, yet, undiscovered. Even to themselves. Those that have to be awakened. Quickened. Extracted from the dirt of disappointment. Exhumed, maybe, from the soil and dredges. The living among the walking dead. They are what it's all for. The very best of the numbered masses.

To harness this young energy is the primary motive. To separate them from the degenerate, inhumane, and backward influences that prevail elsewhere in the prison. To isolate them. Debrief them in order to see what they understand. Initiate an unlearning process to clean out all of the errant, misguided, and destructive beliefs—hard, heart-held beliefs they actually define themselves by. And, finally, to groom them in a way that will promote healthy self-awareness and more accurate objectivity. Ones they can lean on as they seek to redeem the time and choose their own path in life. Once these jewels are properly polished, they will be fed back into the populace. Both prison and society at large. To influence others toward conscious awakening and progressive attitudes.

Rise holds out his hands to calm the murmur of conversation around the room.

"Gentlemen," Rise begins. "Let us start the meeting by observing one minute of silence . . . "

C-Boy and Lil Chris have a workout regimen that they hold to every day without fail. No weight benches in the blocks. No weights, period. Just calisthenics. Push-ups, sit-ups, bend and reach, crunches, and shit.

They're usually right there in the corner of the small cellblock yard. The area where the two fences meet and they can see the comers and goers from the treatment center on one side and the A Building on the other.

This is where they are today. Getting their stretches in before they kick off their 30-minute jog. It just so happens that the guard shift is changing.

Lil Chris really ain't payin' attention, though. He's goin' through that phase where he's so resentful about his incarceration that he hates everything and everybody that represents the system. Especially the correctional officers who are marchin' back and forth on the walk right before them. Besides, security is go'n do what they do, anyway. There are more pressin' matters on Lil Chris's mind. The package lady brought legal mail to the cell the other day. His appellate lawyer let him know that the circuit court denied his direct appeal. Something, also, about the state supreme court, but he didn't really understand it. He's just hopin' somethin' good happens. Eventually.

Then, there's Wayne. Damn . . . Wayne.

C-Boy, on the other hand, is on some real voyeurism shit. "Ooh, did you see that? . . . Lil Chris—"

"Man, I'm not into that. Stop calling me."

"I'm sayin', brah . . . a'ight. G'on head, trip then," C-Boy whispers, sharply inhaling through his teeth.

C-Boy goes quiet for a moment. You can hear the flies buzzing around them.

All of the sudden, Lil Chris feels the impulse to look up. When he does, he almost bites a hole in his lip trying to stop from saying sump'n. No question. All he saw was the back of her head, but it was her . . . he's sure about that. *Damn! The Blocks!*

"Say, check, I . . . I don't know which one of us she was watchin', but that look in her eyes got me messed up . . . Peep. I'm finna go tell the freeman let me on back in the cell, brah," C-Boy finishes.

Lil Chris isn't really hearing him. "Man, quit trippin'. What about the laps we gotta jog?"

"Kid . . . " C-Boy says. Lookin' as serious as a heart attack. "Straight . . . I need some solo time."

Rise walks slowly around the classroom. The club members are paired off and seated at small makeshift tables with chess boards set up to show games that have already progressed to various stages of play.

"The object of the game for the serious player," Rise stipulates, "is to obtain swift victory with minimal casualties. Does everyone understand me?"

He pauses. No one answers. He knows they are hearing but not necessarily appreciating him. "Again. You wanna win as fast as possible. But you wanna do so while using a strategy that will cost you the least amount of pieces."

He pauses, again. Makes eye contact as he steps through the virtual maze of seated bodies. Okay. He sees understanding blooming on a few faces. "How do we do this? How do we obtain swift victory with minimal casualties? Good question! We think! That's what we do. We think . . . what? At least four or five moves ahead. *This* is the key to the game. Forethought. Thought precedes action. Know what you're about before you move. Don't be sloppy. The only way to obtain swift victory and do so with minimal casualties."

Someone raises his hand. Rise doesn't stop. "If I am speaking over your head, then you are in the wrong meeting. You—are—too—slow—for this body. You need to find somewhere else to spend your time and energy."

The guy that raised his hand gets up and storms out of the room.

Lil Chris has been jogging for 25 minutes now. His lower back is tight and warm. His legs are sore. His knee and ankle joints are almost numb. His shoulders have this dull pain. But his chest is wide open. It feels good. His head is clear. At least most of his mind is focused on bending his aching body to his will in order to press on. There is only a corner of his attention still holding on to her . . . Veronica. Veronica Havoc.

Alright, just a little more. Just a couple of minutes left. Come on, now. Focus! Put your mind on what you're doin'. Stretch it out. Push every step. Stay mindful of where you tryna get to.

As Lil Chris sprints out the last seconds, he notices that someone has pulled up on his resting area. Taking a seat and placing a stack of books right next to the C'ster's shed clothes.

He slows to a snail's pace and then begins to walk. Finishes his last lap, steadies his breathing. This isn't his first time peeping this dude. Staring in Lil Chris's direction is too vague. He has learned not to sweat misdemeanors. But stoppin' by his rest area is a felony. This guy has come out there. Stepped, uninvited, into Lil Chris's world. Now, if he out there sideways he go'n to get dealt wit'. No ifs, ands, or buts about it.

The C'ster is silent and alert as he pulls into position, standing over the now-sitting intruder. He says, "What?"

"Oh, what's happenin', brother? You mind if I chill for a minute? I got something I wanna kick to you."

Silence.

The guy continues. "I been peepin' ya style. I feel like you a pretty solid dude. You got a lot of influence with most of these youngstas. I also see you stay to yourself. You stand in a small circle. These are good qualities. You could *be* someone if you willin' to work."

Silence.

Lil Chris crouches down in an OG bucket. Stays on his feet. Stretches his arms out to rest the back of his arms across his knees. Now he's eye to eye with this cat. Stares him down.

The guy doesn't seem perturbed.

Lil Chris asks, "What do you want wit' me, man?"

The guy smiles. "It's not what I want from you, it's what we want for you," he says.

"What we?"

"Da One."

"Da who?" Lil Chris's patience is getting short.

"Da One," is all the dude will say.

"Check this out," Lil Chris begins in a controlled even tone. "Don't . . . play wit' me. You ain't got but a few more seconds before I'm through talkin'—"

"Nooo! Brother, don't get defensive. I'm not here for that. You've been chosen by a family, which is called Da One. Our mission is to help you build. My job is to help you in your process of reawakening, brother."

Silence.

The intruder continues. "I know you live hard. We all do. Ain't no chumps in my fold. Believe me, we can identify with your anger. We just tryna help you understand the reason behind the madness."

Silence. The C'ster is thinking, now. Tryna make sense of what's being said. The intruder sees that as his opening and presses forward. "Look. My name is Mansa. I already know yours. As for today, I came to drop this material off on you. You can read it, tear it up, or throw it away. That's on you. Just know that there are no secrets in the penitentiary. We'll know what you did with it. From here on out, I'm

your contact to Da One. You wanna holla . . . you get at me. Mansa."
Mansa finishes talking, gets up and leaves. He walks off toward the
other end of the yard and begins walking the narrow runner's path
around the perimeter of the abbreviated prison yard. He never looks
back.

Lil Chris picks up the book that Mansa left sitting on the grass beside him. He reads the cover. *Before the Mayflower* by Lerone Bennett,
Jr. A paperback. The cover's artwork is a trip. It's got all these kinda
freaked-out colors. These crude shapings of men. One has a hammer
or something.

Lil Chris just sits there looking at the cover of the book. Tryna
process what just happened.

Suddenly, a whistle sounds, startling the C'ster from his musing.
Yard call is over. The prisoners line up in twos next to the walk to be
counted and shook down before filtering back into the cellblock unit.

Contemplative.

Always contemplative, ever contemplative. Rise sits in the classroom after the P.C.P.A. meeting. Basically digests what transpired.
Keeping up with the times. He categorizes the characters. The drifters.
The strategists. The agent provocateurs. The prodigies, the brothers
who will soon mature into the guiding lights of this prison population.
The number is very small, indeed. And, of course, there are some significant personalities that the scouting committee has failed to pull in.
Regrettably, most of these will end up corrupted and stagnant under
backward doctrine.

Rise has been hearing about the recent resurgence of Da One.
A lot of his brethren are worried about this development. However,
Rise, ever the strategist, believes it could be a good thing. Of course,
their confrontational lean is going to push S.O.G. into a new position
of visibility. The uncontrollable and inevitable consequences of there
being two opposing schools of thought.

Yet, on the other hand, Rise has another angle on the situation as it develops. These two rival doctrines aren't so much opposing as they are simply distinguishable from one another. Which, in proper context, is a good thing. Rise knows the struggle is all about perception. How you perceive a thing. *We create our own realities*, Rise reminds himself, and this is a key fundamental.

There are no real secrets in prison. Too closely situated for that. Only well-kept truths. Visibility is not a threat when your house is in order. Conflict is good, also. It generates interest, opinion, position. Pick a side.

Rise will discipline the soul-jahs who stand in the forefront. They will answer the negative aggression of Da One with strength, wisdom, ideology, and execution. Of these, execution is the most crucial. Credibility is the fruit of consistent practice.

Lastly, key to Rise's angle on the matter is the notion that truth will abide and right thought will overcome. What the Egyptians called *maat*. All those that the S.O.G. misses will hopefully be pulled in by Da One. Still more will be attracted by the chaos of voice and movement. This, too, is a good thing. No matter how they get there, or why they come, the power of perception is key. The third eye sees. All concerned approach the table. Da One could even draw the majority and it would be of no consequence. The objective would be to disarm their prejudices and present truth. Once truth and untruth are matched before them, once the contrast is perceived, if not understood, then each will choose intuitively what is right for him.

Rise is certain that S.O.G. is on the righteous path.

"Say . . . check," C-Boy speaks up as soon as Lil Chris walks into the cell.

Lil Chris leans back into the corner at the front of the cell where the bars meet the wall just inside the celldoor. "What's happenin'?" he questions.

"When I come in from the yard, Fast Eddie stopped me and said homeboy in the cell wit' ya boy Wayne fucked up. Check, dude been sendin' down the walk all day tryna get a knife"

It's always strange to hear C-Boy talkin' serious because so much of what comes out of his mouth is bullshit. But right now it seems everything inside this little box they're sittin' in is still. Even the TV droning on the tier recedes to the background, and nothing exists but the two of them. This moment, this conversation. At times like this, there is this crazy sense of how unfair and absurd prison is. Trapped in this place. With these people.

Lil Chris grabs his notepad and tears out a small piece of paper. Digs out a pen and scribbles a quick note to Wayne. His friend is seven cells down, but that could just as well be seven miles. They are both locked in.

He folds the note, peels the label off his deodorant, and uses it to seal the message. He still can't be sure that it won't fall into the wrong hands, but the most important thing at the moment is alertin' Wayne that there's a chance he's about to be ambushed. He stops the first pair of legs to pass by the cell and sends the note down to Wayne.

Wayne is sitting in the top bunk with his headphones on listening to the TV. Some guy—they're all strangers to him—stops in front of the cell bars and extends a folded note. As Wayne takes it, the guy says, "Lil Chris," and walks away.

Wayne peels the letter open and reaches for his glasses. His cellmate stands up and peeks at Wayne in the top bunk before stepping to the toilet to take a piss.

As Wayne reads the note a shiver runs up his spine to the crown of his head. He refolds the missive and turns his head back toward the TV. Knows his cellie is likely watching him in the mirror mounted on the cell's back wall.

When his cellmate reaches over to flush the toilet, Wayne turns, says, "Excuse me," and tosses the note in the bowl like he would any other. This done, he forces himself to lay down as if he's really into the television program and tries to make sense of what he just read.

Lil Chris and C-Boy sit up half the night waiting for the telltale bumpin' and rumbling that would indicate Wayne and his cellie clashin'. It never comes.

Some time during the early hours of the morning, Lil Chris sets down the copy of *Before the Mayflower* he's been reading since he came in from the shower. He's covered a considerable portion of the book and he's somewhat aggravated. Understanding is startin' to bud. He's gettin' a picture here. He needs more. He craves more.

He's angry.

He rolls over, pulls his mattress back, and grabs a pen. He doesn't feel like jumping down out of the top bunk, havin' to wrestle with slidin' out his footlocker to fish out his note pad.

After feeling around under the mattress for a minute, he finds an old sick-call form. He turns it over to the back and folds the paper in half. This done, he begins to write:

> *One score*
> > *Or somewhere close*
> *My journey brought me to the moment*
> > *When I wrote these words*
> *Mourning. Anniversary of my dearly departed.*
> > *Nobody knows my pain*
> > > *Nor saw my strain*
> *Managing, though I heard*
> > *Ain't no refuge*
> > > *For the brokenhearted*
> *Mangled in manacles*
> > *Eighteen inches*

Retrospect of my middle passage
(my) Native sons and daughters sold for naught.
(but) Guns, rum, and molasses
For cowrie shells, duly discarded
Make me wanna holla! . . .
Mutiny!
T'was my brothers who did it.
Used to be hardheaded
Forgive and forget it
Retribution fo' real
Won't accept what you do to me
Questioned by second-guessers
What do I do with these half-steppers
My infirmity
A-ffirmative Ac-tion
Got my fac-tion pacified . . . Denied the
Mule and 40 acres you had no intention of givin'
Preoccupied
Am I to break this cycle we livin'
Margaret Garner
Gathered her family and fled
Dry-mouthed informants in the big house
Master, Master!
The field niggas is runnin'
Margaret murdered two of her children
To protect 'em from recapture
How can I be happy here?!
Man, I was born black and proud o' my skin
But, I got problems within
When you hear me

Say I wanna be free
Peep the issue
   Damn the physical bondage
    Liberate my mentality!

By the next morning, Lil Chris is irate.

Well, more like smoldering. His intellect and imagination were aflame all through the night. His young mind went to so many places. So much to think about! The past. The present. The future, still looming so far out of reach. The needs of the day, though, the morning, the moment, are the only thing that's real. The only thing that can be.

The cell bars rack back and prisoners step out onto the tier for work call. Lil Chris fights back the impulse to go straight down to Wayne's cell to question him about why he would spend the night in that cell. With that dude? How crazy is that?

He can't keep fightin' for his boy, though. That'll only make matters worse. Lil Chris understands that. PowwWoww said the same thing in the letter he sent him the night PowwWoww got transferred to a satellite camp up North.

For that reason, Lil Chris keeps his distance while they file out of the cellblock and into the sallyport for role call. The whole time, he watches Wayne's cellmate, though. The prick is really no bigger than Wayne but he looks stronger. Brown-skinned with heavy shoulders and small legs. Stands over there with other 'victs. And they all fit the profile. Well-worn, state-issue clothing, sleeves ripped off, faces shiny from Magic Shave and baby oil. Tryna look young. Wolves.

Bunch o' samboes. Damn shame. Nothin' but Black men in this senseless situation. Where did that thought come from?

Whatever the case, they picked the wrong sheep.

No tools this morning. The line pusher sets them in line and they walk for about 30 minutes. They walk so far and for so long that an ice truck has to drive up with the water coolers. They move over flat ground down dusty roads, their dragging, exhausted steps, whether in work boots or wet boots, kickin' up fine clouds that envelop them. Between that and their sweat, it looks like they've been playin' in a sandpit.

When they finally approach the worksite, they're met by an old rusty trailer left beside a dry ditch on the roadside. Piled high with dirty five-gallon paint buckets. Beyond, what looks like endless rows of okra bushes that stand as tall as the line pusher mounted on horseback.

"Say, say, mayne. Check," C-Boy chuckles. He and Lil Chris exchange a look. "Not cool," he drags on. "We go in that stuff, we go'n be itchin' fo' days."

Both of 'em only slept in spells through the night. The growth. The green. The mass. The smell of it is vaguely invigorating.

"Mayne, they shoulda told us to wear long sleeves," someone else complains.

"We ain't just gotta put up with this shit. Nigga need to buck," another voice urges.

A lot of people start talkin' at once. The line pusher doesn't look worried in the least. Some cats sit down, take off their boots, and start to rip open the bottom seam of their socks. Makin' sleeves. The vast majority of them simply move to the trailer, grab their buckets, and wait for the headline to count out what row they'll be working. They're catchin' they cut.

Lil Chris uses the cover of confusion to pull Wayne deep into the okra patch. Once they're duly isolated, he wheels around and confronts his friend. "Mayne, what's hap'nin' wit' you?"

"What are you asking me?"

"On't ac' like you crazy, you ain't even that lame!"

"Wait a sec—"

"—You stupid muthafucka," Lil Chris cuts him off. His voice is high pitched. "You slept in that cell wit' that dude after I sent and *told* you he probably had a knife in there. Tell me you didn't get that kite!"

"Hold your voice down!" Wayne looks around to see if anyone's close.

"Enough for that pussy-ass nigga to jump on yo' back and put that blade to yo' throat," Lil Chris finishes, incredulous. "That's what you want?! You sleepin' on yo' stomach in that muthafucka?!"

Wayne's whole body is shaking. His mouth is clamped shut.

Lil Chris pushes him. Hard. "Fuck is wrong wit' you?" He shoves him again. This time with so much force Wayne stumbles back and almost falls down.

Wayne gathers himself and pushes him back.

Lil Chris shoves him again. Wayne grabs two fistfuls of Lil Chris's shirt.

C-Boy comes out of nowhere. "Say, mayne, both o' y'all trippin. Lil Chris, you act like you lovin' this nigga."

"What you go'n do, mayne?" Lil Chris asks, again. Breathing hard. "Wayne?"

"I just wanna be left alone," Wayne answers, his voice hoarse. Tears stream down his face.

In the distance, they can all hear the line pusher's horse movin' through the okra bushes.

"There it is," C-Boy says. "You cain't make him be something he ain't," he tells Lil Chris. "Leave 'im alone."

"Man, I don't bother anyone," Wayne speaks up. "I stay to myself. I mind my business. None of this makes sense."

"Check," C-Boy says. Talkin' breezy. "You from Houghton, first of all. You a young nigga. You ain't got no homeboys down here. You ain't got no money. And, worst of all, you too civilized."

C-Boy bends down to pick up his bucket. "I forgot one. You ain't my problem. Say, Lil Chris. You see this nigga weak. Let's go. This okra not go'n pick itself."

Lil Chris stands there, red-eyed. Looks at Wayne. "What you go'n do, Wayne?" he asks again.

Wayne shakes his head. "Go pick ya okra." He turns and stalks off by himself.

Lil Chris and C-Boy just stand there for a moment.

"Well," C-Boy says. "You heard him."

Wayne works methodically up and down the rows like he has a homing device in his back. He finds them sitting in a clearing they've made. Whatever they were doing, when Wayne steps into the open, he heads intently for them.

His cellie stands up off his improvised bucket seat. "What you—*ooaah*!"

Wayne caught him right in his solar plexus. "Go 'head. Breathe," Wayne urges him. "Soon as you catch your breath I got some mo' for you."

When it looks like he's just about caught his breath, Wayne wails and catches him flush in the side of his neck. When he doubles over, Wayne drives his elbow down as hard as he can in the small of that boy's back. Dead center.

He walks around the prone figure, looking for soft spots, like he's picking okra. Finally, he falls on him and knees him in the kidney. Drives him hard into the ground. Pins his shoulders and head-butts him in the side of the face.

By the time Lil Chris and C-Boy step into the clearing, Wayne is biting that boy in his face. Gotdamn!

Every time one of dude's homeboys tries to pull Wayne up, he shoves them off and falls back on that boy's head with his elbow. His cellie ain't even fighting back. He's not even screaming for help. He don't even fold up. He just grunts and takes it.

When they finally manage to pull Wayne off him, his cellmate just vomits and lays in it.

Lil Chris is so stunned by the scene, he doesn't come to himself until Wayne walks over and whispers, "Where's the line pusher?"

C-Boy starts to laugh.

Lil Chris just stares for a second. Realizes they're so deep in the okra the line pusher doesn't even know what's going on. He looks over to where they're tryna shake Wayne's cellmate back to consciousness.

He grabs the wire handle of a bucket half-full of okra and runs over with the bucket cocked over his shoulder. Two of the dudes shuffle out of the way. Lil Chris catches the third 'vict, brings the bucket down hard on the guy's head and back. Kicks him in his ass as he stumbles out of the clearing.

By the time the line pusher finds the inmate dry heaving in a puddle of his own vomit, C-Boy, Wayne, and Lil Chris all have buckets at least two-thirds full of okra. Gotta fill that quota.

CHAPTER THIRTEEN

Speak about this

In conspiratorial tongues

Look here!

Spiritual ones

Tote ya' crosses

Ay yo! Sport ya' choices

Note ya' losses

Broken voices, whisper

Foolishness

I bear fruit

New to this?

No! Please

I got nothin' to do with these thieves

I'm a go-getter

Thirty-first degree

Keep an ear
> *To the streets*
>> *Feed.*
Speak what I see
> *Don't doubt me, Sun.*

THEY STAND AT THE BARS eyeing each other. Why is it that they can't get along? Why the friction? Lil Chris has been waiting for him to come back around. He doesn't respect the way Rise jetted out the last time.

Still, Lil Chris has been reading. So affected by *Before the May-flower*, he read it twice. The funny thing is, he has never seen as clear and vivid a picture as he has gotten from this book. Not even when he took Black History in high school. He intends to speak on what he's picked up from it all, but first, he and Rise have issues they need to be about.

"You got something to say, lil playa?"

"You know what? You too comfortable with me," Lil Chris observes with menacing nonchalance. "You need to check that."

Rise laughs. He really digs this brother's spirit. Even now, he's feeding off him. He's also been walking around and talking to different people. Trying to see what can be done to pull the lil brother out of the blocks.

"What your case look like?" Rise asks him.

"Huh?"

"Where you at in court?" Rise persists.

"I . . . ah, my lawyer ah . . . "

"He don't know," C-Boy puts in from the bottom bunk, with the covers over his head.

"Shut up. What I told you about gettin' in' my business when I'm at these bars?"

"Hold up!" C-Boy sits up a bit. "What you mean 'what you told me?' You don't control what's said down here, playa. You got the game fu—"

"—Wait a minute," Rise interrupts. "I'm gettin' at something far more important than them strength games y'all playin' with each other in that cell."

Turning his attention back to Lil Chris, Rise says, "You mean to tell me you been here, ah . . . how long?"

"I been here going on three years."

"And you ain't on top of your law work?" Rise says, as if he can't believe it. However, he's not at all surprised. He's just feigning disbelief to add import to the notion that Lil Chris is major tripping, being in prison this long and not knowing law. The truth is it's commonplace for youngsters much like Lil Chris to come to prison and slowly get involved in everything *except* the primary thing that will guide them back through the front gates.

Of course, it's not hard for them to forget law. Most are struggling with the idea of walking these 18,000 acres of farmland for the rest of their lives. Most get into everything else to distract them from the painful thoughts associated with the front gates. Most are usually devoid of proper education, period. They lack the intellectual tools necessary to even consider the strategy of a legal angle to challenge their imprisonment.

That all comes later. After they have settled in. Acclimated. Once they can see the prison experience for what it is. That it's not what they're trying to make it.

When they first get to prison, at least for the first few years, most are content with leaving their law work to the indigent appellate project attorneys. These are appellate lawyers who more often than not will file a templated direct appeal, just to have the deal done. For appearance's sake. These lawyers usually leave these young men hanging after direct appeal, without even a letter to notify them that they've received their final state court denial. That their limited time to file a critical post-conviction relief application is already ticking away. It is for this exact reason that most of these brothers are procedurally barred from pursuing appellate relief. All this before they can even get around to opening a law book. For once, they are finally following their parents' advice, but still their time limit for filing an appeal usually runs out while they are on their knees praying to be released.

These truths weigh heavily on Rise's mind as he leaves the tier. The sergeant working the unit, looking for a chance to relax, rushes Rise off. Understandable. Rise has trained himself to deal with what comes, however it comes.

He's found out what he needs to know, anyway. For the next couple of weeks, Rise's primary objective is to get the lil homie pulled out of the blocks and into the law library.

Even if it costs him a few boxes of cigarettes to get it done.

It's 11:30 p.m. Showers just ended. The TV will go off in 20 minutes. C-Boy is already dead to the world. Lil Chris watches the last sitcom rerun of the night. He has another book. *Roots* by Alex Haley. He'll get into it once the TV shuts off.

Really, he smells her before he sees her. The tripped-out thing about it is that, when she comes into view, she steps in front of the cell lookin' as much like Elise Neal as the chick on the TV screen.

Beautiful. A smooth chocolate. Dime piece. But not as cultured as the actress. Nawl, she ratchet. This one is a real live wire.

She leans up against the bars and asks, "Yo' name Lil Chris?" in a conspiratorial tone.

"Who wanna know?"

Silence. They size each other up.

"Ooh, my girl said you a smart ass," she says, smiling.

He's not. "What you want wit' me?" The C'ster stares right into her hazel contacts.

"Roni says she miss you and she mad you ain't never call that number she gave you."

Lil Chris shuffles out of the top bunk. Jumps down to the floor with a thud. Steps eye to eye with her. Only the bars between them. "Oh, yeah! I know who you is!"

"Boy, be quiet—"

"You Ms. Roperson."

"Cynthia."

"How you get in here? Don't you work on the day shift?"

"You know the sergeant working this unit?"

"The young dude?"

"Yeah. That's my ole man."

"Damn, you don't look happy about that."

"Get you some bizzness," she says. Her words have a foreboding undercurrent.

"Yeah. I thought I told ya girl never to put people in hers. One o' y'all weak broads'll get caught up and tell God on Jesus," Lil Chris puts in. Watches her closely.

"But anyways," Cynthia rolls her eyes. "It's obvious you don't know who the hell you talkin' to."

"Man, come on wit' the theatrics—"

"—Um, Roni wanna know if the inmate counsel filed a' appeal after D.B. court downed you?"

"Ah, yeah, yeah. I guess he did," Lil Chris says. Don't sound too certain.

"Boy, you don't know?"

"Look, you go'n have to kill that 'boy' shit. You know a man when you see one?"

"When I see one I'll holla," she caps back with a knowing smile.

Lil Chris frowns. Then mugs. The boot starts to come in. He 'bout to say something ugly.

"Man, I was just playin'. Damn. That girl know you to a T."

"Look o' there. You can't even keep y'all business to ya'self. So y'all been talkin' about me, huh?"

"Man, look!" She's frustrated. He's satisfied.

"Tell her I wasn't even trippin' off all that. Why?"

"Don't worry about it. You got anything else you want me to tell her for you?" An irritated scowl takes up her pretty face. Good.

"She know all that," Lil Chris says, smiling.

"Wi' cho' smart azz. I'll see you later."

She leaves as suddenly as she came. As she walks away, the TV flicks off. Only the sweet smell of her perfume lingers.

C-Boy never so much as even stirs. Of course, he was up ear-hustlin' the whole time.

About two weeks later, Lil Chris gets farm mail from Legal Services. His disciplinary appeal has been granted. He will be returned back to population housing and given a job as an education building orderly.

He and C-Boy spend their last night in the cell together eating a tuna fish hookup with oysters. Fish steaks, honey, and all them shits. They even send some down to Wayne and his new cellie. A penitentiary feast. They wash it all down with concentrated iced tea mix and stay up all night running eps about the hood. They've really come to be as close as brothers in this lil cell.

The next morning, while C-Boy is gone out in the field for work call, the people call Lil Chris to pack his things. Push out. As he leaves, he turns around and looks at the cell as the door eases shut behind him. He was on the floor praying for wisdom and knowledge like Solomon's when the call came down. He leaves all of the food products he had in his box on C-Boy's bunk.

He'll never forget the time he spent in these blocks.

CHAPTER FOURTEEN

Do everything you can
Then stand
Give it all you got
Then stand, Mr. Man
Come before me
I'll make you ill, again
Listen to me
I'll make you feel again
Stand before me
I'll make you real, again
. . . Just what you can
Then stand!

THIS IS NOTHING.

No sound. No movement. No feeling or sensitivity. No conscious thought. All is black. Black is the bosom of creation. All that is comes through black. Is from black. Black is the bosom of creation. And black is nothing. Ain't that something?

Blome, blome, blome . . . Clank, blome, blome, clank . . . Clank, clank. . .

The bed is sha—no, the bunk is—no, this is a cot, the cot is jerkin' under me. Damn, I'm in jail, man. . .

Clank, clank . . . Blome!

Man, what the— Lil Chris pops up on his elbows. He was lying on his stomach. He shakes the thin white sheet off his head. Looks around trying to see what's happening.

Blome, blome!

He jerks back and swings around, scowls, ready to—*What! Damn! Boy, that's cold-blooded!* He frowns, gets a menacing look in his eyes. Focuses on his unlikely tormentor.

"Boy, is you go'n get up an go to work or what?" she says with a smart smirk across her pursed lips. Squinting her eyes.

"Oh, you wanna play, huh, lil girl," Lil Chris says. He thinks, *Damn, what's this gal name again?*

"This ain't no game. It's almost 8:30. You need to get up."

"Cynth—Sergeant," he stammers. Sitting up, but still in no rush. "A'ight, you got that."

He watches her as she walks away. So fine. Damn.

Prison is an exercise in crime against nature. Simple and plain. Lil Chris has gotten used to the likes of C-Boy's ugly mug being the first thing he sees when he wakes up, hollerin' 'bout, "Say, man you need to get yo'self up. You go'n eat that bacon?"

Now, to wake up and see Cynthia Roperson standing over him in them skin-tight ass-grippers. *Damn, she pimpin' that uniform*, he thinks to himself. Aggravated.

As Lil Chris swings the corner coming into the education building, Rise approaches him.

"I'm glad you decided to join us."

"What's happenin', my ni—my man. Excuse me."

Rise gathers himself. "No, it's cool. I'm glad to see you tryna get that out of your system."

"I read something that gave me a new perspective. Ya see where I'm at? That got me feelin' some things."

"Yeah, alright. Well, go ahead and check in with Ms. Angelwing, she lookin' at you kinda crazy. Then come upstairs. My man Kunta go'n show you how to work your drop. I want you to hurry up. 'Cause after you finish, I'ma show you a couple of things in the law library."

They dap off and Rise moves out. Lil Chris walks over to the security station and checks in. The woman ain't even trippin' that he's two hours late. That, in itself, got him trippin'.

As Lil Chris climbs up the last couple of steps, he spots this dark-skinned brother. Muscular frame. He's extremely neat. His appearance speaks of a man with a sharp eye for detail. Designer sideburns. Snow white teeth. Precisely-shaped mustache and beard. Starched and ironed blue jean shirt and pants. Spit-shined work boots. The immaculate white handkerchief hangin' out of his back pocket is even pressed. The dude could be anything but an orderly.

"What's happenin', my man," he greets Lil Chris with a broad-faced smile. "They call me Kunta."

"Alright, now," the C'ster says, shaking his hand. "My name Lil Chris."

"You the biggest lil man I ever seen. How you get that name?"

The question is one that Lil Chris usually shrugs off with silence. But there is something about this cat that's . . . well, kind o' cool.

"People been callin' me that since I was young. Well, real young I mean," Lil Chris says. "So what's up with this work?"

"That's what I'm finna show you. Your area is go'n be easy. You just gotta stay on top of it." Kunta steps out of the doorway to let Lil Chris onto the second floor. He already has a mop bucket with pine oil and bleach water made up.

Lil Chris steps into the main hallway and grabs the mop

Kunta continues. "The free folks make their rounds twice a day. You just make sure that when the brass come down it ain't nothing that they can just see wrong and point their finger at. You feel me?"

Lil Chris nods.

Kunta goes on. "The best thing about it is that Sergeant Angelwing. Brah, she ain't 'bout no trouble. And she ain't go'n sweat you. Oh, she might call you from time to time to get her something. Or to handle lil knick-knack stuff. Especially if she dig you. But if that's the case, you'll know it. See where I'm at? Other than that, ain't nobody go'n say nothin' about what time you get here. Long as you beat the brass to work. Then again, if you late I'ma hit ya drop for you. Just like I expect you to do for me. We keep the ranking officers out the sergeant business, that'll keep her out our business.

"Now I'ma give you this lick on how to hit your drop every morning when you come in. Other than what I'm about to show you, unless they call you specifically for something, like clearing a room or waxing the floors—and nine times out of ten you'll know about that ahead of time—besides that, your job will be basically to stay out the way. You get it? You got it? Good."

With that, Kunta walks off. Lil Chris follows.

Half the day is gone. Security just dismissed Rise's morning class. For the moment, Rise is sits up and thinking about Shonda. Wishes he could be out there with her. She's never known exactly how much she's come to mean to him. Rise is too strong-willed to bind her to him. Expressing the true sum of what he feels for her. Damn. If only . . .

"To touch without feeling is the ultimate sin."

Rise doesn't even have to look up to know who this is. He responds, "Far worse than blasphemy." Pushing out from under his desk, he stands to embrace Gary Law.

"How's the brother?"

"I'm straight."

"How we looking in P.C.P.A?"

"This new group is developing well," Rise explains. "I've had to flush one or two undesirables out, but other than that we're pretty much familiar with most of these dudes. Those we don't know directly are cool. They been around. We got a pretty good feel for what they're about."

"Well, I've heard that Da One is starting to stir the pot. Have you considered the implications of their operating this close to us? With this destructive mindset they propagate?" Gary is trying to hide it, but he's visibly concerned.

"I know this much: we're too preoccupied with what we're doin' to be trippin' off them."

Rise's intuition tells him that now is too early to expose his hand. Not even to G. But he definitely has a game plan.

G senses Rise's reluctance. He presses, "I see we got a new orderly in the building. That's ya homeboy, huh?"

Rise lifts an eyebrow. Chooses his words carefully. *G kinda nice wit' his. Can't forget that.* "Yeah. He came on today." *Say no more than necessary.*

"Has he been fingered for development?"

"Why would you ask?"

"Well, because I know you went out of your way to get him released from the blocks."

"I do that for a lot of people, not just prospects and homeboys," Rise shoots back.

"So you're saying that there is nothing significant about your giving the brother a hand up? Remember the constitution."

"I'm aware of the constitution. Well aware."

"Well?"

"Well, the people I talked to didn't move. Apparently, the lil brother had more than one well to draw from."

"How could that be? He almost beat that other brother to death. How did he get out of that—wasn't he in the fieldline? How did he get another drop?"

Rise frowns. "Are you questioning his integrity?"

"I'm merely asking questions. Relevant questions."

"Institutional appellate process."

G is sits there looking dumbfounded. Then he takes a deep breath and says, "Talk to me, Rise."

"What, G?!" Rise is exasperated. "Whadaya wanna know?" G looks back at him, expressionless.

"Okay, man, look . . . " Rise stops. Inhales deeply. He considers himself. Then he straightens up and says, "I never told anyone what I'm about to tell you."

He stops to peep G's reaction. Stonegrill. Gary Law's face is a mask. Rise continues, "More years back then I care to remember—I'm sure you can relate to that—about two years after I started this joust—"

"—You mean when you were in juvenile, right?"

"Look, don't interrupt me, G. Just sit there and vibe wit' me for a minute, man. Yeah, when I was in juvenile, I had this cell partner. His name was . . . well, we called him Playa C. Now, at first he and I didn't get along. I don't know. I guess he felt like I was a square. A buster, or something. I thought this dude was conniving, selfish. Self-centered. Anyways, I believe we jousted for four years together. I was three years older than him. But, by far, he was the most influential of the two of us. Admittedly."

Rise chuckles. His eyes sparkle with the light of the memory. "Man, he kept me in foolishness. Either he done took somebody stuff, or owed somebody he refused to pay. Or he done punched someone's cousin down. It seemed it was always he and I against everybody. We went from being down by default, to down by law.

"But we didn't care, though. I mean, obviously he didn't and I know I didn't. They knew if they was at him, I would be involved. Man, I remember this one time we were comin' back from workshop.

Like 14, 15 kids came at us. I believe their beef was that Playa C had punched they boy in the face for some reason or another. Anyway, the people, they were corrupt in that place. Two or three security personnel knew what was about to go down, but they had been given Skoal and chewing tobacco to turn a blind eye. I stepped in front of Playa C. Lookin' more confident than I felt, I told 'em wasn't go'n be no crowd play. But if they boy wanted to go toe-to-toe wit' my lil brother, we could do that. It was a cat name DaddyHouse. Him and Playa C went into a mix for a minute. C dropped him.

"His boys ain't like that. Especially with me jumpin' around and talkin' trash. Playa C ended up droppin' that boy three times. I mean scufflin' him up. So, one time, the last time, he puts him dead on his ass, right. Playa C was finna start stompin' him. I stepped in and pulled him back. But I was too late. They rushed us, the majority came at me. I was in a circle of 'em. Just swingin' wild and shit. I had lost sight of Playa C. When they crowded me, I just grabbed the closest one to me and pulled him down wit' me. The more they pounded me, the more I worked him over.

"Then, all of a sudden, there's this loud clap. I kinda thought it was a gun. Everyone else must've thought so, too, 'cause they let up a bit on me. Come to find out, it was Playa C wavin' a shovel spade. Swinging it with wild abandon. I saw him crack two of 'em over the head. He was aimin' wit' the edge, too. I don't know how they survived with their domes intact.

"Still though, the thing about it that I'll never forget is how it ended. A couple of our boys had come to our aid in the melee. Once we had run 'em off, we turned back . . . " Rise's voice catches. He goes on like it didn't. "We're out of breath. Heavin' and gaspin'. Most of all, laughin' . . . at least, we were until we came up on Playa C. Dude was sittin' on the curve with the shovel layin' to his side. With his head down. He was slouched over cryin' like a baby. I was like, 'Man, what's wrong wit' you?' He looks up, with tears rollin' down his face. Sniffin' and shit. He says something that we can hardly make out. So, I sit down and I ask him again if he's alright. He looks at me, I swear, and says, 'Them fools jumped on my brother.'"

Tears run down Rise's face too. "It took me a minute . . . to realize that he was talkin' about me. That really shook me up. I told him, 'Come on, get up, kid. I'm a'ight. I'm straight.' And we got up, and . . . he and I were really brothers." Rise stops and just stares at nothing. G doesn't say a word. Rise closes the classroom door. Then he turns around and looks at G.

"The crooked officer," Rise presses. "And he was crooked. The one that got killed in the riot. He was not my kill. I won't go into details, but the buck just kicked off. Somebody refused to accept that. No one could have called it, but before long there was rioting everywhere. Only a few people know what actually happened." Rise looks Gary Law square in the eyes. "I was falsely accused and convicted, and I never said a mumblin' word.

"You know, for a long time I've only focused on what I felt was the injustice done to me. That Victim Awareness course I took last year changed all of that. Man, those survivors . . . you gotta be made of stone not to feel them. No matter how wrong that officer was, I'm aware that there is a mother or child that survives him. The ripples from the pebble in the pond.

"Anyway, Playa C got out about a year after I came down here. His grandpa, his legal guardian, passed shortly after that. My moms adopted him to keep him out of the system. Now we was brothers for real. He gave Momma 'n 'em hell, though. In and out of trouble. Fist fights and shootouts. The same pattern. He'd start shit, trouble, and no one would know about it until it came back around full circle. My family worked with him, though. More than put up with him. Playa C ended up getting his G.E.D. and even takin' a few months of junior college. He ended up meeting this chick. Before long he was doin' the family thing. He was working his way through the madness."

Rise exhales deeply. Closes his eyes. Continues. "He jousted me. Did the time with me. Made sure I had commissary and clothes.

Literally became a resource. I mean *really*. For about four years or so. I don't know where he was getting' the money. He was finding a way to touch me. I didn't struggle too much with creature comforts. For my part, I was encouraging him. Tryna keep him progressive. I really wanted him on top of his thing."

Rise takes a breath. "He and his girl had that graveyard love," he nods. "They swore love for life. That only death would do them part. And, I don't know about her, but he always kept his word.

"His step-pops was like mine. He was violent. This was one of the main things Playa C and I had in common. We hated our stepdads. We both swore to never be like them. Shocked doesn't describe how shook I was to find out he was fighting his babymomma. Man, it was awful. All messed up. They argued all the time. I would talk to him on the phone and he would be in this place . . . this place in his head. He'd go on and on about how much he loved her. We never talked about the fighting. Maybe I should have . . . I knew even then that it was killin' him. To be like his stepdad. To do like him. It got to the point where I would call and he wouldn't come to the phone. I never really thought much of it. I figured he was just trippin'." Tears stream down Rise's face. "I would pray for him. For the whole family, but for him in particular. His real name was Chris."

"I know, man," G says.

Rise gets up and walks to the window. He stands there, the same blank look on his face. "I dunno. I don't care. You know, it's been almost four years and he's still on my visiting list." Rise gives a dry laugh. He wipes his face.

"I don't know what to think about it," Rise says with resolution. "I wasn't allowed to go to the funeral. I used to sleep hard after that. A dreamless sleep. I thought I had pushed the whole thing to the back of my mind. And, maybe I had."

"Until you met this youngster that started working up here today."

"From the time I first saw him. His demeanor. His attitude. So familiar. This young cat's swag—I mean, even his name. And from the first time I saw him at the A.U. orientation, I began having these, I don't know, visions. I'm not sure . . . but whatever the case, they seem real. What I'm saying is meeting him triggered a process. Ended up making me confront my issues with the whole situation. My brother's suicide. I'm resolving those issues—in my own way."

"And, so," Gary Law cuts in, "You see this little guy as your second chance at, what, a lil brother? Is that why you are so drawn to the idea of developing this boy? And don't gimme that 'He hasn't been fingered for development' crap. I know you, Rise."

"Yeah, I'm thinking of pulling him in. Okay . . . so, isn't screening and expansion my area?"

"My sources tell me he's already been recruited by Da One."

Rise refocuses in an instant. He comes completely out of his melancholic haze. He looks at Gary Law intensely. Eye to eye. "So what?"

Later that afternoon, just before evening chow call. The door stands open to the law library. Lil Chris has been finished with his drop for some time now. He took to Kunta's program in no time. The work is really mindless. He walks around just to see whatever it is to see. Learn the terrain. One of the main concepts he picked up from a little handbook he read while he was in the blocks. *The Art of War* by Sun Tzu.

This is about the third time he's passed by the law library today. This time, as he looks through the window, the desk clerk waves for him to come in.

Lil Chris sticks his head through the door.

"What? You need me to do something?"

"No, come in, please. My name is Gary Law."

"Oh, my name Lil Chris."

"Why do you call yourself Lil Chris?"

Question kind of caught the C'ster wrong. He doesn't answer.

"How long have you been in Angola?" G asks.

"A little under three years."

"Do you have a lawyer?"

"Oh, I ain't here on law library callout. I work up here."

G smiles. "I'm aware of that. I work as an inmate counsel."

"Well, why you as—"

"Because, it's my job to make sure your law work is straight," G provides. Not entirely truthful.

Silence. They stare at each other. Eye to eye. You never know what people's intentions are in this place. Careful, now. They both know this.

"Yeah," Lil Chris says. "I got a lawyer."

"Paid?"

"Ah, court-appointed."

"Where does your appeal stand?"

Lil Chris thinks. "I just got a letter saying the Second Circuit denied me. So, I guess that means I got 14 days to file for rehearing. Thirty to go to the next court." Lil Chris feels pretty good. Those law books he started sending for after he had that talk with Rise really helped.

"What you go'n do if he don't file your writ on time?"

Damn. Another good question, Lil Chris thinks.

"Well, while you thinking about that, could you tell me what collateral review is?"

"No."

"Well, what are you going to do after you leave your state supreme court? You do know that after that you won't have the appointed lawyer anymore, right?"

Silence.

"Have a seat, youngster. Let me explain something to you. In case they haven't told you, your job is actually to first make sure that things look neat when the rank come through, and, secondly, to be invisible. You follow me?"

Lil Chris nods.

"Now, there is something about your situation that you need to understand. The prison system is a racket. When we go out and commit criminal acts and get caught, we fall into a well-planned net. A trap. From that point forward, it's we, the offenders, who are usually victimized.

"They already know that the large percentage of us don't know the law—let alone our rights. This problem is compounded by the fact that most of us can't afford competent legal assistance. We're given a court-appointed lawyer who not only doesn't have adequate resources, but also can't properly defend us even if they did have the resources. They're being called to defend too many clients at one time.

"This is the backing we have when we step into the courtroom to face an assistant district attorney who's more concerned with winning than with uncovering the truth. The whole concept of justice in this sense is a sham. The objective isn't to punish us for what we've done—most of us rightfully so, mind you." G raises his eyebrows. "The name of the game is to convict us of the harshest law violation they can match to our actions, and to then give us the largest possible number of years for it. They aren't concerned with us coming back home some-day. The prison owners get paid two ways off us: first, they get a set amount of money per head per day; then, they also get free labor to produce products that they turn around and sell for profit.

"I need you to *understand* this, youngster. Once they place you here, they are not concerned about whether you are innocent or un-justly convicted. Once you get here, they intend to *keep* you here. What they do is play the time game with us. You have so many days to file for review to each court, right? If you or a lawyer representing you misses a deadline, *that in itself* is grounds to keep you from getting any relief on appeal.

"Once you come out of state supreme court, your court-appointed lawyer leaves you to fend for yourself. You don't have but a year to go from state-direct appeal back to your state district. That's co-lateral review. Get it? Double. Up. Two chances. If you go *a day* over the time limit, your case is dead. Some say you have two years. If you wait two years, though, you're dead. Your best chance really won't come until you get to the feds. But if you mishandle the state leg of your co-lateral review . . . that's right. You're dead. This is the situation we're all in. Matter of fact, most of the guys that get held in the parish jail for two and three years after they are convicted are already dead—barred out of court by the time they get here, because of time violations.

"What I'm trying to tell you is that you don't have time to waste on foolishness, son. These people aren't playing. When they say life, they mean life. A lot of brothers have a real uphill battle. It doesn't matter if you have a paid lawyer or not. You have to know the law, no matter what. You have to know your issues. How else are you gonna know if this person you're paying is working for you, or just taking you fast? You gotta keep up, lil brother. Help yourself.

"This is free game I'ma give you. Take it. Please. And grow it. I'll teach you how to use this law library to your advantage. Don't let one of these other chumps that work in here convince you that you need them to do your law work for you. I can already tell that you got a good head on your shoulders. You know how to listen. That's the most important thing. Law can be hard, or it can be simple. Research, analysis, synthesis, litigation. So, as I believe you youngsters say, are you down or what?"

Lil Chris stands up and shakes Gary Law's hand. Looks him in the eye and says, "Let's do this."

THIRD VERSE

One year, six months later

CHAPTER FIFTEEN

This is for my people
    Who feel snake-bitten
For real
    I'm feelin' ya' pain
Hopes decimated
    Contemplatin' ya' situation
Compelled to get in the game
    Who know the score!
No rules
    They makin' 'em as they go along
        Play us like fools
I'm factin' wit' you
We winnin' to lose
    Who know the answers?
These people that we read about in newsletters?

Newspapers tellin' us lies
The truth is
   Often we been misrepresented
Invested efforts brought us no returns
   Dis-service like augmented
      Still we return
Faith in politics?
   Politicians are not concerned
      Still no return.
But struggle we have
   And struggle we will
Till our ultimate destiny is fulfilled
      Liberation
I speak these words for confirmation
   What's yet to come
And condemnation
   To all who chose to betray the chosen sun
Let this music ride the backs of oppressors
   And promise breakers.
We refuse to be what you make us
   What does that make us . . .
      Chumps or victims?

HE HAS JUST ABOUT MEMORIZED the material. C-Boy carefully folds the typed handout and slides it into his pocket. He and Wayne stand at the West Yard gate waiting for Sergeant Evansworth to yell for the Education Building call-outs to come through. C-Boy has been up since 4:00 a.m. studying for the political science class the big homie T. Guy teaches for the Angola Special Civics Project.

C-Boy has been doing the same thing since the course started five weeks ago. He lets the whole week go by without picking up the handout. Then, he gets up early Saturday morning to memorize the material before going to class for the weekly quiz. So far, so good. Up to this point, he's been making nothin' but 100-percents on all his exams and quizzes.

Wayne shakes his head. He long ago came to the conclusion that it is futile to explain to C-Boy that he's only registering the material in his short-term memory. Really defeats the purpose of taking the course in the first place. C-Boy is exactly the type of person Wayne usually chooses to avoid when at all possible. The only reason he's dealing with this obnoxious character is because of Lil Chris, to whom he agreed to tutor this imbecile.

Depending on how you look at it, things have been relatively hard *or* easy. Crucial or privileged. At least for Wayne that is. He has learned that prison is the wrong place to be civilized. Sometimes you just have to do things that defy reason. Trying to rationalize every move has always been his Achilles heel.

It really got bad after the skirmish. Wayne was well aware that wolves tend to wait in the shadows. To circle in on the weak one who's caught out there by himself. Backward-minded prisoners are no different.

Not so for Wayne. Word has slowly gotten out that for all his questionable tolerance, Wayne will fight if backed into a corner. As a result, his standard of living—in terms of how other prisoners treat him—has improved.

That's all Lil Chris needed to hear. Now, provided that Wayne makes a showing for himself, the C'ster makes sure that the homie henchmen have his back when the drama is too much for him to handle alone. Wayne didn't have any friends, so when the brothers started stepping up on his behalf, it didn't take long for him to figure out the root of his supply line.

With this added backing, Wayne has put together a proper joust. A comparatively better existence in this place. Not only is he in the Bible College now, he also works in the visitation shed on weekends. It's not much, but at least now he's been hooking the homies and their families up with free food. A small token of his appreciation. He's finding a way to keep his head up.

Another one of Wayne's problems is that he thinks too highly of himself to just come out and say thank you. However, he is extremely loyal to Lil Chris. This is why Wayne went ahead and signed up for this class that Rise's folk, T. Guy, put together. Lil Chris wasn't getting visitins, and this way they could kick it. He hadn't banked on Lil Chris being so serious about the curriculum. It was at this point Wayne decided to at least try to help Lil Chris's cohorts.

"Alright, come on, ah . . . A.S.C.P.," Sergeant Evansworth finally called. "All you boys that's tryna learn about the government. Yeah, you ah, politicians. Come on here. Hey, hey . . . ah, Calvin English, ah, French—whatever yo' name is—C-Boy! You know I'm talkin' to you. Whatever they call you. Yeah, just stand there and pull them britches on up around ya' waist like a decent, ah, convict. Yeah, what? You lookin' crazy, huh? Well, g'on on back to the dorm and put on some jeans that fit you. Yeah . . . g'on, now. Hurry up, for you say I'm makin' you miss ya callout. You didn't wanna go, anyway. That's for smart people. Come on through, Wayne. No! I don't wanna hear it! That boy stuntin', anyway! He'll meet you up there, later on. He didn't really wanna go. He know how to come up to this gate when I'm working. What?! Y'all g'on on now!"

C-Boy heads back to the dormitory. Wayne heads toward the Education Building. He shakes his head. These are the type of people Lil Chris is so drawn to and down with.

"Question three: what was the problem with the Articles of Confederation?"

As Rise finished writing the question T. Guy just posed on the chalk board, Lil Chris collects his thoughts. *I can't get none of this wrong.* He and Rise have some kind of a grudge going. Rise, who volunteered to help T. Guy, is willing to accept nothing less than excellence from Lil Chris. Their relationship has really developed over the last year and a half, since the C'ster came back from the blocks. Although they stay at each other's throats, they make it an unspoken rule to never disagree in front of an audience.

"Question four: what was the difference between the Virginia Plan and the New Jersey Plan?"

Wayne jerks his paper and slouches further down on his desk to shield his answers with his left shoulder and elbow.

"Say, mayne, wuz happenin'?" C-Boy whispers harshly, forgetting himself.

"Is everything alright over there? C-Boy? Wayne?" T. Guy asks.

Manipulator starts snickering. Taco kicks his foot.

Muse says, "Oh, excuse me, brah. I got gas." Everyone laughs.

"And, for your last question, explain both The Great Compromise and The Three-Fifths Compromise."

A low groan emits from the student body. All except Lil Chris. He drops his head and begins to write.

"Brothers," T. Guy begins. "The thing that we need always remember about the U.S. Constitution is that it is only what we call the framework of government. It does not specify each law that we should live by. What it does is simply provide the parameters, or boundaries, within which the laws should fall. You gotta give it to 'em. Yeah, yeah, yeah, they were an assembly of hypocrites who fought to shake off enslavement by one nation only to enslave others. But never let your resentment blind you from acknowledging a very, very important truth: these men, most of 'em young, in their twenties and thirties, put together a truly timeless document. Laws will always change and develop with the times, swinging moral values, new belief systems, and growth customs. But the constitution provides the scope. Okay, look, it's like a basketball court. Think of all the—"

"Man, come on," Manipulator says. "We know what scope is."

"No, Nip. *We* don't. So, for the benefit of those of us who don't know . . . I know we're all men, and men sometimes have a problem admitting they don't know. Let me finish. Anyway, like a basketball court, the Constitution provides our baselines. I mean, think of all the amazing things that go on on a basketball court. Yeah, the rules are subject to change. Safety concerns, game expedience, and advancements in skills and abilities, but . . . *but!* All of that has to take place within the baselines, or outlines, of the basketball court. Are y'all gettin' the picture, now?"

"Yeah."

"Yeah, we can dig it."

"We got it."

"Now, I'm not a basketball expert, but the same court measurements that Bill Russell played on are the same court measurements that Shaq and Kobe have won basketball championships on. Of course, the rules have changed along the way. They've added the slam dunk and the three-point line. There are goaltending and illegal defense violations. They say these changes were made to do everything from make the game more exciting to preserve fair play. Negotiating the challenges presented by the amazing physical skills that have developed in ballplayers over the years," T. Guy explains.

"Believe that. I bet they ain't have nobody flying from the free-throw line when Russell was playing," C-Boy puts in.

Everyone chuckles. T. Guy capitalizes on their open minds. "That's the same situation we have with the Constitution. No one back then could have imagined the wealth of the robber barons or Apple. The complications of the Great Depression. What to do with freed Black folks, evolved women, and alcohol. The Constitution's articles simply establish what's in or out of bounds. Although there is a deeper history, it's still as easily understood. Since 1788, the framework has been in place. And, almost immediately, they began to make changes. First major change, the first ten amendments, were in place by 1891. Then they began to lay down the intricate laws. Through the course of time, they have changed over and over again.

"Brothers, always remember, a nation is a state of mind. It isn't a body of land, or a group of people. It is the understanding that a group of people share. It is the common understanding I speak of. This is what's embodied in the Constitution. Why is it important that you all should be familiar with this? I mean, what difference does it make?" T. Guy asks.

No one answers.

"Lil Chris," Rise speaks up. "Lil Chris knows the answer to that question. No sweat. Ain't that right, lil homie?"

"Because the constitution, as America's social contract, represents the nation's conscience. It's almost like . . . like a . . . a civil philosopher's stone. No, let me try, again—"

"No, you had your—"

"—Hold up, man!" Lil Chris cuts Rise short. "Now, as I was sayin' before the big homie's interruption—whenever there have been people in the history of this nation, existing under the nation's Constitution, that have felt that their living conditions were sub-par—when people felt like they weren't getting a fair shake, then they would say that their livin' was unconstitutional.

"It's like this," he continues. "The Constitution, especially the Constitutional Amendments, which people call the Bill of Rights, is like a promise. Not a promise that people can have these rights of freedom, or individual ownership, or the pursuit of happiness—the Declaration says we were *born* with these rights. What the Constitution does is promise these rights will be protected. And that they won't be violated."

"Yeah, that's right," Manipulator puts in. "That's why when they had movements and whatchamacallit, ah . . . ah, mass . . . mass protests! When they have mass protests, the first thing they do is throw the Constitution in them fools' faces."

"What fools?" T. Guy asks.

"The, ah, government. They go to the government with the Constitution."

"But wait a minute. Didn't y'all just tell me on y'all quiz answers that the form of government in America is democracy? Government by the governed. Rule of the people and all that," T. Guy shoots at them. "It's a lot of people in America. You mean they—"

"Nooo!" Taco puts in. "They tah'm 'bout the, ah, Congress!"

"Okay, now we are a little bit further ahead of what we've covered in this course so far. But I wanna go wit' this. What's Congress?" T. Guy asks.

"The, ah . . . House."

"Repa—"

"The Congress is politicians and shit."

"Ha, ha. Come on, man. No cursing during class."

"The Senate and the House of Representatives," Wayne says. Involved, in spite of himself.

"Yeah, that's what I was saying at first," Manipulator says. "I was sayin' that when people feel like they being messed over, they go to the government, Congress, or the legislature, which is the same thing."

"Okay, well, what are some examples of protests?" T. Guy pushes.

Muse says, "The Civil Rights Movement was a protest. And, the, ah . . . women's right to vote."

"And, they fought with the Constitution?"

"Yeah."

"Was the legislature, or Congress, the only government body, or branch, they approached with their grievances?" T. Guy asks. "Nip, help me out?"

"Nawl, they go to the courts, too," Manipulator says.

"The judicial branch. That's right. And there are several other resources wronged people will approach with the Constitution as their backing. We'll break all of these down later in the course. However, the reason why we went down this road is because I wanted y'all all to see why studying the Constitution is important to you."

"It's because the Constitution is what we have to fight with to get out of jail," Lil Chris cuts in. "Whether on the state or federal level, we stand in front of the courts with the Constitution as our weapon and our protection."

T. Guy looks at Rise. Rise smiles and shakes his head.

"Yeah, Lil Chris. You're right. This is one reason. Right now, probably the most important reason why we should know the Constitution in and out."

Ironically, C-Boy has learned how to beat the security checkpoints by reading a book written about the prison's warden and his unit management security strategy. The book, *Cain's Redemption*, has all kinds of fly lil tidbits that helped him get a better understanding of the controlled chaos that has been his prison experience for more than a decade.

Now, having easily made it through the network of locked gates, he has a couple sugar bags in his pocket as he turns off the East Yard walk and onto the yard. He takes a left, followed by a right by the back basketball court, and spots Lil Chris sitting on the far end ledge, talking to the big homie.

"What it do, soul," Lil Chris greets him.

Rise nods and asks, "You a long way out of pocket, huh?"

"Check . . . c'mon, Rise. It's good. I'll be back on the West Yard before the whistle blows."

"Had to come kick it wit' ya' folks, huh?" Rise observes. "I can dig it. I'll see what I can do about getting you moved over here. Looks like Wayne could get it done on his own."

"'Preciate that, big homie."

"It's nothing," Rise assures him. "Okay. I'ma leave y'all to whatever you're about."

With that Rise pushes.

"Rise don't really be hangin' out, huh?" C-Boy observes.

"He coolin'," Lil Chris puts it. "His head on his court order right now."

"Word," C-Boy says. Excited.

"I know he prob'ly anxious as hell. Boy! He 'bout to see that free world!"

"You ain't neva lyin'," C-Boy replies. "So, you still smokin' or what?"

"What," Lil Chris chuckles. "Askin' me that crazy. Mayne, roll that up."

C-Boy fishes the two sugar bags out of his pocket. "This dat purp, right here. This shit go'n knock yo' socks off."

"You walkin' around with that in your pocket?" the C'ster queries, slyly.

"Say, mayne. Check," C-Boy caps back. "Don't try me. I 'on't be finger fuckin' myself like dat. Them niggas crazy!"

Lil Chris laughs.

C-Boy finishes rolling the two squares. He fires one up and passes the other one to Lil Chris. "There. That's you, to da head."

They smoke in silence for a spell. The smell of the potent herb wafts up and around them, enveloping and stimulating.

"It feel like . . . "

"You feel that?"

"Hell yeah," Lil Chris says. "I'm sayin' . . . it feel like . . . this shit cleaning my mind."

C-Boy cracks up. They both snicker.

"I know you high," C-Boy says. "Nigga tah'm 'bout the weed cleanin' his mind."

"For real, mayne," Lil Chris assures him.

"Just airin' ya shit out," C-Boy says. A deep throated giggle. "Cleaning yo' constitution," he whispers.

They burst out laughing.

A few weeks later, Lil Chris and C-Boy meet up at the gym to get a workout in. As they begin their routine, they peep No Love walking in with someone Lil Chris hasn't seen in some time.

"Man, that's Mansa! Look out! Over here! Come holla!" Lil Chris is instantly amped. Mansa looks up and walks over with No Love.

"What's happening, young man?"

"Mansa Musa! You named yourself after a African king from Mali."

"That's good. You been doin' your research. In the future, you want to refer to his state as the Empire of Mali, respectfully."

"The old Mansa was Muslim. What, you a Muslim?"

"Don't worry about that. That's the way we've been conditioned. To classify everything. It's that Americanized file-and-rank tendency. Control that."

"A'ight, you got that," Lil Chris says, irritated at being corrected twice.

"Kid, I remember a time when you would've been ready to bump if somebody checked you like that," No Love observes.

"He didn't check me, homie. He corrected me. It's a difference. Besides, I ain't trippin' like that no more," Lil Chris says.

"Them books done civilized him. Don't let the information kill your beast, young man," Mansa warns.

"No, never that. But I do know how to control my beast. No one provokes me. I determine when and when not to move. C-Boy, I'm finna go over here by the bleachers with the homie 'n 'em right quick."

"Say, say, man! We just got started. You go'n break up the routine. You can always talk to dem," C-Boy protests.

"Balance, lil brother. It ain't good to be one-sided. Okay, you working on your body. What about your mind? Ya spirit? Mind, body, and soul, young brave. You need to come over for a minute, too."

"Man, who is you s'posed to—"

"Come on, C-Beasley," Lil Chris interjects, tryin' to get C-Boy to chill. "C-Beesalini. Come mob wit' me. It ain't go'n set us back but—"

"A'ight, a'ight, man. But, say, say, look . . . Man, I'm sayin'—"

"You got that, yo," Lil Chris finishes before he can start. Mansa and No Love look at each other like, *What the hell?* The four of them walk over to the bleachers flanking the ball court.

"Spit somethin'," No Love urges.

"Hold up, Love. Nawl, Mansa. I wanted to tell you I appreciate you. You pointed me in the right direction when you gave me that book. I hate you ended up gettin' caught up on the—what it was? Twelve sugar bag play?" Lil Chris says.

"Don't sweat it. That's the joint. One minute I'm in this spot, the next minute I'm over there."

"Say, say, say, Lil Chris. Won't you g'on 'head spit somethin'. Hold up." C-Boy pauses to lean on the bleachers and beat out a rough drumline. "Check this out," he says. Then he starts humming the bass part to that old-school Mase, "Why You Over There Lookin' At Me."

"Man, this kid stay amped up," Lil Chris says, exasperated.

"Go'n head, lil homie. Bless ya people," No Love puts in as the O.G. homies Charlie Brown, Don Smiley Loc, and El Wil come over to see what the deal is. Next come Flick, B-Geezlehop, Wacc, and the A-town homie, Poison.

The C'ster looks over his audience. *Mostly for-real hoodfellas. Gotta hit them wit somethin' deep. Something gangsta, too, though . . . Okay, I got somethin' sufficient.*

"Ah yo, ah yo, peep
   Mumblin' incantations
      Whispered in foreign tongues
  Mass prostration
    Tribal migration
 Children sweep the camp and come on
    Know that
    The oracle sees
       The comin' of cannibal nomads
        They search for pasture
At arms
  Young warriors, mind you, listen
    Un-sta-ble situation
      Unstable tactics
 Hang back
  We mashin'

Reactionary strike

Guerilla war fashion

We outnumbered

The government is playin' politics

Desert fox in Baghdad to bomb

Combat brief, had that

Iraq was holdin' back

On weapons inspections

But was it

Really necessary that we bomb

Saddam

A million second-guessers

Ask that question

Wow

They kicked our sisters off welfare

Say that they lazy

First they

Sentence us to life

Now, they starvin' our babies

Really, this livin' done done it to me, mayne

These shackles is real

See me livin' behind bars

I struggle to chill

See me stressin'

Oh! The scandal

Too hectic to handle

Jealousy!

They lied on me

When they came to dismantle me,

Why!

Barbed wires

And cell bars

God!

Where I'm from, it was hard
But, I'm numb in these jail yards
Survival! Is all I'm thinkin'
Live homie
Get out in one piece and make a meal
Homie!
Keep it real!
Ob . . . a . . . man! I fell off . . . "

Lil Chris trails off.

"Man, come on!"

"Ah, man!"

"Yo! I don't wanna hear no more. He da coldest on the river."

"Yeah, man. Kid nice, for real."

The crowd starts to slowly disperse. That's how most of the real hoodlums are. They ain't go'n sweat any one person. They give Lil Chris his props, drop pounds, and move out.

C-Boy is straight now. He leans back and chills. Lil Chris is secretly twisted 'cause he fell off. But it was still a nice showing. No Love is silent. Entranced in his own thoughts.

Mansa turns to speak to Lil Chris. "That was some nice work. No, you ain't just been studyin'. You've been researchin'. There's a difference. A major difference. The question is, how deep you dug?"

"At first, I was just into history. Really ancient history is still my thang. The Egyptian—excuse me—Kemetans. The Assyrians, the Babylonians. The Greeks. The Romans. You know, your progression of world powers. But then my reading took me deeper into Africa. Besides what you gave me, most of the stuff I was reading was out of high school text books. I didn't feel like I was getting enough on the Motherland. So, I started going to get it. West African Empires. Mali. Songhay. Hausaland. Ashanti. Yorubaland. It was real hard to come across that deep history on the interior and sub-Saharan regions. Then, too, most of the deep stuff I got on that Northern shore was about the Roman provinces—"

"—Yeah," No Love says. "We been gettin' used up for a long time."

"But, you see, the good material I ran across was about the leaders." Lil Chris's eyes gloss over at the thought. "Man, I read this book of letters. Personal letters. Written and received by Kwame Nkrumah from his six years in exile. This cat, man! This book . . . it literally changed me. I mean, the dude, he was like the first true president of Ghana before he got overthrown in, I think, 1966 by a military coup. And, picture, he's taken in by his homeboy who is the president of the country of Mali. He sheltered him there until he takes sick. Anyway. He stays there for about six years, until 1972, and this book . . .

"Man, this book, it gives you his personal letters. I'm tah'm 'bout uncut. Straight butter.

"Most of the good stuff was either to or from this chick June Milan, or something like that. I would be sitting there reading those letters and it seemed so real. The man, this great man, seemed so human. It made me realize that beyond all this media mumbo-jumbo, most of these major figures are just like us! They deal in doubt. And hope. And cope with the breaks. Man!" Lil Chris shakes his head. He's on one. "I even got C-Boy to read about some o' dem cats."

"Yeah, yo," C-Boy jumps at the chance to put his two cents in. "I read, ah, *Long Walk to Freedom* by Nelson Mandela. Then, too, I read all kinda stuff, like about Du Bois and Garvey and of course, you know I had to holla at my people. Martin Luther, the King." C-Boy being C-Boy.

"What do you think about MLK?" Mansa asks Lil Chris.

"I think he was a great man," Lil Chris says.

"Yeah, these people got a lot o' y'all trippin' like that, too," Mansa says with disturbing arrogance.

"Check . . . wha—what you mean, trippin'? I know you ain't go'n say Martin Luther King—I'm tah'm 'bout da Doctor! I know you ain't sayin' he was sour. I can't respect that," C-Boy declares.

"Look, lil man, I don't expect you to feel me. 'Cause I ain't go'n tell you what's in the books. Some time you gotta read between the lines."

"Ah! Man, g'on head," C-Boy fights. "You tryna give me your opinion—"

"—Hold up, lil homie," No Love sets in. "Just check him out. He might just put you on something."

"The thing is this; right now, he fighting 'cause there is a slim chance that I might say something to undo that trash they been feedin' us. *All* of us," Mansa emphasizes. "That's these demons of ignorance they done implanted in us. Agents of darkness will always fight the light. Try to control 'em, young man. You might learn something. You see, what a lot of people won't admit is the Civil Rights Movement was a middle-class movement. They didn't carry the ghuttah. Believe that. Your precious Dr. King wasn't poor. He came from money. His people had money. The Civil Rights Movement was a protest by the Black middle class to be accepted by white middle America. King didn't care about the Blacks that were strugglin' in the ghetto. He didn't even understand our pain. He was never there. Matter fact, when he brought that nonsense about nonviolence to the Chicago slums, they turned him around. Ain't nobody in the hood growed up slangin' and throwin' them thangs wanna hear nothin' he was sayin'. No! What King did was get a lot of people bruised, beat up, molested, and killed. So we could take our money and patronize white establishments. That's why the white folks love him. *That's* why they constantly push him in our face. He showed them where they was slippin'. 'You know what, Bob? That there boy's right. Let's let them coons in here and take they money.' Yeah, that's what the deal was. King and his people wanted to buy into White America. Better the living conditions of those few who were allowed to be able to afford it."

"Man, this fool crazy!" C-Boy says as he hops up and storms off toward the weight pile to finish his workout.

Mansa and No Love turn to look at Lil Chris. Lil Chris is off into his own thoughts.

They begin to speak with him about joining Da One.

"Say, mayne, check," C-Boy throws 195 pounds on the rack and sits up from the flat bench. "Don't be no fool. You know that shit dude spittin' ain't right."

"How I know that? How do you?" Lil Chris says with more calm then he actually feels. "How you so sure?"

"'Cause anybody wit' sense know that Martin Luther King was one o' the realest niggas ever did it!"

Someone behind Lil Chris starts laughing. A deep, rhythmic rumble. It's infectious. Before long the majority of the men under the weight pile are either laughing, snickering, or smiling. Lil Chris isn't one of them.

"He just come from over there talkin' to Mansa," Monster, the smooth grit of his voice like sandpaper on good wood, observes. He does find it funny.

"Nah," says the guy who started it. "I was just laughin' at how this dude called Reverend Martin Luther King, Jr., a real nigga."

Another round of laughter.

Lil Chris doesn't think the shit is funny at all. C-Boy does, though.

"Say, mayne, check," C-Boy addresses the guy, an angular red-skinned dude with chiseled features. "Ah . . . What's yo' name, brah?"

"I ain't nobody to be knowing like that," the guy says.

The statement catches Lil Chris's attention.

"Never mind all that. Check, do you think the Civil Rights Movement was a Black middle class movement?"

The guy looks at C-Boy, as if he's considering his response. "Well, I've never known Mansa to hold such a belief," he finally says.

"Well, he do," C-Boy says. "He tryna make it like MLK used up po' black folks so rich black folks would kick it with—"

"That ain't what he was sayin'," Lil Chris puts in. "Not all of it."

"Well, I think he right," says Monster. "I mean—"

"Mayne, y'all Black-ass niggas!" C-Boy exclaims.

Another round of laughter.

"Y'all ain't seeing the whole picture," C-Boy continues. "Mayne, we was doin' bad back then. They was handlin' us bad as a muthafucka back then. Ah, MLK ain't have to march with poor folks to get them *fucked* over. That was happenin' anyway. Martin did what he did so it would stop happenin! Y'all got that man bad."

"That's just what you was taught to believe," Monster rebuts. "You must not be hip to Selma."

"Mayne, please," C-Boy bickers.

"Well, then you know that it all was game then. Martin used them people to get ahead," Monster reasons. He looks genuinely thoughtful. His mom's name tatted on his forehead to honor her memory. One tear tatted beneath his right eye. "It was all politics, and that mayne was just playin' the game."

"Say, brah," Lil Chris addresses the red-skinned dude.

"His name is Joseph," Monster says.

"Joseph," Lil Chris says, as if trying to remember if he's heard that name before.

"I think both of y'all are right," Joseph responds. "Or, at least, I don't think neither one of y'all are wrong."

"It's all a matter of opinion, then," C-Boy says. "And his opinion can be wrong. That jus' go back to what I was sayin' at first."

"That man gave his life for what he believed in," Joseph stresses, as if life and death is something he finds familiar, is comfortable with. "You can't just gloss over that part."

That got their attention.

"I think it comes down to your personal constitution," Joseph adds with a smile.

C-Boy and Lil Chris share a look. "You mean each of our own understanding . . . of the facts," Lil Chris reasons.

"No, you gotta—" Joseph stops. Considers. "Not necessarily just understanding. I mean your personal values. Everybody knows what happened. You never hear them arguing the facts. Them don't change. It is all based on values when you pick it apart, though. If you value life over death, then you'll see it one way. Probably blame Martin for the lives lost. But if you think a few lives lost for a higher purpose, the greater good, is worth it, if you value progress that much . . . Well, that's your personal constitution," Joseph concludes matter-of-factly.

CHAPTER SIXTEEN

She bore the features
Of a true woman
I'm feelin' somethin'
The vision cut through my heart
Like a knife
My first impulse
Was to make her my wife
I recognized her from another life.
From a little bit past the jungles
Off the West African coast
I'm short o' my rib, y'all

LIL CHRIS MADE IT TO the Education Building early that morning and posted up to wait on Rise to come through. He is more than a little anxious. He feels good about being a part of today's events. It's an accomplishment.

The C-ster is looking penitentiary sharp. He has some Sean Jean jeans on he got from Lil Ron. Some wheat and cornflower suede Gucci loafers he got from the homie Hip City. A sky blue t-shirt Rise gave him and a button-down, blue jean shirt. And blue-tinted sunglasses he gaffled for a while back—he's still tryna remember who he got them from. He's got his hair in two underhanded braids going to the back, the plait tucked under. He even got the N.O. homie Project to shape up his peach fuzz for him. When he made it to the building, Rise peeped out the C'ster and just shook his head. The lil youngster is definitely on some "other" stuff, but he fly.

Rise, on the other hand, had walked up looking *so* every-damn-day-ish, Lil Chris thought. State-issue blue jeans. A white t-shirt. Blue and white Adidas shelltoes. Of course, his hair is shampooed, oiled, and air dried. The nappy look. The two of them hooked up and walked the rest of the way to the A Building together.

Lil Chris watches as Rise hits one of them square cats he runs with. They do that characteristic embrace and whisper. Rise ignores his question about what he "Be doin' with those marks," which leaves the C'ster feeling a little twisted. He makes a skullnote to step to Rise a little later and press him on what he and them dudes be whispering about all the time.

Time enough for that later on. Indeed. At that point, wasn't but one thing on Lil Chris's mind: the annual A.S.C.P. College Seminar.

He and Rise wait in the A Building for about 45 minutes. But just as he starts spoiling over the big homie's nonchalance, in comes the students from S.U.N.O., followed by the ones from Tulane. Then Grambling comes through the door. The biggest group of all were the pre-law students from Texas Southern.

What Lil Chris doesn't understand is that Rise has his mind fixed on the order of the day: educating these pre-law students about the number of backwards elements of the dysfunctional criminal justice system, in which they will soon be launching their careers. The room fills up with about 140 or so students, mostly women, and Lil Chris's mind goes elsewhere, fast.

From the carnal perspective, it is pure joy to just stand there and watch them walk to and fro. And that's basically what T. Guy's poli-sci students have been doing. Pathetic. Most of these students are the same age. Even Lil Chris, with all his boasting and bragging about how much he has to say, freezes up.

"And, what's your name?" a short redbone with two afro puffs asks as she stops in front of them. They pause, unsure who she is referring to, so Rise takes it up.

"Rise—*oop*," he stops. "It's Oschuwon."

"Noo," she sasses. "You said Rise?"

"Uh-uh," Rise shakes his head. "This is a formal affair. Don't you let anyone hear you calling me that."

"Well, we can go with Oschuwon. That's cute, too. I'll just call you Rise on the under."

"Straight. What's your name?" Rise asks. Starts to regain his bearing.

"Yolanda."

"Well, Yolanda, we've got some responsibilities to make good on. But I definitely will get with you later, or whatever. Is dat cool, sistah?"

"Yeah, you make sure you do that," Yolanda says, kind of spicy-like. She walks off to her group's table.

As Rise was turning his head to Lil Chris, the C'ster said, "What? That easy?"

"Yeah, that easy," Rise assures him, and himself.

Rise spends the morning working the room, going group to group. Pushing the viewpoint. Feeling the response. Fielding. It's still early, but there have already been some memorable exchanges. Like when Rise gets trapped with two over-talkative juniors. Young ladies, of course. He ends up calling C-Boy, who has been playing the wall all morning. Rise introduces him as one of A.S.C.P.'s Political Science graduates. It's these students' third Angola Legal Seminar, and they are obliged to pull C-Boy into their web of words. Last time Rise checked,

C-Boy was still nodding his head and saying things like "Oh yeah? I never thought of it that way."

Rise laughs to himself about it before Lil Chris breaks his train of thought. "Damn," Lil Chris says, hitting Rise's shoulder so hard his herbal tea spills. "What you did to that chicken head over there?"

"Watch your mouth," Rise replies. "These are sisters. You go'n have to discipline yourself, lil brother." But then he turns his attention to where Lil Chris directed it, toward a sister sitting at the head of one of the student tables.

Time stands still. Yes, she stares directly at Rise. What's worse, she's got the look of a woman who's used to getting what she wants. He holds her gaze for a moment. She doesn't turn away. Rise narrows his eyes. Tilts his head just a little to the left. Like, *What up?*

One side of her nice lips pulls girlishly up and she lifts her brows. She sits a short distance from where Rise stands. Rise steps out in the *other* direction.

An hour passes. Rise works his way around the room of students. Turns as blind an eye as possible to the fact that these are some of the most attractive sisters he's been around in a long, long time.

"Trust me, I've studied many of the same books you all are studying, right now," he explains to a group by the hobby craft station. "The only difference between you all and me is that I'm trapped in this system we're all studying."

"You . . . what's your name?" He asks one woman. She wears no makeup on her oval face. She's got dark eyes that seem to bore into Rise.

"Rashonda." Her voice is soft.

"And, you're a what—sophomore?"

"Junior."

"T.S.U?"

"No. All of us are S.U.N.O . . . Oh! And Dillard. I'm sorry, y'all." She says the latter to some of the other students situated at her sides.

"Do you think it's unconstitutional to deny an imprisoned person the opportunity to pursue a writ of habeas corpus?"

"Of course it is," Rashonda says, assertively. "Habeas corpus is a right afforded to any imprisoned person who wishes to have their case examined to determine whether their captive status is lawful and just."

"Okay. That's what my book teaches me as well, but are you familiar with the A.E.D.P.A?"

"No." She looks perplexed. "What's that?"

"The Anti-Terrorism and Effective Death Penalty Act," Rise specifies.

Rashonda is visibly clueless.

"Yeah, there was anti-terrorism legislation way before the towers fell. President Clinton signed off on a bill that declared myself and others like me—everyday brothers off your block—to be urban terrorists. Picture that. And because of this bill, there are several conditions fixed to what is supposed to be our right to pursue federal habeas corpus. Conditions that function to deny us the legal rights the Constitution has promised.

"Let me lay it out for y'all," Rise continues. "The books we read that tell us about all of the rights we supposedly have: the right to legal assistance, the right to fair trial, the right to appeal—there is no such thing in the real world. At least not for everyday people, people with no resources. No means. No connections. No power."

Rise pauses. "No. In the real world, these rights are no more than words on paper. To be maneuvered around. 'Interpreted' is the word they use. How many of you have taken a sociology course yet? Deviance is behavior that is, at first, generally acceptable. Acceptable behavior is not a social problem until a segment of the people deem it such. Well, when our government officials interpret these rights, usually they do so in a way that systematically denies these safeguards to those of us who need them the most. Clearly deviant behavior, from our perspective. But they claim their actions are committed in the interest of the people. Well, when is a segment of the people going to deem their actions a social problem?

"Of course, we learn in sociology that people from different backgrounds will view problems and solutions differently. All that sounds well and right, but for the more than two million incarcerated individuals across the nation, who constantly witness interpretations that seem to disregard their rights and safeguards, we have to ask exactly what segment of the people our leaders serve with their present approach to criminal justice."

Rise's voice trails off. He's found himself looking into very wide-eyed, very confused faces. They don't get it. Yet, more importantly, he sees something else. They are fighting to stay with him. They want to understand. Good.

He tries another angle. "It's kinda like when someone says, 'He's gettin' on my nerves.' Have any of you ever had to say that?"

Chagrin, amusement, curiosity, and anticipation flash across their faces. His change in course has jolted them. Exactly what he intended. "You see. There's no benefit in saying this, other than . . . well, sayin' it. If you want to do something about the problem, you have to articulate the causes. Only once you identify what's going wrong can you begin to fix it, right?"

The students nod.

"Well, the same thing is happening with criminal justice. We all know that 'lock 'em up and throw away the key' isn't working. I mean, they're gettin' on *my* nerves," Rise allows himself a smile here. "Our books even admit that. But, what exactly is wrong? What are the viable options? Once we can all get on the same level in viewing the causes, then we can begin to eliminate the problem.

"You are all about to enter this dysfunctional system. What are your intentions? To get in where you fit in? To correct the situation? Your position on the board is enviable. You have the opportunity to collect the facts, to study the impact, to inform your opinion, then begin to contemplate workable solutions. It all starts with information, sisters. Over there on the table are some pamphlets our research committee has prepared. I encourage you to take one. Add it, along with the letters you receive from the individuals you meet at this seminar, to your bank of prisoner perspectives. I'll talk to some of you later on in the program."

As Rise turns, he finds himself looking into the same pair of almond-shaped eyes that were staring at him across the room earlier. Without thinking, he grabs an empty chair, straddles the seat backwards, and sits. Like, "What's happenin'?" All in one smooth motion. He never releases her gaze.

"What are you doin' here?"

Her accent is very feminine, very pleasing, almost nasal, from somewhere else. "What you mean, 'What am I doin' here?'"

"I've been all over the room and most of these students are clueless as to why they are actually here. They think they're on a field trip or something."

"I know. On the way up here, they were joking about maybe y'all were gonna have on a ball and chain or something. Somebody asked me was I scared. I told 'em hell nawl. I'm goin' to see my brothers."

With this, she claims a piece of Rise's heart. A heart he didn't even know could still feel. It isn't exactly what she said, or how she said it. It's who her statement showed her to be.

Rise plunges forward. Not really knowing where he's going. Just vibing. "I'm surprised to hear you say that. I noticed you earlier. I had you pegged for some ladies first, women's lib type."

"Oh, never *that*."

"I'm saying. Do you? You ain't gotta front on me, or for me," Rise says.

"Don't play," she says. "I don't ascribe to their theory of equality. I'm not with this whole I-can-do-whatever-you-can concept. A sister has her place and a man has his place. We're codependents. We both bring very different and . . . ah . . . "

"Distinct," Rise ventures.

"Yeah, distinct plates to the table. Heaped with different entrees."

"I'm feeling that. You kinda good with that, yeah," Rise says, smiling.

"What?"

"This whole tell-him-what-he-wanna-hear thing."

"Boy, please!"

"I'm sayin' . . . " Rise grins. "Hold 'em up." So smooth. "Go 'head on, get hostile. That's kinda cute"

"Oh, he got jokes," she replies, trying to temper her emotions.

"A'ight, that's better. We dealin' with the uncut, no pretense. Something tells me we ain't gotta do the chill factor thang to get what we want from this exchange. Follow my lead," Rise says. Still doesn't know exactly where he's taking this. Just going with it anyways.

"What?"

"Uncut. No pretense," he says. Like a challenge. He holds her gaze. Her eyes speak to him. They both laugh. "You kinda flavor, you know that?"

"Yeah? Which kind?" she teases.

"Oh, we on some other shit, right now. Ain't we supposed to be discussing criminal justice and the need for penal reform?" Rise asserts. Or, at least, tries to.

"Okay, but somebody issued an 'uncut no pretense' edict, and right now I'm not focused on . . . "

Rise leans back, aghast. Slack-jawed.

She smiles and continues, "Uh huh, that's right. She can be bold."

"What's your name?"

"Kaylina Muhammed."

"Oh, you Muslim?"

"Nation," she stipulates.

"Okay, now I'm startin' to catch up."

"And what's your name?"

"Oschuwon. My people call me Rise," he says. Slipping yet again.

"Okay. Well, why Rise?"

"I feel a person's name should say something about who they are."

"And you are Rise," she puts in. Forceful. Determined to have her say.

"That's right. I've been called a lot of things. Rise is the first name I actually chose for myself." He looks around the room. Recalls where he is and what he's supposed to be doing.

Kaylina just sits and watches him. As if searching for something.

"They should be callin' y'all for your mini tour pretty soon," he says, kind of smooth. "I'll be interested in hearing what you have to say after you've seen some of the prison." He stands to leave.

Kaylina tilts her head up. "Umph. Rise, huh?" She whispers, more to herself than to him.

As the students file out for the mini tour of the institution, Lil Chris is feeling the moment, but also a twinge of nagging curiosity. He spies Rise over by the serving counter and decides to pull him over and press what he was asking him about earlier. He takes an indirect approach. Be strategic.

"Rise," Lil Chris begins. "You know what No Love and 'n 'em was saying in the gym the other ni—"

"—Who is No Love 'n 'em?" Rise asks.

"Oh . . . ah, you 'ont know him. A dude named Mansa."

"Mansa Musa?"

"Yeah, you know him?" Lil Chris feigns surprise.

"Uh-huh. Go 'head."

"They said the Civil Rights Movement was a class effort. That it was a push by the Black middle class to be accepted by white middle America. And that Dr. King hurt us more than he helped us."

Rise thinks. He knew what page the C'ster was on when he saw him coming. Perhaps it's time to entertain him. He takes a breath to think a bit more about his reply. The main thing at this juncture is not eloquence, or sounding smart. Rise needs to make sure Lil Chris feels where he's coming from. Coherence.

"Well, first of all, lil brother, we really have to be sensitive to how and when we criticize a man's life work. Yes, it's our right to question its effect and consequence, especially when we have to live with the consequences, but we have to handle such a thing with respect and reverence for the what the man devoted his life to."

"Even if the spin-off proves to have a negative effect on me?" Lil Chris is visibly standing on end.

"Especially. This man gave his life for what he believed in. More importantly, he had enough courage to live his life practicing the rudiments of that belief. That's to be respected. Now, I'm not going to deal with the intent behind the movement. Depending on who you talk to, anyone can put their spin on that issue. The raw truth, though, is what we see every day. What we can touch and lay our hands on. That part that we've been entrusted to pick up and carry to the next level."

"Well, let's deal with that then. Spit, man."

"Patience, lil brother. Just listen to me. Be cool, I'ma give it to you. The thing that hurts us the most, as a direct effect of the Civil Rights Movement, is the way our people, or at least the majority of us, view success. In all of our music, our books, our everyday conversation, our main thing is to get out."

"Huh?"

"Yeah. We wanna get out of the 'hood. We wanna get away from the place where we started. The people we're fighting to catch up with have used this warped perspective of success to paint a false sense of equality. And, we as a people have bought wholeheartedly into this. In short, we've focused on inclusion rather than reparations. Because of this, the movement was crippled from the start. They were focused on the wrong thing. *In my opinion*," Rise stresses. "Now, a lot of people will say that America has what she has because of our people's blood, sweat, and tears. But, come on, now. Black blood, sweat, and tears was only one element of the resources that were employed. Just as critical was how those resources were put to use. Look, those of us from the streets understand that they put down their hustle to get what they got. What they amassed. They did that. We can't hate on 'em. I mean, come on, now.

"Review the problem. The problem was that the two communities were unequal. They had more than we had, and they were using it against us. The most obvious solutions would have been to pursue public policies that would even things out, let us build our own thing up. There would have been efforts to strengthen our own institutions. Better schools. Debt forgiveness. There would have been more done to strengthen our economic situation by patronizing our own businesses—where, incidentally, we could always enter through the front door. On a level playing field, we could have specialized, we could have retained ownership, and we could have sold to the white community. The same way Americans sold their goods to the British, competing in the marketplace to work out from under their yoke.

"Instead, though, our people turned to a Civil Rights program. In essence they were saying, 'Hey, it ain't all good over here. Y'all should let us come over there with y'all.' Me, I don't believe this was some diabolical plan by the Black middle class. Hindsight is 20-20. I believe our leaders chose what they thought was the path most likely to succeed.

"And, what did it lead to, this path? It led to us sacrificing our children—more significantly, our women. America, by nature, is based on competition—the *individual* pursuit of happiness. In this context, the movement splintered into individual efforts to be accepted, chosen, by the white establishment. When we lobbied to buy into their game, everything else that came with it was the proof of purchase. Including the pronounced stratification of Black America."

"So what do we do? Where do we go from here?" Lil Chris asks.

"That's the question." Rise sighs. "The answer to that question is no different for us prisoners than it is for Black America as a whole. Most of us have been sentenced to unbelievably absurd amounts of time. We walk around daily with the pressure. We laugh and socialize in ways that a lame would not believe possible under the circumstances. But there is a dark tax. And a lot of us are paying it without even knowing."

Rise stops to study Lil Chris' young face. Knows the lil brother has no clue as yet of the demands that long-term incarceration will draw from him. Hopes he never finds out. Understands that he'll have to, in order to be better.

"It's like that serenity prayer," Rise continues. "We focus on what we can control. And, of those things, becoming the best men we can possibly be is foremost. There is a deeper, darker reality to this thing we call doing time. And we negotiate it, we carry it with our aspirations."

He stops again, considering. "This is the reason for all the dialogue. The history. The politics. Breaking down the facts and moving toward a civic philosophy. It's like we're working our way through a maze, and the walls—the very boundaries—are our ability to perceive what's real. To be objective. To gauge the truth of it all. To truly understand how we got to this point."

This time he stops because Lil Chris is nodding. "That's why it's so important to call it like it is," Lil Chris says.

"Right," Rise smiles. "To call it accurately. To shake off the distortion of bias and the feeling of having been victimized. The irony of these awakened offenders who've left so many victims in our own wake. There are two phases of reality, Lil Chris. A static reality. Something more than still-life, but less than motion. The static is the separation from our family. The locked doors. The cages. The life sentence.

"The second phase, though. The movement. The evolving situation. The building is what we are about. And the people we engage in this discourse. Those that are attempting to redeem the time—they need the part we play in this. Those incarcerated, and that mass of confused and struggling souls that are only doing a little better than us in society. The work we do to enable ourselves. To inform our perspective. To concentrate all of our efforts in this music we have and give is how we infuse this incarcerated life with worth. It's how we give our individual lives meaning. This is us saying, 'Yeah, over here, too. This life matters.'"

Rise stops again. So alive in the moment.

Lil Chris smiles. He's following him. "The music, huh," the C'ster says. Nodding once more. "This life matters."

Rise collects himself. Prepares to move on.

"This is the age of information," he says. "That's what's so important about the music at this particular phase of the struggle for social improvement. The issues need to be articulated. The people need to be given a clear and honest picture of our situation as it is. Not griping about the decision, but rather, understanding our options now. Understanding how best to play our position now. We speak that reality to them.

"Lil brother, unlike any other kind of music, hip-hop has the potential to communicate the complex principles of politics, empowerment, and self-enrichment. Because of the length of each verse. The *wordiness* of it all. The singsong fashion that teaches and informs, usually without the listener being mindful of the process . . . this is crucial in our predicament. Because the more people we enflame, the stronger we all become."

"And people learn faster when they don't know they're learning. I feel you." Lil Chris is starting to peep game.

A little later, the college students come back in from their mini tour. Rise and Kaylina get at each other and shuffle through more conversation. Rise knows that the odds are against anything ever coming of it. Such is a reality of prison life. He and Kaylina exchange addresses, kick it for the rest of the day. When the seminar is over, they part ways.

Then life resumes. The moment passes.

Rise and Lil Chris walk out of the A Building and head back down the walk towards their respective dormitories. Soon they pass the sliding cast-iron bars of the MPO. The Education Building. They encounter No Love and Mansa. They move toward Rise and Lil Chris, headed to the treatment center.

"What's happenin'?" Lil Chris calls out as they approach.

The tension between Rise and Mansa is immediate, obvious, and palpable. They eye each other acutely. With studied stances, they front one another. Mutual respect and distaste is scribbled all over their features.

Rise speaks first. Tactful. "How long you been back in population, Mansa?"

"Why ask me a question you already know the answer to?" Mansa is straight and direct. That's not always a good thing.

"Say, man! Why y'all ain't wait on me?" C-Boy catches up with the crowd. Pulls his baggy jeans up and reaches for the rolled-up Bugler cigarette behind his ear. He glances at Rise and Mansa, who are still staring each other down. Then turns to Lil Chris to ask for a lighter.

"Say . . . " C-Boy drags on the square as he touches it to the lighter's flame. "Check . . . " He exhales, blowing a stream of gray smoke. "Did y'all look at the bulletin board in y'all dorms this morning? They got open mic night comin' up."

"What's happenin' with that?" Lil Chris asks.

"Lyrical Warfare," Mansa answers. At this, he steps away.

No Love daps Rise, Lil Chris, and C-Boy off before he turns to leave.

Rise strikes out walking in the opposite direction. He never looks over his shoulder. Lil Chris and C-Boy are left standing there. Tryna figure out what the deal is.

CHAPTER SEVENTEEN

One Revolutionary Zion
    (stress that)
Words of a visionary Lion
    (we said that)
Come on
    Speak directly
Now hear from your affiliate
    Nawl, hold up
    See y'all
        Go'n respect me

THEY COME TO IRON HIM up early. About 5:45 a.m. In the cool of morning, a quiet hope at the base of his throat. His belly all but empty. Can't eat. Eyes wide open.

Riding solo in the back of a white state van with tinted, reinforced windows, a man and a woman up front. Regular prison personnel, both Black. Maybe mid-30s to 40s. The mood easy. Hip-hop and R&B on the radio station, and he made sure to sit far in the back by the rear speakers so as not to hear their quiet conversation. And to be alone with his own thoughts.

They take the ferry out of Angola. This sense of eerie beauty and awe as they shuffle across the strong flowing waters of the Mississippi. The dotted white froth of its currents.

At the back of his mind is the thought of sinking, handcuffed and shackled, locked in that container, and he can't swim. But, just as quickly as they drive up on one bank, they drive off on the other side.

After that, it is the dawning horizon, the treelines and empty pastures. Southern crop fields and rural homesteads. The steady rhythm of the tire treads over smooth black backroads and the passing miles.

For miles and miles, he doesn't think of the courtroom and what lies ahead. Oh, he tries to drill himself at first. On the issue, ineffective assistance of counsel. And the precedent, Strickland. Teague. The supporting statutes and case law. But his mind won't hold it. He knows he knows it. Has drilled it enough already, by himself and with Gary Law. That circle of inmate counsels. He's well prepared. And the sights, the landscape are too much to ignore. Been too long since he's seen the like. Traveling. Instead of marking step on that prison farm. So as the miles pass he drinks it all in.

The rhythm of the road beneath them changes somewhat as they turn onto I-49. The steady bump of the interstate, the slate course ahead. The officers turn the radio up a bit. The free world begins to welcome them. The upbeat DJs and traffic reports sizzle in and out as they move through Louisiana's more populated parishes. The hustle and bustle. You can just feel the pulse of it all speed back up. Like returning to civilization.

They arrive at the courthouse in Monroe, its stacked red brick and flat top. Intricate horticulture. Bushes trimmed low and neat, lined in orderly rows. It's like he can feel the weight of an indifferent world close back in on him. The air becomes compact, stifling. Cool.

Yet there is a difference from the last time he experienced this. He's grown now. And well enough in tune with himself to recognize the humanity of the people he passes as he moves through the ordered halls. It's no longer foreign and mysterious. He sees the drama for what it is. The social roleplay walked out by people that are really no different than him. All reasoning with life's choices. Some careful, and others careless. The arrangement the same. A scene he's held in his mind's eye for more years than he cares to think about. Though, really, it's all he can think about.

Just as I knew it would be, he thinks as he steps toward the courtroom. Its frivolous decor. The sounds of well-worn wood on wood, hinged on metal. He can feel the moment's escalation. Embraces it. He lays eyes on the judge, mindful of what's at stake. Knows how chancy and subtle, how sensitive the opportunity. Knowing he has to rise to it. In that moment, he is who he is. Everything he is and all it took to become. More than simply Oschuwon Hamilton. In that moment, he is Rise.

Then it is over. In and out, like a warm breath. He is out of the building, back in the van, and on the highway before he can really mark the passing. Like swimming up through the deep, only to break the surface for a heartbeat before being pulled back. There just long enough to live. He hopes it was enough.

> *Umm, sagacity*
> > *Won't you yell*
> > *Rise, brother, one struggle*
> > > *When you call for me*
> *We are*
> > *Worldwide mob figures*
> > *Go-gettahs*
> *Ever heard of a smart gorilla?*
> > *We herbal healers, huh?*

I migrated to the isle of
                    Madagascar
        Colonized cultivatin' berries
                    And figs
My base addicts pimp your rigs
        Eight CCs of true enlightenment
                    Mainline it smack it and dig!
                    Bang it!
Man, I wanna make a play on how it feels when the high first hits you,
Chris thinks. *The narcotic lift-off. Tie that in to a music-gets-me-high
concept. Ahhh, let me see . . .*

Let the rhythm get inside.
        Set your mind free . . . mind gone . . .
Na, I don't wanna use mind twice, he thinks. *Least, not like that.
Try this . . .*

        Let the music beat a rhythm
                    Wit' your heartbeat
No, No, No. Hell no!
Let the rhythm mark time
        Wit' the motion
                    My melodic self-love potion
We will survive
        And that's more than a notion
Nawl, too corny. He thinks. *Needs some edge . . .*

"Rise! I know you heard me callin' you," Lil Chris is more anxious
than angry. "You got that chorus I asked you to write to?"

"No, it's somewhere in the dorm."

"Did you write to it?"

"I'm writin' right now."

"Oh! Okay, lemme hear what you got?"

"Stall that. This is somethin' else."

"What else?"

"Some other stuff."

Lil Chris's patience just snapped. "Man, come on with the bull-shit! Why you playin' games?"

"Kid, I told you. This ain't a game—"

"Yeah, but you ain't *told* me nothin'," Lil Chris shoots back. Insistent.

Now Rise is getting agitated. "Not now, lil homie. I'm zoning."

"Man, break bread. I'm through just understanding. I wanna know what's happening. 'The board.'"

Rise lifts his head and looks at Lil Chris. A question in his expression. Refusal in the set of his jaw. Agitation in his sitting posture. But, there is resolve in Lil Chris's stance. He ain't going nowhere. "Break bread," he reiterates.

He was so involved in what he was writing, Rise only now really takes in the scene around them. Tries to come up with the best way to respond to the lil brother.

The sky is clear-cast. Real sunny. A few sections of roaming fluffy whites. Beneath, the horizon is lined with trees as far as the eye can see. The woodland enclosure reinforces the notion that they have been separated from the rest of the world. Isolated. Closed in, in the middle of nowhere. Damn.

From his position on the dormitory ledge, elevated about four feet off the ground, Rise looks past Lil Chris. Farther out in the prison yard, several different sports team practices are going on.

On the other end of the second football field, a circle of old cats are exercising. Doing their aerobic thing. Toward the fence, the Wolf-pack, the prison's only all-white sports team, is practicing their brand of volleyball.

This ain't livin'. They're just trying to stay healthy. To survive these dark days. To last until better days come.

"What's the primary purpose of leadership?" Rise asks all of the sudden.

"Huh?"

"What's the basic function and responsibility of leadership?"

Lil Chris thinks. "It kinda seems to me like you're asking a, ah . . . you know, that thing when you already know the answer to your question—or a, a question you not lookin' for an answer—"

"A rhetorical question."

"Yeah—"

"Well, look. You might be right. Check this out. I just wanted to hear what your perception of the subject is. But check, the people never really pay attention to the true causes of their struggles."

Rise eyes Lil Chris. "Just think about that statement." He pauses. "People don't even take for granted that their leaders have their best interest in mind. They simply don't think about it. The whole concept of political action—and the process of moving and shaking that goes with it—is foreign to our thought process. It's not that we don't care. The fact is, the majority of us, especially our family members on the streets, are so caught up in simply making it from day to day that we don't even have time to consider politics. Yeah, Momma kept food on the table, but she was so preoccupied with keeping her head down. With keeping her grind on. She rarely had a chance to stay up on what those people were doin' that were standin' over her head—"

"—Alright," Lil Chris interrupts. "I'm feelin' that, but what that got to do with what I asked you? Come on, man. Break br—"

"—How many times I have to tell yo—"

"—How many times I gotta tell *you* 'bout callin' yo'self talkin' down to me?" Lil Chris holds his ground.

Rise just looks at him. Lets the silence separate them from the budding altercation. "Listen, there is a very distinct difference between having a strong will and being obstinate. Watch how you handle the information you come across. Now, think about that on your own time.

"Leaders not only have the responsibility of leading the whole of the people in a direction conducive to change and progress. They also are responsible for keeping up with the government that stands over our community. Doing whatever they can to work not with, but between the two groups to create a political climate that allows the governing body to control just the parameters of the community, not the lives of its people.

"This leaves the people open to take advantage of reasonable opportunities to better their day-to-day living. The stronger the people get in a democratic society, the stronger the government gets. The stronger the government gets, the better it will be at regulating and assisting with the problems the community faces. In other words, the people's standard of living is based on their productivity. Good leadership arranges their surroundings so they can be as productive as possible. This done, a productive people empowers their government to better serve them."

"Okay. That's the same shit that T. Guy was teaching us in political science class. It's like a cycle." Lil Chris already knows all this. He makes his statement with a dismissive air, bordering on arrogance. He leans casually against the ledge, gazes out past the fences toward the treeline. He pulls a blue-green pack of Bugler tobacco from his pocket. Hand rolls a cigarette right quick. So damn cool.

"Listen, I'm trying to help you make the connection. I'm playin' you to pocket these conversations," Rise pushes. Attempts to assert a moment of clarity. "Most of us steal, kill, and sell drugs not just to survive. We commit these seemingly senseless acts for a reason. They make perfect sense when you factor in the raw need to provide. For our young families. For our dysfunctional families. Disabled, disadvantaged, altogether unfortunate families. Often, we make these dire decisions before we know enough to understand our needs. Even though all we know is raw need, before we understand why we're in need in the first place. The reach for fast money only proves how immediate these needs are.

"The prisoner usually gravitates towards economics, politics, and leadership in general in an effort to understand raw need. To get to the root of it. To understand what happened to us. Before us. Why there's all this need in the first place. Having made what we believed to be rational decisions to address raw need, finding ourselves in prison, we wanna finally know—why were our choices so limited? More importantly, what can be done to change that? This is what sends the conscious criminal mind to politics. This is what pushes us to get involved. Our own brand of activism. We ain't posturing. This ain't playing politics. This is us identifying and addressing the contributing factors. This is us learning how to answer the call of raw need."

Rise watches him. He's becoming a soul-jah before his eyes, every day. Still, he's just cruising. Lil Chris is not developing half as fast as he could be. The trick to the process is consciousness. When we are conscious, we get a picture in our head of the world around us, who we are, what we are, and who we need to become in this proper context.

This picture becomes our road map. By knowing what we're aiming for, our decisions come faster, more definite. This is what speeds the process up. The benefit is a solidified growth. You not only get there, you know how and why you went there. And where you're going.

"Lil Chris," Rise says. "I'm sure you've heard it said that God looks after two—"

"—Little children and damn fools." He cuts Rise off.

"Yeah, but did you know how they are provided for?"

"Shhh, I don't know. Ahh, what it is . . . ah, divine intervention," Lil Chris grimaces.

"Yeah, but how?"

"He makes a way for them."

"How?"

"I don't know. How?"

"Man, he works through people." Rise pauses to let that soak in. "The people who don't know become the responsibility of those who do."

"Oh, I know that."

"No. You knew it once I brought your attention to it."

"Man, I—"

"Look, stop fighting me. Focus. Think about what I'm saying. Yeah, the understanding that God works through people was in you. You just didn't know it until I directed your attention to it," Rise says. He studies Lil Chris for his response.

Lil Chris nods. He slowly begins to get it. It dawns on him. It just bit him! "Yeah, yeah. I feel you," he says. Starts to smile as he exhales gray cigarette smoke from his precious young lungs.

Rise starts in, slowly . . .

"Don't wanna stray
    Stricken strabismal. . . strategy straddled
Strenous streams strangle my strength
    I'm straight, but I straggle
My stratagem structure stretches
    Strafes when it strikes
If you can hear me, Listen
    Laugh when it bites
        Anger black as the night . . . "

Lil Chris's smile broadens into a grin. He bursts out laughing nervously, then hysterically.

Rise joins him for a heartbeat. The short reprieve feels good. But he straightens up. Reins in his emotions. Bears in on Lil Chris. *Yeah, it's good that he gets that little morsel, but now let me offer him the plate. Try to get a breakthrough.*

"And, that's what the deal is, you feel me," Rise begins. "You wanted me to break bread, right? Well, what just happened here is what's *really* goin' on."

"Huh?" Lil Chris is perplexed for real now.

"The purpose of this whole affair—"

"What—"

"The Lyrical Warfare thing they got comin' up. The reason why I'm on some other stuff right now," Rise puts in, insistently.

"The Lyrical Warfare?"

"Yeah. The war is for credibility. We're fighting for attention, for real. We ain't on no ego-clashing shit. We—well, let me explain somethin' to you. Out of all the people that's gonna be spittin' mad flow that night, they will all be representing two primary factions. The battle will be for your ears. Each one of us will be straight-up talking to you through the music. Each of the two groups has a common message. We strugglin' for power, for real. To win has nothing to do with us outdoin' each other. To win is to become the voice that the majority of the people will choose to listen to. Over all the rest."

"Man, that's deep!" Lil Chris's eyes are ablaze.

"That's power," Rise says soberly.

Both are momentarily lost in their own thoughts. Lil Chris speaks into the void.

"You said 'each of you.' You were talkin' 'bout S.O.G. and Da One . . . "

Rise nods.

Lil Chris is at him. "Tell me about them. What's happenin' with them two squads? What's up with y'all?"

Rise hops down off the ledge. "I'ma lace you. That's what page I was on when we first started this conversation."

"Yeah, but why you always gotta take the long way around?" the C'ster puts in. Frustrated. "Damn."

Rise folds his gray hooded sweatshirt and sets it on the ledge, over his notepad, to stop the pages from flying off in the wind. He turns to Lil Chris and says, "Let's make a few laps."

The C'ster agrees. The two of them strike out walking. They keep a relatively slow pace, follow the prison yard's perimeter toward the razor and barbed wires. Except in a few spots where construction has left the lingering smell of burnt tar, the air is otherwise clear and seemingly clean. As they make their way across the field, leaving the dormitories behind, the grass is like thick carpet underfoot. Once they reach the fences, the ground is more unyielding.

Like two brothers walking together, they are close-mouthed, each alone in his own thoughts, taking in the panoramic view: the expanse of land, hills, and trees beyond the fences. The correctional officer's quarters are a little farther up, the guard towers loom at each corner of the fenced-in area. Ultimately, their eyes rest on the hundreds of inmates amusing themselves at the yard's various sporting events.

As they walk, Rise breaks the silence. "You know, all of 'em's just waiting for somebody to step up and tell them what to do. Most of them are craving an answer to one question: 'How do we get out the joint?'"

"And, from what I can see," Lil Chris observes. "Those dudes that do step up don't do nothin' but throw movie nights. They take in the money our families send us and sit on it. That is, until the warden comes along and takes it to buy a slave bell, or some shit."

"Hold up," Rise cuts the youngster off. "The warden ain't doin' nothin' but his job. He's—"

"*What?!*"

"Listen, man!" Rise frowns. He hits Lil Chris with a look that says he's about to bug up. "You gettin' your head together, but you're still wild. But, I'ma give it to you from the shoulder. Damn what it sounds like. Digest it. Don't make a habit of spittin' up the real. That ain't good. This is good game I give you. Lemme help you understand. The warden is exploiting business opportunities, no doubt. He's a man, too. And, a man go'n get his hustle on. Just like you would, too.

"Don't practice looking at life from a singular perspective. You gotta have negative capability, hold more than one perspective in your head. If you don't, you'll miss something. That's how you come up short. In order to keep a good understanding of the situation you have to be able to look at it through the other man's eyes. You don't have to agree with it.

"This warden wasn't put here to be your boy. He's not your friend.

He's your keeper. Understand where you at. He was put here to run this prison and he does *that* well. In his world, there is no correction in corrections. Life means life. We are convicts. His job is to contain us as threats to society.

"Now, he could have done that by brute force, but he on some space-age pimpin'. He manipulatin' us. Straight institutionalizing us. Peep game. Security has total control over the prison." Rise pauses, briefly, then plunges ahead. "All these cats that have been here 20 and 30 years have had to forge a lifestyle, right? They swept up all the revolutionaries and political-minded prisoners a long time ago. That left a small number of strong, predatory prisoners and a large number of weaker ones.

"Security, being the only organized presence on the prison farm in the midst of the madness, was able to gain control. How? When knives were drawn, it was the prisoner's code to not get in the next man's business. It was security that came to stop the bloodshed. They established themselves with the weaker ones as their protectors.

"From there, the weak began to rat more frequently. Security used this information to put the clampdown on all illegal activities. Both the strong and the weak prisoners who were violators had to suffer or else play ball with the uniforms. This means drugs and other contraband flowed through the security.

"Remember, all the free thinkers and purpose-driven prisoners were in cells. Three-fourths of the remaining prisoners were gay. This was population. This created an illusion that became a comfortable distraction. The security came with the fences and the barbed wire to put down this unit-management scheme. To break the population down to workable numbers. They began to control how many gay prisoners were released into each camp. The ugly truth. They were the main ones turning out fresh fish, fresh off the bus.

"Now, when they wanted information, all they had to do was come around and pick all the punks up. Keep in mind, back then there were no women around. So, again the seemingly strong had to break along with the weak. They all worked with the security.

"It was around this time, the 60s and 70s, that Angola became known as the bloodiest prison in the nation. This wasn't soul-jahs or revolutionaries. This was a bunch of booty bandits challenging each other for their manhood. And the free folks were the ring leaders, the instigators. That's how dudes would kill with impunity. Shit, the security was doin' most of the killin' theyselves! Facts.

"Meanwhile, state legislature drops the bomb. They took away any possibility of parole for lifers. And jacked up the minimums on other crimes to make long sentences mandatory. That not only paralyzed the prisoners that were already sentenced to life, but now it slowed the killin'—'cause few dudes were dumb enough to catch a fresh life sentence.

"The prison population was left numb. The freethinkers, having been languishing in the cells, were by then obsolete. They were non-factors. And they were the only ones truly paying attention! So, with no one to organize them, in the 80s, the 90s, the prisoners bathed themselves in drugs, sex, and prison sports. And, now, church. And, check 'em out. Think about it. Each of these primary lifestyles are totally dependent on security personnel." He gestured. "No power."

Rise stops to look at Lil Chris. He can't really tell if he's been listening. The youngster is just walking with his head down, his hands clasped behind his back. Rise says a silent prayer that he's listening and continues his talk.

"When I got here from juvie over a decade ago, the folks was routinely making sweeps to scoop up any inmates that showed signs of true leadership qualities. They then chose our leaders from whoever they were willing to speak to. On whatever terms they dictated to them. Usually, weak or ignorant prisoners that they propped up. Grateful recipients make loyal agents.

"Inmate clubs had already been around for some time. But more and more, security made it a practice to rig inmate club elections, to set in puppet leadership—they couldn't let us pick our own leaders. This is how most of our hip-hop generation found the prison when we got here toward the end of the 90s. At about the same time we got here, female correctional officers started trickling in. Women being less likely to put up with security's corruption, security had to stop all the underhanded killing and dealing they were caught up in and clumsily covering up. They, in turn, then got distracted with sex rackets set to snare and entrap the lady officials. This gave hustlers and freethinkers, the truly strong prisoners, an opening to re-surface and start doing foundation work. The warden we have today also came in around this time, in 1995. During the stalemate. The religious manipulation became his thing. Opting for a more subtle grade of oppression and mind control. Facts.

"Oh, you can trust and believe, I was just like you. Wild as hell, but I wasn't stupid. No fear, though. Ignorant, to an extent, to grown-world reality. But, with the ability to understand. Just like you. This was 1997. I used to smoke bud half the day and spend the other half rappin'. It was my way of crying without shedding tears. A lot of us did that. Hell, No Love and Mansa Musa were here doin' it before me. No Love was already a legend when I first touched this ground."

At the mention of names he recognizes, Lil Chris looks at Rise. The lil brother's face reads deep concentration. He's been taking it all in. This invigorates Rise.

"You see, we was all riders. So energetic. All we did was get into shit. Getting moved back and forth from camp to camp. From cellblocks to population and back! While in the cellblocks, some of us came across those same true soul-jahs who had been separated from the rest of the population. People like the Angola Three: Woodfox, King, and especially Hooks. By then, they had already been in those cells for decades. A testament to their strength that they were still sane. They touched us with the game. Commissioned us to carry on the struggle. Not just for release from prison, but also for liberation, for social empowerment.

"By dudes already looking for fly material to rap about, they started putting these socially conscious and cultural messages in the music. There's only so many ways you can talk about the hood, right? Then there were the out-of-towners. Like Too Short, Fresno, and Wack. Mostly west coast gangbangers who got caught up enterprising down south. OG Smiley Loc and 'em. They got with Charlie Brown and the OG homies from up North around our way—Shreveport, Alexandria, Monroe, and such. More gang mentality in-state hotspots. Cultures more susceptible to group-think. They started the painstaking process of instituting this whole Cali concept of organization. But, modified to account for this prison's realities. Machine in motion, among the young hardheads. By security being so well entrenched in day-to-day life, it was real touch-and-go. But all of us, myself included at that time, we were all so hooked up on studying Kemet and Egyptology. Greek mythology and the Homer epics and such. So, the natural inclination was toward the underground.

"It seems like everybody had this thing for secret orders. As the children on the prison yard began to mature into young men, what was fashionable became an understood necessity.

"I was already an avid reader before I got here. I was already up on a lot of things that most were just being introduced to. At first, I just stood back and watched them. I saw the hard times make these young brothers either break or choose survival strategies. I saw those practical strategies merge with book studies to form strong convictions about how they saw themselves, their situations, and what needed to be done about it.

"I stood back and watched these secret societies fade out and link up. Eventually pulling the old heads in with their reach and resources. Mostly former Panthers and their ilk. That's when shit really got serious. Until now, when there are only two left . . . "

"S.O.G. and Da One," Lil Chris anticipates.

"Right," Rise says, as they continue around the yard. Yelling and hollering floats over to them on the breeze from the nearby playing fields. "Da One ended up being the die-hard revolutionary camp. They see the world, now and then, through the lens of conspiracy theory. They adamantly teach each other that deception is their best weapon. Their bible is the snake book. They all study it—"

"—I know. I ran across one in the dungeon," the C'ster interjects.

"The thing is, they are so driven by contempt for the system that they have become like the very same thing they claim to hate. And then, there's S.O.G."

"What does that mean?"

"Skies Over Gaza. For me to go into the meaning behind the name would lead to a whole 'nother breakdown dealing with pyramids and astrology and zodiacs," Rise smiles faintly. "Look, I got a book in the dorm called *Message of the Sphinx* that will start you on that path if you want." He waves his hand. "For now, I wanna put you on the S.O.G. stance."

Lil Chris makes a skullnote to get the book later. And holds his peace for the moment.

"We've been accused of being reformist," Rise explains. "To a certain extent, we are. But, we are not accommodationists, which is the tag they try to attach to reform. However, reform for us is not a defining ideology. Reform is what we consider to be the best solution to our common problem. Reforming the state's dysfunctional criminal justice system is a far more practical solution. Remember the Constitution? The Civil Rights Movement? These conversations? Can you dig it? Especially when doin' otherwise would justify the perpetuation of our livin' hell on another generation of deviants.

"This is why this whole Lyrical Warfare is so important. The music is how we speak to the people. True leadership hangs in the balance. Those of us who are conscious tend to guard what comes out of our mouth. The tongue is a powerful tool. It sets things in motion. Those of us with a sense of responsibility know that we are held accountable for our speech and our actions.

"This is why we always, *always*, greet each other with a whispered reminder: 'To touch without feeling is the ultimate sin.' Because once you know the truth, how could you not feel it? As brothers, we respond, 'Far worse than blasphemy.'"

Later, Lil Chris goes in to work at the Education Building. Really, he just wants some time alone to think over all that has been happening.

As he sweeps the floor, he finds himself looking blankly at his watery reflection in the linoleum. The Pro-25 headphones clamped on his head block out everything. He thinks of his momma and sisters. He often does this, though he rarely talks about them. His thoughts of them are his alone, thoughts he chooses not to share with this place. Shit, he has nieces and nephews he's never even met.

He thinks of them in the context of what he's been learning. History and politics. Concepts and philosophies. A whole other world. Very different from the one he was raised in. But he would be lying if he said his studies didn't afford him a broader perspective. His momma's struggles. The earning ceiling holding his sisters back. The mischief his nephews are already prone to get into from time to time. It's all so exhaustive and exasperating to consider. So much to be done . . .

Someone waves a hand in front of his face. Lil Chris picks his head up to see.

"Hey, that song. I know that song," says this tall, goofy looking white dude. A lieutenant, he knows by the single bar on his collar.

Lil Chris pulls off the headphones and the world floods in. A moment of disoriented searching. The officer has this almost childlike voice and manner. There's an air of testing about him. As if to him this encounter is some kind of experiment.

"You playin' wit' me?" Lil Chris questions, indignantly.

"Oh, no, no," the officer denies, with a self-deprecating chuckle. Almost nervous.

The C'ster recoils a bit. *What's with this dude?* He checks the guy's nameplate. Brecheen.

"I was just sayin' I know that song," Brecheen explains. "The one you was just listening to. 'You feelin' kinda limp, nigga. Go'n brush ya shoulders off,'" Brecheen sings. Tryna rap. "'Ladies is pimps, too.'"

Every muscle in Lil Chris' arm flinches with the impulse to lay the mop handle he's holding across this white boy's face . . . no. He jerks around, pulls the mop bucket with him. Splashes soapy water in an effort to create some space between himself and the temptation.

"What?" Brecheen asks. As if he don't know. Following the C'ster. Step for step!

"Look, cracker!" Lil Chris whirls around. Mop cocked like a bat. Water flings everywhere.

"Wow!" Brecheen throws his hands up. "Damn, brah," he chuckles, again, uneasily. "You prejudice or somethin'?"

It's not his tone of voice. This ain't the first redneck he's heard speaking Ebonics. It's his eyes. The utter absence of malice. Like he's approaching the C'ster on the playground or some shit.

Brecheen starts laughing again. "C'mon, man," he says. "Won't you chill out? You gettin' water all over ya self!"

"Lyrical Warfare."

It's the phrase that rolls off of everybody's lips as they stand in line waiting to be summoned through for callouts. Still, very few of them understand the term like Lil Chris does. He stands in line with the hoodlums and hooligans, engulfed in his own thoughts.

It's not about being scared to move, Chris thinks. *Sometimes you gotta let go and back out of what you've accomplished in one pocket. In order to get farther up the path. To win is to negotiate the passes in times of decision.* With this, Lil Chris steadies himself. Much-needed balance.

Rise thinks to himself, *Don't play with me, mayne. Dammit, I'm fly for real. You all are really not on my level.*

He is the very picture of confidence. He's in his element.

The one thing that nags him is the white envelope folded in his back pocket. He picked it up from legal mail on his way up to the A

Building. He knows it's the court decision back from his court order and appeal.

It always happens like this. He puts in all those long hours studying. Sees the sense and logic in his argument. Recognizes that it is in concert with standing precedence recorded in the relevant case law. He has a budding hope that a ruling will be granted in his favor. And, slowly, that hope solidifies into concrete faith. So many long nights writing into the morning without sleep, with faith in his purpose. Faith that makes his actions, his sacrifices, his commitment make sense. Only to have that same faith crushed by one sheet on typed stationary. Abbreviated text that culminates in one word: Denied. Stamped on it.

No. Not tonight. He won't play their head game tonight. Tonight, his thoughts are of what needs to be accomplished for the whole of his people. He pushes his own issue to the back of his mind. He goes about contemplating the business of the night with a single-minded focus.

The people begin pouring into the A Building. Mostly hardheads. Younguns, penitentiary sharp. Booted and suited up to come get with their homies. Vibe with them. Kick around some game or something. Above all, brothers is anticipating what's going down tonight. Every man in the room feels like it's a big thing to be in the building. Yeah, they sweating the microphone. Ain't nothing but penitentiary legends on the roster of performers tonight. Most notable are No Love, Poison, J-Rocc, Shady House, Heroin. Rise, of course. And young Lil Chris.

Mansa Musa and them mob past the check-in counter at the entrance looking like, "And what?" If you don't know who they are, you don't notice them. They've perfected the art of blending in. Invisibility even. Da One is not a name that's spoken by everyone. If you know about it, you know to keep it low, though. They ain't playing.

Even more mystic are the suns of the Skies Over Gaza. S.O.G. These are the older cats. Oldheads. The majority of which you'd never even assume had any stakes in the events of the night. But, oh—they're definitely paying attention.

In an instant, a memory unbidden siezes Rise. Déjà vu, even. A right brain feedback triggered by the scene unfolding before him. There was a night much like this one a few years back. An open callout that had pulled him to the chapel for its promise of live music. The place had been packed with an older crowd. Dudes from an era of eight-tracks and guitar gods. They had billed it as a "gospel explosion." A line-up of convict bands from all over the prison farm, featuring a Who's Who of legendary bassists, drummers, and singers. Supermen who otherwise posed as Clark Kents in the law library, the laundry, or in the bowels of the kitchen. It had been their night to revisit their passion. To get a fix of that crowd adulation and hero worship that is every performer's secret drug of choice.

His eyes search and rest on Lil Chris and Gary Law where they stand at the other end of the building, but his mind vividly recalls that night so long ago. Those gray-headed performers, the colors faded in their t-shirts, their jeans threadbare, but their outfits starched and pressed all the same. In cowboy boots and big rodeo prize buckles, they gyrated and worked that pulpit like a stage at Woodstock. Moved flawlessly through a playlist of gospel standards. Musical passages they each had taken 20 to 30 years to perfect on this prison farm. Beautiful melodies that the crowd—just as aged and weathered as the performers—cheered and sang along to.

Rise can remember sitting alone in the pews at the very back of the chapel. Tears streamed down his face, his shoulders heaved as he took in the scene. Inconsolable, as the callout's organizer came angrily upon him and asked, "Man, what's wrong wit' you?" Demanded that he, "Get yo'self together!"

He couldn't, though. Rise had been traumatized. He had felt like nothing so much as a child. A child who had stayed up past his bedtime and happened across a movie he shouldn't have been allowed to watch.

A weak moment. He's had his share.

As Rise pulls himself free of the memory, he looks up and spots who but Mansa approaching.

"What's going on, Brother Rise?" Mansa greets.

"Brother?" Rise frowns. "Is that what you calling me, these days?"

Mansa steps closer. Lowers his voice. "You just as conscious as the rest of my brothers. You know I've always tried to embrace you. I've always acknowledged your potential."

"Yeah, when you wasn't busy tryna assassinate my character."

"Hey," Mansa leans back a little. "That was unfortunate. What you thought would happen? You accepted all that information from us, then turned away from the fold."

Rise scoffs a bit. Faces him eye to eye. "I guess I was homesick."

"Uh-huh. Sick for a home that don't want you," Mansa derides him. "You still see yourself as part of a people that have rejected you. I mean, smarten up, Rise. We da ones the world chose to forget."

"And therein is the gist of our signifying." Rise gathers himself to break their engagement. "You willfully see yourself as an outsider. That perspective is dated. Me, I'm simply an outlier. I won't be here for long."

Da Hit Squad is the front group for Da One. Vanguard serves the same purpose for S.O.G. Each one will be pushing their respective team's message through creativity and heat rocks. Although there is no seating arrangement, representatives from each camp split the room right down the middle. Most are at least a little familiar with what type of vibe will be coming from where. There are those who have their favorites. They make it their business to support them when the cyphers kick off on the yard. But, tonight is different in that usually if you ain't feeling the cat you 'on't listen. In here, every man will have his say. He'll be amplified by the house system. Speakers lining every area in the building. The stage area is so hot the dudes in the back of the building can hear what Gary Law and Lil Chris are whispering about. G will be MCing tonight.

"Say, ah, Lil Chris. Since you the only one don't have a click, you go 'head and do you first. So, you'll be back before the shots start poppin' back and forth."

"Oh, nawl, big brother. I'm straight. I just came to check these cats out. I ain't go'n spit," Lil Chris answers.

"Hold up, youngster. They got dudes here that came to hear what you sayin', too. I'll call you in a few minutes."

"Man . . . "

Boom! . . . Doom-doom, Doom-doom!

Before Lil Chris can respond, the system is crunk up. Somebody done dropped that instrumental to Master P. and Scarface's "Homies & Thugs." The old-school "Friends" sample is pushing a bass kick so hard that when it hits, his shirt sleeve vibrates.

G starts in, "Alright, alright, ain't no sense in waiting. We got a big night in store for you. My name is Gary Law. *My* cut-'em-up days was really back in the 70s. But I can still relate. So, I'm go'n be drivin' tonight."

Lil Chris is getting amped up. When they said they would be using instrumentals, he didn't believe they would sound this clear. Not to mention the house mixer is doing a good job on the board of blending in what's being said on the microphone.

Oh, I gotta get wit' this! he thinks.

"Anyway," Gary closes. "With no further ado. The first man up is Lil Chris. Y'all give him a hand."

Claps spark up all over the room. They all feeling the youngster. His reputation is above reproach. Not only is he solid, he's one of the hottest lyricists on the river. The kind of G that everybody knows.

As he steps to the mic, the soundman momentarily fades the music out to cue up the CD player. A few seconds later, the music behind Jay-Z's "Hard Knock Life" flows into the room.

Heads are bobbin' as if in a trance as the C'ster grabs the mic.

"We fall down
>Lord have mercy

This ole livin' shol hurt me

I speak about it every day that
>They work me

I swear the sun's beamin'
>Scorchin' me down. It's so hot

Pushin' myself to give it all that I got

To get up and get on
>Principles I stand on won't let me quit

Trus' that I'm tired and afflicted

I've seen life at high speed

My youth passin' me by

What if I told you
>I'm a luminary

I make my home in the stars.
>You know who we are

The God-sent!

Show me my nation
>If I'm to be the guiding light of
>The lost

Soak me in flames
>Publish my name
>Lil Chris!"

While Lil Chris is spitting, Mansa walks over to No Love, who's standing off to the side. He asks, "Did you just hear that?"

"What?" No Love is irritated. He really wants to hear what the lil homie is saying.

"They got him. They finally got 'im."

"They got who?"

"Come on, Love. You heard him. He said he's a luminary. Soaked in flames—that's a sun! Think about it: the guiding light of the lost. He's tellin' you he's choosin'. He's a sun in the Skies Over Gaza."

"You trippin', Mansa. Don't jump to conclusions. The homie still standing in the middle." No Love is sure of this.

"Look, if he ain't chose, he got the charge." Mansa has already begun to scheme. He returns to his seat amongst his cohorts.

Meanwhile, the C'ster still has the mic.

"Authors of my demise
    Are politickin'
    Plottin' my destruction, but my
Weary eyes have peep the play
              I will survive
My strong network of resources labor
    Unearthing my recourses
        From the dirt and the grime
In the bottom of the pit of struggle
    I know y'all feel, now!
My vessel is bound
    For the higher grounds of Spookville
        Quit whistlin' dixie, boy!
This life we livin' got
Hard qualifications, Lord!
Livin' like a fugitive . . . Burnt!
My indignation
Come and peep the play
    Here's what I learnt
My obligation to shine
    And be a symbol of hope
        For this population
Stay on top of my situation
    And stop fakin'
    It is time for some decision makin'
        Akkhum . . . "

As Lil Chris pauses to clear his throat, the crowd erupts. He

216 | This Life

couldn't get a word in if he wanted to. Mansa is just further convinced. Everybody knows how close he and Rise are anyway.

The thing that is so disquieting about a court trip is that the beauty of the commute doesn't pass. It stays. It sustains and nourishes. Not like a blanketing or coating of the sense. More like a reveal. It feels, to Rise, like a shade has been lifted. Like the scales have been taken from his eyes and everything is so vivid. So striking, intense, and provocative. The world around him has more volume, is expansive. And the nature of it all is more defined and detailed, having been where he's been, seen what he's experienced.

Regrettably, Lyrical Warfare begins to take on another context for him. The effect for Rise is jarring, almost shameful, as he watches the program unfold, courting that blasphemy that his circle so frequently wards off. Their whispered warning.

Gary Law calls another rapper to the stage. Presides over the opening arguments. Rise's heightened sense of awareness pierces the whole exercise. This isn't industry. It's not about how many records these dudes could sell, given the opportunity, or the value their skills would have under different circumstances. It's about *these* circumstances. About the fact that when they imported the men to these rural surroundings, they also imported their culture. About them refusing to surrender who they are in the face of the court's dictates and security's containment strategies. This is hip-hop leveraging culture to answer the demands of the moment. This collective moment.

Still, the truth is they're not a collective, even if they're all subjected to the same reality, the same depraved, barren existence. Rise looks over the soundstage and the crowd, matches many of the faces to the atrocities he's had to stomach during years of case law research. Admittedly, research that has found its way into several of the appeals he's pursued while fighting his own conviction. Including the petition that led to the ruling in the unopened letter presently in his back pocket. As if he's somehow complicit in their acts, having leveraged their case law in his own defense.

Even without questioning to what extent he truly believes a man can be redeemed from his past, Rise considers what he knows of these men today. Their tendencies and values. Their characters and demons. The make of the men. Even if they are guilty as charged, like he is. Or even guilty of the many things he's gotten away with. How much does he really have in common with the worst of them? Rise remembers the man he'd known and befriended for five years before discovering that he was in prison for raping his 11-year-old stepdaughter. Remembers, too, how reluctant he was, even after finding out, to turn his back on a man that had been such a close friend for all those years. How most of his closest friends in here are someone else's nightmare. How he is someone else's nightmare. None of them are here for being choir boys. To what degree can he still identify with them once they no longer have incarceration in common?

Mortified by this realization and its implications, Rise looks up and notices Lil Chris heading towards him.

Up front, Gary Law stands in and calls for a break in the action so security can get the head count out of the way.

Lil Chris is lightheaded. Breathes deeply, his steps sure, he is blanketed in this sense of finally becoming. Finally being able to put the pieces of the whole picture together. How this life came to be. What's possible. He's energized by the notion that the choice is his to make. Where he stands. It doesn't really matter to him that he's had to come to prison to finally grasp these mechanics. Because his new and hard-won consciousness affords vision. He can begin to sense what he's capable of. Kwame Nkrumah! Mandela! He's aware of the infinite potential of one constantly evolving lifespan. At the moment, his life sentence is the last thing on his mind. Hard to convince a sane man in his early 20s that he'll die of old age in prison. Too much livin' to do.

He senses Rise's mood as he steps up, but he thinks nothing of it. This is Rise. He always got it together.

"Wuz up?"

"Nice showing, young man," Rise answers. They share a man hug and a fist bump. "I hadn't heard that one before," he notes.

"You know I never stop writing," Lil Chris shoots back. What's with this Kool-Aid grin on Rise's face?

"Yeah, I know the score," Rise chuckles. Tryin' to tuck this nagging sense of being held up. Like he's missing an event somewhere else. "Hey, heads up. Don't miss your unit, mayne."

"Yeah, yeah, yeah," Lil Chris drifts away, realizes Rise seems barely aware of him.

Anticipation is high. As the prisoners walk back and forth to the security counter, Mansa gets with each of the rappers in Da Hit Squad. Tells them to aim shots at Lil Chris. To destroy his credibility.

His team starts to balk on him, though. There is division in the ranks. Lil Chris is highly respected among the hip-hop heads. Plus, he subject to bug up if the wrong thing is said about him. Mansa manages to convince his team to make the hit. Out of obligation to the cause.

No Love seethes. He ain't about to cross the lil homie. He tryna think of what to do about it, though. Time is runnin' out. Count is almost over.

"Okay, y'all. Let's crank this thing back up," Gary says as the "Friends" sample kicks back in. This time, Scarface's vocals murmur in the background. "We got some artists comin' up from Da Hit Squad. Y'all let 'em have it!"

The crowd applauds.

"Friends" fades, and seconds later a molasses-slow groove with a thick bassline filters through the thick speakers. It's that old-school "High Powered" instrumental from Dr. Dre's *The Chronic*. The beat is so familiar that everybody in the crowd is mumbling, "Seven execution style murders . . . "

Da Hit Squad represeters, Osiris and Horus, grab the mic and start chanting.

"Can . . . you . . .

Recognize

Who I be and what I'm off into

Can you

Recognize . . . "

Damn, what was up with that fake-ass smile the big homie just gimme? Lil Chris posts up off to the side. Rise just scrambled his circuits. Not to mention, No Love is posted up over there by his crew, Da One. He's been pickin' up bad vibes from those numbers ever since they called count. And not once has No Love came over and holla'd. Something's gotta be up.

Lil Chris's impulse is to go over and get at Rise. See what's what. *He must think I'm leaning toward rockin' with Da One.* The thought makes Lil Chris grit his teeth. *If that's the case, knowin' Rise, he wouldn't tryta talk me out of it. Pro'ly wouldn't change nothin' between us, either. Mayne, Rise trippin'.* His present line of thought is more than makin' him angry.

He looks over and spots Wayne and C-Boy. C-Boy heavy into the music. Da Hit Squad is gettin' it in. Though they haven't looked his way once, he could've swore some of those one-liners were aimed at him. *Now ain't the time to get paranoid . . .*

Just as Lil Chris is about to look away, Wayne taps C-Boy and gestures in Lil Chris's direction. C-Boy looks over; he and Lil Chris make eye contact. The homie gives him a nod of recognition, and that's enough.

The C'ster knows in that moment he's where he needs to be. By his lonely, standin' on his own two. Plus, he just made his mind up.

On the other side of the building, No Love slides into Rise and whispers something in his ear. Rise gives an almost imperceptible nod. Signals two of his rollies to pull in. He and No Love discuss some things.

When the gathering breaks, Rise heads toward Lil Chris. On the way to him, he hits Gary Law in the ear before pushing to the lil homie.

Mansa, who's been in the seating section across the room, has been on top of the play from the word go. He's more than disappointed that he's lost Lil Chris, but he had to make him pick a side. His influence was too detrimental to just leave him standing in the middle. No Love crossing is what he didn't anticipate. Since there is no way of intimidating No Love, Lil Chris, or Rise, all Mansa and his people can do is sit back and watch the night slip away from them.

After Da Hit Squad's first set finishes, Gary Law steps to center stage with a little more pep in his step for real. The "Friends" sample kicks back in to hold him down.

"Yeah, it's about to get thick in here. Y'all ready for the jump off?!"

The crowd roars.

"I know y'all didn't think it had already jumped off, did you?"

Mumbles. Grunts. It gotta be more to it.

"Nawl, it ain't yet. But, it's 'bout to. First though, we got a surprise for you. That is, unless y'all have any objections?"

Silence.

Anticipation.

"We go'n bring Lil Chris back up! To—"

Gary Law can't finish. The crowd amps out. They wildin' in the A Building tonight.

"Well, we go'n bring up Lil Chris. Better yet, he says now y'all can call him . . . The Sun o' Man!"

There's more yelling. Beating on tables. They feelin' this young cat.

"Following him, we go'n bring the newest mystery member of Vanguard right on through."

Silence. Brothers is looking crazy with this one.

"Y'all hold that under your hats, though. For now, let's see The Sun o' Man. Lil Chris!"

Crazy applauds erupt as Lil Chris steps back up to grab the mic. The "Friends" sample fades. This complicated bass lick and drum kick floods the room. It's the instrumental beat behind Biggie Small's "What's Beef?" Yeah, they bobbing they heads. Wow. It's on.

The C'ster steps to the stand and takes the mic. Clears his throat and releases.

"I feel fire burn cold
>Heated seven times, a tragedy untold
>>Say what? . . . Criminal mind
Adolescent but heavy
Now, you know you gotta
>>Cook the blood out
>Seasoned in simmerin' *hot* grease
Intentions speak *loud*, homie
>>You wit' me or what?
>Actions *talk*, now . . . Speak up.
>I'm for *peace* but when I *speak*
>>They are for war
Duppies got game, galore
>You *despise* my witness
>>What for?
Yeah, you would slay me
>If you thought you could take me
>>But, you ain't tryna see
Really, apprehensions speak volumes, playa
Listen for the still, small, voice
>Not in the wind
>Not in the earthquake
>But, after the fire . . . "

As Lil Chris is rappin', two soul-jahs in black hooded robes step up to either side of the stage. Heads down. Identites concealed. They began to sway in rhythm with the music. The C'ster draws to a close with a fever.

"Until all of eternity
>Condense to one point in my mind

Ghetto ghost of Ashanti
I feel you, Witherspoon
Thoughts burst
    Searching for room
Gas and dust
    A coon for the stars
        Big Bang Theory
I'm for *peace* but when I *speak*
    They are for war!
Troubled seeds
    Shakin' the curse
Tryna get off they knees
    Dyin' of thirst
Thoughts ooze . . . Unforgettable
    Permeatin' minds
    Take this, as a sign of the times
        We've all learned!
Sunrays got me *burned*
    For the Love o' *God!*
    Bake me deep chocolate
        I'll wear it wi' pride
Tough times got
    Blood in my eyes
Yeah, we *all* know this livin' is hard
    Why we actin' surprised
I'm for *peace* but when I *speak, really*!
    They are for war
The most vicious kids I ever saw
I'll say it again like I said it before
I'm for peace but when I speak
    They are for war.
That's self-explanatory, mayne,
    My story goes . . . "

Boom!

All the sudden, the beat changes. The hyperactive highs and synthesized sound of Jay-Z's "Dirt Off Your Shoulders" comes pumping through. It got that hop to it. It's pickin' 'em up.

One of the brethren in the black, hooded robes, the one on the right, steps across the stage and takes the mic Lil Chris hands him. They both stand there a moment, heads bobbin'.

Lil Chris makes as if he's brushing dirt off his shoulder. Then, with both hands, he wipes down his shirt. Like he's brushing the lint off or something. He pats the thighs of his jeans and each knee to shake his pants leg off. All in sync with the drums. Flossin'. Fly showmanship. He getting' his thing on.

The cat in the robe turns toward the crowd. This guy is amped already! As the beat rolls around, Lil Chris pulls the hood off his head . . . It's No Love!

He looks up and eyes the crowd. Choices. He's just taken the stage as Vanguard. No turning back now, whatever the fallout.

He makes brief but certain eye contact with Mansa. Then spits these words:

"Inclined to the best
But, yo!
A hidden essence
Ten compromises. One forbidden message
Married to everything known
As esoteric
From ancient B.C. to modern Man's presence
Modern Man's blessin' is me
The Don DaDa
Call me Manotha
The German head rocker
Like the finest kind o' wine
My homies define time
One time for your mind . . .

Hum . . .
Wake up! Call brothers.
    Young Tommy is back!
Yo! Attackin' cats
Like we engaged in combat
Scriptural knowledge wit' Egyptians
    We done that
At war wit' these heathens over lyrics
    We won that
What the hell with these cats
    Engulfed in actin' hard
Define the word, retard
    Scandalous lil' boy!
Never been worthy for brothers to call you
                  Lord

Hatin' your religion
    Ignorance, your god
Imagine a cat who destroys
       With ram rods
Your hormones is next . . .
      What you? Y or X?
Have you seriously
    Contemplatin' your chosen sex.
Yo!
    Throw you out the game
          For a foolish tech
The only thing that I want
    Is your head on a platter
Don't even much matter
    I like it raw
It was ripped from your neck
    Wit' my Lion's paw
There's a rule in the jungle

Don't ever! Roam alone
Snatch you out your home
    Split your dome
It's Vanguard to the death
    Whether right or wrong
Cat's enchanted by my psalms,
    Like the 'Song of Songs'
Entire history
    Written on . . . both my arms . . . "

Boom!

Silence reigns.

The crowd explodes into whooping and hollering. Claps and yells.

Then the Lil Wayne instrumental for Cash Money's "Go DJ" starts in. No Love throws his hands up and begins to chant, "Go! Go! Go! Go!"

The crowd joins in and now everybody throws their hands to the ceiling, yelling, "Go!"

The last man standing, his head dropped and hooded, wearing a robe, steps to center stage and stops beside No Love. Stock still. No Love is still hyping the crowd.

Slowly, the figure begins to nod. A deep bob. All in the shoulders. This brother's bobbing is so hard he's almost bouncin', springing up and down from his knees.

He takes the mic out of No Love's hand. The crowd still yells and chants, "Go!"

The figure starts nodding so violently his hood bounces, threatens to come off. Lil Chris walks over and pulls the hood away.

It's Rise.

Sweat pours. Already! Teeth clenched. Lips drawn away in a growl. "What? What!

    Show ya' mind, true liberation
    Young Rise, my profession
        Influence!

Sow blessing for my congregation
    Feeble mind remedy
Spit peace but I garner enemies
                Fake hearts
                    Feel that!

Vanguard go getta!
    Menes was my grandfather
One God worshipper . . . go figure
    Think large, wit' a
           Rod, for ya' guidance
    I'll spank ya, listen here!
Ain't no idiots livin' in here!
    No Love
           Would you make that clear?"
"Aight!" No Love yells.
"The revolution will not be televised," Rise continues.
"Partake. Free ya' mind
    Ask Fredrick Douglass 'bout my life
We been a long time
    At Golgotha!
Resurrect, Brothers!
For real! Where you at, Brothers?!
What the deal? Introspect, Brothers!
Live with these thoughts
    Speak wit' these thoughts
Breed with these thoughts
Look how wrath was wrought
    Monotheism!
Amenhotep the fourth!
Back! Thuthmoses the fourth
Come! Ramses
    Two of these
           Cat's didn't get the memo

Why you immolatin'!!!

Truth!

Poppy gotta get his self in order, huh?

Bring bacon, work harder, huh?

Y'all don't hear me

All hail three kings

Mend broken rings

Hold the noise down!

I'm tryna think!

Bet ya we work out!"

Boom!

The low-end base frequency carries the moment into history. Legend.

Rise, Lil Chris, and No Love all throw their fists in the air and begin chanting "Vanguard, woof-woof! Vanguard, woof-woof!"

The crowd catches on and before long, the whole building swells with one voice, chanting the same battle cry.

After everything settles down, C-Boy, Lil Chris, and No Love are on stage, rocking the crowd.

Rise slips out of his black robe. He walks to the back of the room, where people have pretty much cleared out. As he sits down, he feels the legal mail that's been in his back pocket all night crinkle under his weight.

He lifts up and pulls the mail free.

Just sitting there, he stares at the envelope for a moment. Meditates on it, even.

What the hell.

He tears the flap. Pulls the paper out. Two sheets.

His eyes move with a cold, detached disposition. He looks at the heading. Sees his name on the case title.

He reads the first few lines. All formalities. Yeah, yeah, yeah. Blah, blah, blah. He shuffles and flips to the second page. Cuts to the chase, goes to the last line.

He reads.

Pauses. Takes a breath.

He reads again.

He sits heavily back in the chair. Numb. After a moment, he nods slowly. Tears threaten to fall.

He smiles. Exhales.

He's going home.

CHAPTER EIGHTEEN

What it is that
Burns in my soul
What it is that
Burns in my soul
Could it be Mahalia
That sung the song
 that enflamed my spirit
wrought like magnetic
 the groove was low
   I could barely hear it
Brought like prophetic
Fossil music . . . reclaimed my bones
Estranged from home
Still a caged bird
But, they reframed my tone

This land I roam
In a crowd
But, it feel like I'm all alone
My love is strong
If I say I'm wit' you
    Trust that. It's on
Light
    That was seldom shone
Caught knowledge
    Once seldom known
Couldn't go wrong
    I'm a go-getter
        I won't be here for long
Conflict within me
    Won't let me sleep
I'm on a full-scale revolutionary creep.
                Action!
Confirmation from my faction
Visionary men
These are the suns of men
        Fac' affiliated
Truth stated
    Why debate it?
I'm like,
    'God! Can I move
        It's been propagated
            I'm righteous, Dude!'
One with the Universal
    Atomic Nucleus
Dynamic spirit

Within me. Hear me
That's what it is
That burns in my soul!

HE STANDS AT THE DESK watching her.

Her skin is bright. Reflects the early morning sunlight.

Water drips from his face. He didn't bother to take a towel to the sink with him when he went to brush his teeth. He rubs the fingers of his right hand over his chin. Flicks the water off, carelessly, to the side. He understands this environment so much. To the point that he feels he's in his element now. But his tolerance for ambiguity is low. The consequence of his recognition that the stakes are so high. Life for Lil Chris has become deep waters. He's all in.

"So, what's happenin' wit' you?"

"Don't come over here wit' no foolishness, Lil Chris. It's too early in the morning for that!"

"What makes you think I'm on some foolishness, Cynthia?"

"Boy, don't be—"

"Can't nobody hear me, girl. The fan is too loud. Watch your face. What? You forgot how to play the game?"

"I don't feel like playin'," she pouts.

"Chill out, chill out, man. Don't trip."

"And I done told you," she angrily cuts him off. "I ain't no 'man.' That's what your problem is, anyway." She sits up and begins to shuffle paperwork around on her desk.

"You're right, you're not a man," Lil Chris heatedly counters. "If you were, dealing with you wouldn't be so complicated. And confusing."

Cynthia stiffens. Takes a sharp breath, as if he had just dashed her with cold water.

He realizes he went too hard. Remorse.

"You forgot," she mumbles. Pulls short.

"And there it is," Lil Chris recovers. "You know these circumstances better than I do. If you see I lost it, stop fuckin' playin' and help me remember!"

" . . . How to talk," she finishes. Shakes her head, like, *A damn shame.*

"Look, check this out, Sergeant Roperson," Lil Chris begins calmly, using her formal title with emphasis. He's got her undivided. "Otherwise, why are we friends? You might as well just do your job."

Silence.

"Now, write me a pass to the A Building," he whispers.

"What time?" Her voice is hoarse. Stripped down a bit. Damn.

"8:00," he says, and struts off.

Rise sits alone in the A Building.

He rose early and got there before anyone else was even stirring in their sheets. The weeks that passed since the court ruled in his favor were slow indeed. The prosecution appealed to the highest state court. The original decision was upheld. It took 35 long days, but Rise will be released tonight. At midnight.

He has one last thing to do before he leaves. It's funny how these things have worked out. Six months ago, he appointed Lil Chris to be sergeant-at-arms. The lowest post on the chess club's executive board. Shortly after, his vice president got locked up. Dirty piss test. Then, his treasurer got swung to a satellite camp. When his secretary refused to step up in the order of ascension, it placed Lil Chris right beside him as vice-president of the Prison Chess Players Association.

The order of the day is to step down as president and install Lil Chris as his successor. What better occasion than today? It's the P.C.P.A. annual banquet.

My mind will flow in all kinds of directions, Rise muses as he considers what lies before him. *But my actions will hold true to what I stand on.*

At about 8:30 a.m. the members begin pouring in. A few club

officers come over to greet Rise and get some final instructions for how to carry out the business of the day.

C-Boy and Lil Chris stand over by the security gate. Receiving the club sponsors and visitors as they come in from the streets.

Rise looks over and spots his rolldog. He makes a skullnote to be sure and vibe with Lil Chris before the day plays out. No use in tryna holler now. C-Boy has him hemmed up.

"S-s-say, brah. You see Ms. Sam? That thang off the chain, huh?"

"Look out, man. That's somebody's visit you trippin' on. I ain't go'n pull nobody off you. So, you need to watch what you do with your eyes."

Lil Chris is all business this morning. Guess you could say he's feeling hisself. The responsibility he's about to be entrusted with is weighing down on him. He plans to take his post seriously.

"Look, C-Boy, hand out the rest of these programs for us. I need to go over here and get wit' Rise before we get swept up in what's goin' on this morning."

"Man, what you mean, 'Pass these out for us?' You done went to sounding all political and things already. Don't change on me, kid." C-Boy is smiling, but he ain't playing.

"Don't panic on me," Lil Chris reassures him. "You know we get it on. But we all gotta grow, right?"

C-Boy sobers. "I feel you. I was just sayin—"

"Well, don't be just sayin'," the C'ster says, asserting himself. "That's how things go bad. Just rock with me if you 'just' go'n do anything."

"A'ight, a'ight. I got this, yo. You just go head and holler at Rise." C-Boy takes the rest of the program pamphlets out of Lil Chris's hands. He turns to meet the procession of visitors stepping past the security gate.

Lil Chris turns and walks over to Rise.

The day is fast-paced already. Lil Chris and Rise embrace each other like brothers. After exchanging daps and pounds, they step around the serving counter into one of the back rooms where the refrigeration units are kept. They stop on either side of a low-topped deep freezer and stand eye to eye.

"Have you thought about how important the day is for us?" Rise begins.

"This day," Lil Chris says soberly.

"This day." Rise permits a smile to crease his features.

"Yeah, you hand over the club to me today."

Shit is forced. They both know it. They have to stand off each other. They know this as well.

"It's not just about the club," Rise comments.

Lil Chris starts to speak. Holds his tongue.

Rise grins sideways. Can't help it. "This club is just position. You can lose it. Gain it back." He collects himself. "Man, look at you. Posture. Confidence. That alchemy at work."

"C'mon, Rise," Lil Chris flags his hand.

"No," Rise insists. "You should be proud. You've come a long way. Raised me in the process." He looks him over for a heartbeat. "And, believe this, lil brother. It's not gonna take you as long as it took me."

A security whistle blows somewhere outside the window. Draws Lil Chris' attention.

"Ignore that," Rise holds one hand up. "This us, right now. They business ain't no more important than ours."

"I feel you, big brother."

Rise takes a deep breath. "These last couple weeks I've really been grappling with some things. Questions I won't present to you. They're for a season. You'll come across them in your own time. Find your own answers. You don't have to know everything. But you have the mechanics you need to figure out whatever draws you."

"Like the law library," Lil Chris reasons.

"Right."

"But, that only counts if you stick to your beliefs."

"*Principles*. Beliefs change."

"Constitution." Lil Chris settles on this with the resolve of autumn leaves. "My personal constitution."

Rise pauses again. For pace. Just entirely in the moment. "There will be plenty of people around you that understand what needs to be done. You are the only person that can carry it. The next part I give you plain: never compromise your carriage. Don't get creative with it. Those masks tend to get stuck in place. You will meet a lot of people. They'll cycle in and out like kids on a carousel. Never let a one of them make you feel inadequate. Make sure they all witness your humanity first, whether they choose to acknowledge it or not, and regardless of what you think you need from them.

"Also, there is no altitude in prison. You can't climb your way out. Don't get caught up in the favor game. You work your way out. This is America still. If you know what you want and you're willing to work for it, you can have it. Define your own positive. Know your own forward. Be the kind of leader that you would follow and the rest will fall in place. Step sure.

"Finally, I love you, man. No ifs, ands, or buts about it."

Rise tries to keep a straight face with the last. He fails.

They share a laugh. One final soul-jah's embrace. Then back on their respective squares.

"I know that. Even though I didn't really look at it the way you're puttin' it to me. I'm ready, though." Lil Chris is standing. Shoulders square, chin up. Looks every bit the hope of the struggle he has come to be.

"Well, look," Rise says. "There is no need to prolong this. We've lived with each other and walked together for almost five years, now. Everything you need is already inside you. The only thing left is for you to formally become one of the suns in the Skies Over Gaza. You ready for that?"

Silence.

Their eyes communicate.

Rise lifts his left hand and waves in eight convicts who have been standing right outside the room's entrance since he and Lil Chris walked in. Gary Law leads the number. Most of the brothers with him are at least 50 or older. The old battleships come to surround Rise and Lil Chris at the deep freezer.

Gary Law is the first to speak. "You know that your choice to be a party to this number is a decision that has to be made of your own free will?"

Lil Chris nods.

"From now on, we need you to drop the 'Lil' from your name. Chris is sufficient. The change will be a statement in and of itself. From here on, this is your inner circle. Any one of us would die to protect this circle and the members thereof. Every one of us is actively committed to the freedom, uplifting, and empowerment of our people. We give what remains of our lives to live for this cause. Are you with us?"

Chris utters, "Yes."

"Well then, from here on out, the brethren will greet you with the reminder, 'To touch without feeling is the ultimate sin.' To which you will properly respond, 'Far worse than blasphemy.'

"With this whispered reminder, we acknowledge that no one of us is perfect. We all have done things that would have better been left undone. We've learned from our shared experiences that to live is to be accountable. In so much as we are capable, we must be the answer. This is how offense is recompensed."

At this, Gary and the rest of the circle one by one embrace their new leader with a whispered reminder. "To touch without feeling is the ultimate sin."

And each time, Chris answers, "Far worse than blasphemy."

THE BREAKBEAT

A year and six months later

EPILOGUE

CHRIS IS UP BEFORE THE sunrise. A cup of community coffee, brewed through a stretched athletic sock as a makeshift strainer. Good jabba. Them shits cost six dollars a bag. These days his commissary is straight, though. Rise been sending him a few pennies.

He had a thought early on, while he was brushing his teeth. Anti-cavity toothpaste. Ubiquitous in the prison. The state is still handing it out in generous amounts. Wonder why? Imagine a prison full of bad breath and toothaches. Thought that was funny.

Our Daily Bread devotional, a couple Bible verses, and he's up and moving.

The first spot he hits is the gym for an early morning workout with his man, Hao Nguyen. Hao is Vietnamese. Didn't speak a word of English when he first stepped on the prison farm. That was 21 years ago. Since then he not only speaks English, he also reads and writes it. And he's retooled himself into one helluva chef. The latter being the chief reason why he's up at the crack of dawn throwing around weights with Chris. All that cooking and taste-testing. His short frame and face have been roundin' out. Gettin' kinda plump. Got him scramblin' tryin' to address that. Oh yes, he is.

"I thought you knew that, Chris," Hao is saying. He and his fellow Vietnamese homie, Tran, are recapping some elements of the crime he was charged and convicted of. Particularly the fact that he always maintained that it was self-defense.

"Yeah, I knew that," Chris agrees. He had been speaking about a rape and, wanting to make sure he didn't offend, asked Hao if that was his charge. Somehow, the simple question has tilted the conversation.

Chris's turn has come up in the shoulder routine the three of them are doing. He climbs under the weight, pumps out his number. "On you," he says to Tran, when he finished his reps.

As he and Tran are switching out on the work bench, Chris asks Hao about the Vietnamese community in Houma, the small Louisiana town near the Gulf of Mexico where Hao caught his charge. Hao speaks about his culture. Chris casually listens as they all sweat through the workout. Hao's manner. His tone of voice, the windedness. The pacing, the vaguely uneasy glances at his homeboy. Damn if he doesn't remind Chris of how he and his Black homies would act talking about Black culture in the company of a white dude. The recognition is unsettling.

"I know it isn't your culture," Chris qualifies. "But I just recently got some pictures of Chinatown in San Francisco."

"Yeah," Hao ventures. "There is a Chinatown in almost all the major cities."

"Alright," Chris goes on. "I got a picture of a, ah, Chinese brunch with that, too."

"You mean dim sum?"

"Yeah, that's what my homeboy Zach wrote on the back. A couple bowls of dumplings."

"Uh-huh," Hao says. "*Qoang tha'nh.*" Chris breathes a bit as he sees his longtime friend loosening up. Hao, for his part, explains, "Usually you can pick from a bunch of them. Pork, beef, duck. Hey," Hao says. "You know, ah, New Orleans has a pretty big, ah, Asian community, too?"

"Yeah," Chris jumps in, all enthused. "I used to write to a Asian girl from New Orleans," he shares. His voice gets wistful. Dreamy. "Seray. I'm tah'm 'bout beautiful. And that muthafucka was sexy too. Like gotdamn!" He chuckles.

When Chris refocuses from his bout of nostalgia, intuitively his eyes dart to Hao. Then Tran. That recognition again. *Ah . . . so that's what we be lookin' like*, Chris thinks to himself.

Later in the morning, Chris' next stop is the law library to check with Gary Law before going upstairs to clean his drop.

G likes to ask if Chris has heard anything new from Rise. Always a rub, 'cause Rise doesn't write much. At least, not an actual letter. Kinda feels fucked up to expect more from him. But, even with the money it feels like being left behind. Abandoned. Chris usually says something vague, like, "I heard from him the other day. He wasn't talking about much."

The best thing about hanging out with G is the law work. Once he got used to the language, that is. And that alone took a minute. Now, however, Chris has gotten to the point where he can read case law like novels. Like every syllable is as descriptive as a love letter. Well. Maybe not a love letter. But his mind does tend to hug them shits. To memorize the "keys" effortlessly.

Plus, lately Gary Law has taken to introducing him to bill writing. Imagine that. Him, the C'ster, actually studying statutes, legislator's voting records, task force packages, and such. Part of a team that actually drafts bill proposals that could one day become law! It's one of the things Chris does with his time that he's most proud of.

Dipping out of the law library, he takes a walk upstairs. Kunta has already hit the drop. So, he falls into the little office he and his work partners have set up in one of the old book storages along his work station. Actually, he couldn't control who could and could not visit the chess club's office. So, he gave Kunta and 'em free rein of the club office and in exchange he has his own space. In a restricted area at that.

However, he still can't control all the traffic that comes through. Case in point, as he opens the door he's greeted by the familiar presence of Brecheen, a captain now, slouching in the glow of the television in one of Chris's office chairs. Like a relative who came to visit for the holidays and won't go home. Should've known it was a catch to agree to let the officer stash his video game in his spot.

"Hey, Chris! What up, brah," Brecheen greets him in that childish voice of his. He has brown hair, and is a foot taller and about 30 pounds heavier than Chris.

As he often does, Chris doesn't reply. He just grabs an energy drink out of the mini-fridge, a bag of Cheetos out of the cabinet, and plops down beside the captain.

The two of them sit, as they often do, in silence. Except for the sounds of the PlayStation's game play and soundtrack. Another army/military/special forces number. They seem to be Brecheen's favorite. He's assigned to the Treatment Unit on his regular shift. Yet it seems like every off-day he's sitting here beside Chris. Usually talking about his dream of quitting his job and running off to become a standup comedian. No shit. Can't make this up.

"You know what?" Brecheen says, the first to break the silence. As he often does. "Bourdelon's a real dick!"

That's Major Bourdelon. Brecheen's supervising officer over at TU. This oughta be good. Chris pops the cap on the energy drink and munches a few Cheetos in response.

"Man, there's this little Black chick . . . "

Chris doesn't so much as flinch, though his breath slows as if his air passages are contracting. Totally involuntary. Damn Hao and Tran!

"Well, put it this way. Bourdelon's jealous 'cause I give the lil mamma a ride to work every once in a while. You know, take her home . . . "

Chris, picking Cheetos out of his back teeth, forces his breathing back to normal. One of the main tortures of long term incarceration has been being forced to watch the prison personnel go about living their lives over the years right before his eyes.

"Here's the thing, see," Brecheen continues in his white man's equivalent-of-hip voice. "That asshole's been lovin' her. She's a sweet lil Black thang. Big ass, small waistline. Keep herself up, too."

Here, Chris turns to face him, this flat expression on his face. Brecheen's personal business, as is often the case, is nowhere near what was on his mind when he first turned that door knob.

"Anyway, the shit hit the fan last week. I took the girl home, you know. Like I always do. And I never ask her for nothin' for it. But, I guess she wanted to do something to, you know, show her appreciation." This low echo colors his voice. Like he's forming the words in his chest cavity. "So, we pull up to her crib. Right there in the drive way. Before she gets out of the car, the girl reaches over and—"

"I get the point, mayne," Chris interrupts.

"She blows me, man!" Brecheen just had to get it out.

That piece of shit, slut bitch. Chris' venomous, involuntary thought.

Brecheen is so self-absorbed by now, he doesn't even notice Chris' expression. Or maybe he does. He's married, by the way. "So, the next day, when I get to work, this fat fuck is acting all crazy. Like he's mad at me all of a sudden. He's tellin' everybody I got in his business." A prisoner's slang.

Chris gnashes his teeth so hard his jaws are rippling. "You snitched."

"I told a couple of people, maybe," Brecheen mumbles, like it's nothing.

Chris throws his hands up. Almost upends his chip bag. As often happens, Brecheen has drawn him into his madness.

"Man, yesterday, the son of a bitch wrote me up on a DR1," Brecheen bursts out. "That fat bitch is tryin' to get me demoted. He fuckin' with my money, now. My wife's gonna have a fit if that happens." Here, he starts laughing almost uncontrollably.

"C'mon," Chris says in this flat voice. "I'm listening. Don't go to actin' stupid."

"Nothing more to say," Brecheen snaps back. "I know it's hard to believe. But, yeah, this redneck cracker is pert' near irresistible. Especially to Black women."

Chris still looks at this obnoxious asshole. Who he's slowly but surely, if grudgingly, come to think of as a friend. He would never speak those words out loud. Though there are still things that he would never talk to Brecheen about, and he's equally certain there are things Brecheen would never tell him. Though they are still from two different worlds, and both have to be discriminate with every interaction. Chris looks at this friend—crazy how life unfolds—thinking of his other friend, Hao, and his homeboy, Tran. Chris realizes his goal should be a clarity of principle and concept. Clarity that affords him the confidence to be exactly who he is, no matter the company.

"You know what I think?" Chris finally says.

Brecheen lifts his eyebrows.

"The sistah," Chris continues. "Was probably down on her luck to begin with. Juggling you and that other fat muthafucka was just more bullshit. She be a'ight." He chomps some more Cheetos. Sips a little more of the energy drink.

Brecheen holds out his fist. They dap. And then Brecheen quietly gets up and leaves. Mu'fucka doesn't even turn the video game off.

Chris munches on chips and his thoughts for a while. Eventually, he licks the cheese from his fingers and opens a note pad.

"Rise," he writes. "Remember when we used to speak about the need to have negative capability . . . "

He still has the callout tonight in the A Building. Gary Law mentioned it earlier. Supposedly some pretty important people are coming. He's just looking forward to seeing Saboor.

The chess club's concession is supposed to provide refreshments. He'll need to get up and see to that. So much about his life is still a work in progress. He puts the notepad away, resolves to write Rise later. Negative capability, indeed.

"You know, it's crazy," Chris observes. Looks over the crowd. "How everybody wanna preach about protest, lament, and speak to the wrongs done to young Black men. The injustices. Now, I know there's more than Black folk in here tryna get free."

Applause.

"The thing is, what just occurred to me is how they always wanna say, 'Y'all doin' them wrong 'cause they innocent!' As if to say the shit they do us wouldn't be wrong if we was guilty. Excuse the language."

A few hardheads snicker.

He spies Mansa, No Love, Joseph, and 'em among the crowd. Mansa lifts two fingers to his brow in salute.

"Police even gettin' laws passed: Blue Lives Matter. High-profile PR campaigns to rebrand how we look at and judge what they do. It's ugly, they say. But, they are fighting crime, and these people are guilty! Well, I'm saying I'm guilty as hell, and my life matters, too!"

Applause. And encouragement.

"I mean there's a science to this shit!" Chris decides he'll stand in the moment. "Alchemy, they call it. How do you turn base life into livin' golden? More importantly, if I manage to somehow infuse my life with meaning, with worth, some type of contribution, on whatever level—I'm not sayin' that makes what I've done any less wrong!"

Silence. He stops. Stares at them. Wide eyed and sincere.

"I'm sayin' if I'm livin', I'm changing. And, if that change is for the better, then that 'better' matters."

Applause. They agree.

"I'm sayin' that, individually, if you, or you, or you, do what you need to do to be better, then the same laws that identify your 'bad' should also acknowledge your 'better.' Mayne, from the shoulder. Daily, I work hard as a mu'fucka to be the best me I can be. And, I don't need *nobody* to tell me that this life matters!"

She kicks his prison cot.

He wakes up groggily. She leans over him, her face only inches away from his own. He can still hardly hear her for the fans blowing, but he recognizes her voice immediately.

"Are you go'n get up? You were asleep when I came in before."

"What time—?" *Rise is a free man, now.* Strange waking thought. Even after all this time, he misses his brother. Must be the speech he made earlier. The outside visitors.

He sits up in his cot. Rubs his eyes. Stares out of the dormitory's glass façade into the bleak, black early morning sky. *I wonder where he's at. What he's doing . . .*

He put his feet to the floor. Slips on some dark gray jogging pants, slides into his shower shoes. Grabs a towel, a toothbrush, and toothpaste, and heads for the shower area.

Come a cool breeze

Blow my lows away

She's been working this compound long enough to know that any given moment he could be picked up and swung to another spot on the prison farm. If he were caught up like that it could be years before she would be close enough to touch him again. She wants to touch him now. She's grappling with the urge. They've touched before. That was all good.

At present, she sits at the security desk in the front of the dorm. The fan buzzes steadily beside her, faces the rows of sleeping convicts in their prison cots. Chris comes shuffling back out of the shower. He raises the towel to his face, wipes away the tap water.

When he clears the serving counter and steps around the fan, he comes to crouch down beside her chair.

"What's happening with you, sergeant?" he says casually. "It looks like you've developed feelings for an inmate. Watch it . . . you violatin', now."

"Boy, shut up!"

"Cynthia tell you what I asked her?"

"What, to teach you how to talk to girls?" Veronica smiles. "Or, ah, help you remember?"

"Don't make it sound like that," he grumbles self-consciously.

"You don't need her for that," she mumbles. Insistent. "You know how to talk."

"You ever notice that most prisoners don't look directly at you? And, eye to eye signals an intimate or honest exchange?"

"It's because y'all always bracing for rejection. Even you, sometimes," she says. "Cynthia told me you came back in from your callout and went straight to sleep—"

"I had a long day," he growls. Still a bit groggy. "I was hoping you would be close, tonight."

Veronica figures she doesn't need to say anything to that. She's here. She realizes that's enough. Instead, she reaches out and places her hand on the crown of his head. Scratches the nape of his neck.

"You better always have my back," Chris complains.

"I see and don't see. At the same time, I see without seeing," is her cryptic response. As she looks over the rest of the prisoners in the dormitory, absently continuing to scratch his neck, she adds, "We'll see us together, you'll see me happy, and I'll see you through."

He nods. Yawns.

He stands up to leave. Walks to his cot without looking back. Lays down and pulls the covers over his head. Not really tired. Just restless.

In his frustration, he begins to roll over, but feels the crinkle of folded paper in the front pocket of his jogging pants. One of the few actual letters he's gotten from Rise.

He pulls it out, unfolds it, and gives his eyes a moment to focus in the dim light beneath the covers.

It's a poem.

We stood I and I

Two men beneath the sun

Free minds in a captive land
    Conscious.
He spit when he spoke—
  And a spray of his spittle
    Did touch my lips
      I'm overcome by
My sense of awareness
      He gave me truth.
Rise
Have you any passion inside left
    For this rugged ride
Your proof of purchase ain't an issue
  Perfect your walk,
      Be your . . .
Wages of labor recompensed
  From this system of servitude
  That you've been toiling under
    Trigger my journey over.

Chris refolds the paper. Balls it up in his left hand. Rolls over and crosses his arms underneath his pillow.

He lies there a moment.

Awake.

Thinking. A burning behind his eyes.

He looks through the wall of windows again, the yard full of prisoners. They stand. Some with their state blue shirts opened and blowing in the wind, revealing stained white t-shirts. About four, five homies bob their heads to the music blaring from a Super Radio.

Minutes pass and he sees C-Boy walking toward the ledge of his dormitory. Close to the windows now. When C-Boy spots him, an aggravated grimace scribbles the contours of his walnut-colored features. He motions for Chris to get up. Mouths the words, "Come here."

Chris steps over to one of the screened sections and winds the crank so that a square of tiered glass panels swing up to make an opening in part of the façade. He thinks of the guard's eyes. Her smiling eyes. Through the opened window he can hear the sound of the radio and then C-Boy's voice. "Man, how long you was go'n leave us waitin'?"

Another day. The sun scarcely rising above the treeline, beyond the barbed wire fences. The same sky that makes a canvas for the prison yard.

Perfect your walk, be your . . .
He needs to get dressed, now.
Rise.

~ To Chris ~

I won't forget. I'll never let anyone else forget.

Haha! JaCrystal's just like you!

Life goes on..

ABOUT THE AUTHOR

Quntos KunQuest was born in Shreveport, Louisiana in 1976. Since 1996, he has been incarcerated at the Louisiana State Prison in Angola, Louisiana. He is a musician, rapper, visual artist, and novelist.